Lovers at Heart

The Bradens, Book One

Love in Bloom Series

Melissa Foster

D1280061

"Steamy sex scenes and heartfelt confessions. A satisfying addition to the 'Love in Bloom' series."

-- *Midwest Book Review*

ISBN-13: 978-0-9890508-8-3
ISBN-10: 0989050882

This is a work of fiction. The events and characters described herein are imaginary and are not intended to refer to specific places or living persons. The opinions expressed in this manuscript are solely the opinions of the author and do not represent the opinions or thoughts of the publisher. The author has represented and warranted full ownership and/or legal right to publish all the materials in this book.

LOVERS AT HEART
All Rights Reserved.
Copyright © 2013 Melissa Foster
V1.0

This book may not be reproduced, transmitted, or stored in whole or in part by any means, including graphic, electronic, or mechanical without the express written consent of the publisher except in the case of brief quotations embodied in critical articles and reviews.

Cover Design: Natasha Brown

WORLD LITERARY PRESS
PRINTED IN THE UNITED STATES OF AMERICA

A Note To Readers

Lovers at Heart is the fourth book in the *Love in Bloom* series, and the first book of *The Bradens*. While it may be read as a stand-alone novel, for even more enjoyment you may want to read the rest of the *Love in Bloom* novels. If you have read the first three *Snow Sisters* books, then you have already met Treat Braden and Max Armstrong. If you haven't, then buckle up for an emotional ride. These two characters have a special place in my heart, and I hope you fall in love with them as much as I have.

Melissa Foster

For Russell Blake, a talented writer, a treasured friend,
and a fierce and worthy competitor.
You're a hell of a guy, skater shoes and all.

PRAISE FOR MELISSA FOSTER

"Contemporary romance at its hottest. Each Braden sibling left me craving the next. Sensual, sexy, and satisfying, the Braden series is a captivating blend of the dance between lust, love, and life."
—*Bestselling author, Keri Nola, Psychotherapist (on The Bradens)*

"[LOVERS AT HEART] Foster's tale of stubborn yet persistent love takes us on a heartbreaking and soul-searing journey."
—*Reader's Favorite*

"Smart, uplifting, and beautifully layered. I couldn't put it down!"
—*National bestselling author, Jane Porter (on Sisters in Love)*

"Steamy love scenes, emotionally-charged drama, and a family-driven story, make this the perfect story for any romance reader."
—*Midwest Book Review (on Sisters in Bloom)*

"HAVE NO SHAME is a powerful testimony to love and the progressive, logical evolution of social consciousness, with an outcome that readers will find engrossing, unexpected, and ultimately eye-opening."
—*Midwest Book Review*

"TRACES OF KARA is psychological suspense at its best, weaving a tight-knit plot, unrelenting action, and tense moments that don't let up, and ending in a fiery, unpredictable revelation."
—*Midwest Book Review*

"[MEGAN'S WAY] A wonderful, warm, and thought-provoking story...a deep and moving book that speaks to men as well as women, and I urge you all to put it on your reading list."
—*Mensa Bulletin*

"[CHASING AMANDA] Secrets make this tale outstanding."
—Hagerstown Magazine

"COME BACK TO ME is a hauntingly beautiful love story set against the backdrop of betrayal in a broken world."
—*Bestselling Author Sue Harrison*

Chapter One

TREAT BRADEN didn't usually charter planes. It wasn't his style to flash his wealth, but tonight he needed to be anywhere but his Nassau, Bahamas, resort—and missing his commercial flight had just plain pissed him off. He owned upscale resorts all over the world, and he'd been featured on travel shows so many times that it turned his stomach to have to play those ridiculous media games. Most of the pomp and circumstance surrounding him had begun to irk him in ways that it never had before meeting Max Armstrong. It had been six months since he'd seen her standing in the lobby of his Nassau resort. Six months since his heart first thundered in a way that scared the shit out of him.

He'd tried to ignore her, but it seemed that everywhere Treat went, she was destined to appear. Treat wasn't a Neanderthal. He knew he had no claim on her. Hell, he hadn't even given her any indication that he was attracted to her. But that hadn't stopped his blood from boiling when he'd seen her with Justin Barr, one of his employees, and it hadn't stopped him from acting like a prick when he'd seen her the next morning standing in front of the elevators at his resort, wearing the same clothes she'd had on the night before.

Meeting Max had sent his heart and mind into a wind tunnel of regret. He was thirty-seven, and it was high time that he settled into life and cast away the fears he'd carried around his whole life due to his mother's untimely death and his father's grief. *I'll fall in love and she'll be stolen away. I'll be as heartbroken as Dad.*

If he'd had to look at the lobby of the Nassau resort for one more second, he might have torn the place down. As the plane landed, Treat knew that getting away from resorts altogether and spending a weekend with his father at his ranch was just what he needed. Being with his family would center him, and Hal Braden had always been a calming influence on Treat. After his mother passed away, it was his father who pulled him and his five siblings through those tumultuous years. His father had constantly pounded a strong work ethic and sense of loyalty into his and his four brothers' heads, and that had enabled them all to be successful in their careers. His younger sister, Savannah, however, was the most ruthless businessperson of them all. The thought of his gorgeous, albeit cutthroat, sister brought a smile to his lips. He'd have to remember to call her while he was in town.

WESTON, COLORADO was a small ranch town with dusty streets, too many cowboy hats, and a main drag that had been built to replicate the Wild West. It was everything Treat remembered as he sat in his rental Lexus SUV on Main Street. The traffic he was stuck in was not at all typical, and it wasn't until he crawled around the next curve and saw the balloons and banners above the road announcing the twenty-second annual Indie Film Festival that he realized what weekend it was. *Damn.* He had forgotten about the festival.

His cell phone rang, and he picked it up while he waited for the line of cars to turn off the main road toward the festival grounds.

"I can't believe you didn't call me before you came out."

Savannah. "Hi, honey. I miss you, too."

"You big oaf." She laughed. Savannah was a ballbusting entertainment attorney, but to Treat, she'd always be his baby sister. "I'm at the festival with a client. When will you get in?"

"I'm here now. I'm on Main." He hadn't moved an inch in five minutes.

"Yeah? Come to the festival and see me. I'll call Dad and let him know. I'll wait for you at the rear entrance."

Even though his sister had issued an order rather than posed a request, Treat smiled. All he really wanted to do was to reach his father's five-hundred-acre ranch just outside of town, but Treat knew that if he didn't see Savannah right away, she'd be disappointed; and disappointing his siblings was something he strived not to do. His father's words rang through his mind. *Family knows no boundaries.*

"You sure you can get away?" he asked, knowing there was nothing that would stop Savannah from making time for him.

"Who are you kidding? For you? Hell yes. Come in the back gate. I'll wait there."

"I'll be there as soon as traffic allows. Hey, don't forget to call Dad." The thought of his father waiting for him worried Treat. After he ended the call with Savannah and waited through two more unbearably long traffic lights, he picked up his cell and called his father, just in case. He didn't like to cause his father undue worry.

"Hey there, son."

Hal's slow, deep drawl tugged at Treat's heart. God, he'd missed his father. "Dad, I'm here, but I'm gonna stop at the festival first, if you don't mind."

"Yup. Savannah called. Treat, spend some time with her. She misses you."

His father was always looking out for them, and it warmed his heart to hear that things hadn't changed. "See you soon, Dad."

Chapter Two

MAX ARMSTRONG donned her most comfortable jeans and her usual festival T-shirt on opening day. Her boss—and owner of the Indie Film Festival—Chaz Crew had created so much buzz over the past few years that they were expecting a crowd of more than forty thousand attendees during the two-day festival. The festival grounds covered one hundred acres a few blocks from Main Street and boasted five new theaters. Also on the grounds were restaurants, gift shops, and a high-class hotel. Hotels in neighboring towns were booked a full year in advance of the festival.

Whether there were twenty or fifty thousand attendees, Max was ready. She was nothing if not efficient and supremely organized. She'd been organizing the festival sponsors and logistics for almost eight years, and there was nothing that could throw her off her game. At least that's what Max always thought—

until six months earlier, when she'd met Treat Braden at Chaz's wedding.

Max had worked with Scarlet, Treat's assistant, for months via telephone calls and e-mails, coordinating logistics for the double wedding he'd hosted at his Nassau resort for Chaz and Kaylie, and Treat's cousin, Blake Carter, and his new wife Danica—Kaylie's sister. She'd come to know Scarlet so well that Scarlet now recognized her by voice. But she hadn't been prepared for meeting the six-foot-six darkly handsome god that was Treat Braden, with his seductive voice, and the way every inch of him screamed of adrenaline-pumping, heart-fluttering masculinity. He'd knocked her so far off-kilter that she'd lost her ability to speak, along with her mental faculties.

Now her stomach clenched just thinking about the way he took her hand in his and kissed the back of it with those warm, sensuous lips, or the way he'd looked at her as though she were the only woman in the room and then, in the next breath, had arrogantly blown her off. Who was he to judge her personal activities? Sure, she'd been in the same clothes she'd worn the night before, and yes, she'd been out on a date with one of his employees, but she was a single woman. She had every right to do whatever she wanted to do with whomever she wanted—without judgment. *Why do I care what he thinks anyway?* That awful look he gave her was in such stark contrast to the impeccable manners that he'd otherwise exuded; holding doors, thinking of the needs of her and his other guests before himself, taking extra steps to ensure that every little detail of his cousin's wedding had been taken care of. Before that look, he'd paid full attention to every word she'd spoken, and the way his eyes trailed her every move did not go unnoticed. Her pulse sped up just thinking about it. Max couldn't let those things sway her resolve. She'd been mistreated, demeaned, and judged by a previous boyfriend, and she swore she'd never go down that road again—not even for too-sexy-for-his-own-good Treat Braden. She'd tried to avoid him after that interaction, though she'd been far from successful. After Nassau, she'd walked away and never looked back. Well, maybe a few times, in the darkness of her bedroom, when it was only her and her sexual fantasies.

She'd learned her lesson. Max forced herself to fall right back into doing what she did best: focus on her work. And it had paid off. This year's festival would be a huge success.

It was warmer than it should be in Weston that afternoon, with temps in the mid-sixties. She was glad she didn't need her parka, as she had during other festivals where the weather had taken on a freakish Arctic chill. The afternoon films ran without a hitch, and so far, the celebrity speakers had made their appearances without any wardrobe malfunctions—a trick of the trade for gaining media exposure. Max ran a tight ship, and she was quick to nix any wayward thoughts that celebs might conjure up.

Max spoke into her earpiece as she drove over toward the rear gate. "Heading to the rear gate now. I'll check on Dean."

The ruckus between the celeb's entourage and the media was already creating a shit-storm of confusion. Photographers surrounded Connor Dean's limousine and the two accompanying SUVs. She should have known this might happen. Dean was a local celebrity actor turned millionaire, whose reputation had exploded since they'd booked him eight months earlier. She'd been wrong to think the Hulk-like security guards could manage a little drama. As she neared the scene, she rolled down her window and surveyed the ensuing nightmare. Shouts and threats were tossed around like candy to children, and no one was making any headway. *What on earth is that woman doing with her body halfway out of the limo?*

Max parked right in front of the first SUV, threw open her door, and stepped from the car. She'd hoped to create a long enough pause to get the crowd's attention, and when that didn't work, she moved to Plan B. *What is that woman in the limo shouting—legal jargon?* Max groaned as she climbed onto the roof of her car and raised her hands in the air. With a quick flip of a switch on the control panel on her belt, she flicked on the intercom mounted above the gate.

TREAT PULLED up to the back gate behind a mass of media surrounding a number of cars. He rolled down his window and was met with too many shouts to decipher. It was obvious that no one was going anywhere anytime soon. He pulled into the parking lot outside the fence and decided he'd run in, say hello to Savannah, and tell her he'd catch up with her later at their father's ranch. The last thing he needed was to deal with this type of headache.

He heard Savannah's voice and swiftly scanned the crowd. *If anyone touches her I'll—* Savannah was standing with her body out of the limousine's moonroof, shouting God knew what as the media peppered her client with questions. Connor Dean, Savannah's client, was an actor who was quickly climbing the ranks of fame. Savannah had been his attorney for two years, and whenever he had a public engagement, he brought her along. It wasn't a typical attorney-client relationship, but for all of Connor's bravado, he'd been slandered one too many times. Savannah kept track of what was and wasn't said at most events—by both Connor and the media.

Treat couldn't see Connor Dean, but by the way the media swarmed the limo, he assumed Connor was inside fielding questions from behind the slightly open tinted window.

Treat leaned against the entrance to the gate, crossed one foot over the other, and watched his little sister in action. Her long auburn hair looked like fire against her narrowed, serious green eyes. She was the only one to have their mom's coloring—and their mother's spitfire spirit also came with the genes. He and his brothers were all dark, like their father.

Savannah glanced up and their eyes caught. Her scowl morphed into a warm smile as she scrambled onto the roof of the limo.

Treat pushed away from the fence and headed in full protective mode toward his sister. She might be mouthy, but she could be easily injured by those media animals as they pushed their way forward.

"Treat!" Savannah called.

Treat moved into the crowd, parting the media like flies. His six-foot-six frame naturally commanded more space, and one look up usually sent smaller men scrambling away. The ones who remained, he gently persuaded with a cold, domineering stare—a stare he hadn't needed to rely upon since Savannah was a teenager, when he and his brothers had spent countless hours keeping the horny boys away from their precious sister.

Treat reached up and caught Savannah as she jumped down. He spun her around and, as he set her on her feet, his eyes landed on a woman standing on a car in front of the limousine. His breath caught in his throat. *Max.*

"OKAY, THE SHOW is over." Max ran her eyes over the crowd as her voice boomed into the raging crowd.

"Let's give Mr. Dean some space to continue driving through. He'll be signing autographs and answering questions after his appearance." Max's gaze landed on the handsome man towering above the crowd, with a gorgeous woman in his arms and a smile on his lips. She froze as he spun the woman to the side and his face came into view. *Oh God.* Her pulse soared, and—damn it—the butterflies in her stomach that she thought she'd annihilated six months earlier roared to life with a vengeance. She stumbled backward, and one of the security guards was quick to grab her until she found her footing.

"Max! You okay?"

The security guard's voice wrenched her back to the chaos. She tore her eyes from Treat and whomever the woman was that he was holding as if she meant everything in the world to him, and she blinked away the unexpected tears that threatened her steely reserve.

"Clear a path or you'll be removed from the premises for the rest of the festival." Even she could hear the difference in her voice, the weakness. *Damn it.* Her eyes darted back to Treat, who was staring at her with an incredulous look on his face. Suddenly painfully aware of her jeans and T-shirt, the ponytail in her hair, and—*oh God*—how she must look like a crazy woman standing on top of the car, she clambered down to the ground as the crowd surprisingly obeyed her orders and began to dissipate. Threats of eviction usually worked.

She turned off the intercom and fumbled for her keys. Treat was heading her way. She wouldn't be caught dead speaking to him after the way he'd blown her off six months earlier. The woman he was with now was stunning, and obviously well connected, and it was abundantly clear by the way Treat looked at her that she was exactly what he wanted.

"Max," he called.

His smooth, deep voice was enough to send her heart aflutter. She cursed under her breath as she started the car and navigated around the crowd. She glanced in her rearview mirror, grasping the steering wheel with trembling hands. Damn him for having this effect on her. Treat stood alone in his dark suit, watching Max's car, while his beautiful companion looked on with a confused expression on her face.

Chapter Three

"WHAT THE HECK was that all about?" Savannah asked.

Treat couldn't believe his eyes. *Max.* After all these months, he'd thought he had squelched the need she stirred within him, but seeing her standing on that car like she could command the world—all wrapped up in an adorable five-foot-five, one-hundred-ten-pound frame of brown-haired beauty—all those urges came rushing back. Treat saw right through those jeans and that T-shirt. He'd seen the sexy woman beneath, the one she tried so hard to ignore.

Damn it. How could he have been so stupid? And now Savannah was looking at him like he'd lost his mind, and he wasn't so sure he hadn't.

"Nothing. I thought she was someone I knew." What the hell was Max doing at the festival—standing on top of a car? Of course Max was there, he realized. The other groom in his cousin Blake's double wedding had been

Max's boss, Chaz Crew. Chaz owned the festival. One phone call six months earlier would have told him everything he'd ever wanted to know about Max, but he hadn't made that call. His only goal had been to forget her—and now Treat wanted to know more.

"That was more than nothing, bro." Savannah flashed a sly smile. "Let me tell Connor I'll catch up with him, and we'll go grab some coffee and chat."

Treat couldn't put anything in his stomach if he wanted to. It took every bit of his focus not to run after Max's car, or ask the security guard where he could find her. He didn't want to make a scene, and it was obvious that she didn't want to talk to him. He was frozen, locked into place between what he wanted to do and how quickly Max had fled. The thundering of his heart was too strong to ignore, and now, with the hope of forgetting her gone, he accepted what he had feared all along—the thundering was his heart's way of telling him not to let her go.

TREAT BRADEN. Oh God, Treat Braden. Max drove as fast as she could into the underground garage that was reserved for the festival's staff. She slammed her car door shut and paced the concrete floor. *What is he doing here? Is he doing this just to torture me? Is this some sort of game to him?* She thought she had hated him enough after the way he'd treated her that she'd become immune to even the sight of him. But the way her heart melted with one look from his piercing dark eyes convinced her she was wrong. Boy, was she wrong.

Get a grip.

A voice came through her earpiece. "Max, I need you by Marquee One."

Damn it, Chaz. Now? "Be right there," she said into the earpiece. There were thousands of people milling about. What were the chances she'd run into Treat again? Not much, she decided. She felt a pang of disappointment, then chided herself for it.

Max hurried to Marquee One and flipped through her planner to make sure there were no issues with it that she hadn't taken care of. She found Chaz staring up at the large sign.

"Max, come here." Chaz motioned her over with a flash of his pearly whites. His hair had lightened from the sun during the summer, and he still carried a copper tan, giving him the look of a twenty-something surfer rather than the thirtysomething director and owner of the festival. "Look at that. What do you think?"

She squinted at the sign, having no idea what she was supposed to be seeing. Maybe she just couldn't focus because her heart had yet to settle down. "What?"

"That there." He pointed again.

"Chaz, sorry, but you've lost me." She pushed her earpiece to her head and answered another request. "Yeah, no problem, Grace. Sure."

"I think we can have Joey maneuver something right along that wall, in that divot of the sign, to create another major sponsor location. I looked at both sides, and they match. What do you think?"

Leave it to Chaz to find more opportunities for

sponsorships in the middle of the festival, when Max would give anything to hide beneath a rock. There he stood, smiling and pleased with himself at the chance to sell more sign space and bring more funding to the festival. Max could easily be annoyed with him for his bad timing, but she had no siblings and he'd become the brother she'd always wished she had. After so many years of working together, they bickered like she imagined siblings would and cared just as deeply about each other. Chaz's wife, Kaylie, had become one of Max's closest friends.

"I think you're a pain for calling me out here for something like this." She smiled, and he crossed his arms, trying his damnedest to look angry. "You know I'm right. Why are you even looking at this stuff right now?"

The screening was letting out, and people streamed out of the theater entrance. Max and Chaz stepped to the side, listening to the patrons as they talked among themselves.

"Incredible," an older woman said.

"Loved the dramatic flair of that one character. Winston?" said another.

"Oh, I hated him. Too full of himself," a short, stocky woman said with a wave of her hand.

"Hot, though. And talk about commanding an audience! That Connor Dean is amazing."

They could have just as easily been talking about Treat. Just the thought of him made her mind ache. Why was she torturing herself like this? She should just disappear into the office and stay there until there was a real emergency.

"Hey, Max, look!" Chaz waved. "Treat? Over here. Hey, buddy. How are you?"

Max turned her back, frantically running excuses through her mind. *Sick? Need to go help the crew. Lighting, yeah, that could work.* She turned with the excuse ready on her tongue.

Treat's eyes locked on hers.

Max's mouth went dry.

"Chaz, Max, how are you?" Treat asked in that wanton voice that made her legs turn to wet noodles.

Please go away. Please go away.

She couldn't focus on what Chaz was saying. All she could do was stare at the woman who had her hand on Treat's shoulder. *God, she's pretty.* Max hated her already. *Oh no.* She was reaching her hand out toward Max.

"I'm Savannah," she said.

Savannah. What kind of name is that? She must be a model or something. Without thinking, Max looked down at her own attire and cringed.

When Max didn't acknowledge her, Chaz stepped in. "Chaz Crew, nice to meet you. This is Max Armstrong."

She gave Savannah's hand a quick shake and tried her best to flash a feigned smile, then buried her nose in her planner before the woman—or Treat—could strike up a conversation.

"Max." Treat moved to her side while Chaz talked to Savannah. "How have you been?"

So much for looking busy. Max kept her eyes trained on her planner. "Fine. Why are you here?" *What is wrong with me?*

"Max, I've been wanting to say something to you."

Go away.

"I'm sorry for what happened in Nassau."

Why do you have to sound so sincere? Why was he being so nice? She wanted to hate him, to run away and never look back, and here he was, standing next to his ridiculously gorgeous model girlfriend, apologizing for being the ass that he was.

Max held on to her resolve by a thin thread. "I have no idea what you're talking about." She lifted her gaze and saw the hurt in his eyes.

"I...you...I'm sorry," Treat said.

In his expensive dark suit and finely pressed white shirt, just as he'd been wearing almost every time she'd seen him in Nassau, he brought memories tumbling back. She nodded, unable to speak.

"Come on, Treat. Let's get some coffee and catch up. Then we'll go see Dad," Savannah urged.

Treat held Max's gaze a beat too long. She felt her cheeks flush with desire. She wished she could tell him it was okay—even though it wasn't—and take his gorgeous, chiseled face into her hands and kiss those luscious lips of his. God, how she wanted to taste his tongue in her mouth, feel it—

"Treat?" Savannah's eyes darted between Treat and Max.

"Right. Um, Max, may I call you?"

How can he ask me that with her *standing right there?*

"Dad's waiting," Savannah said in a singsong voice.

Dad? "Dad?" The word slipped from Max's lips before she had a chance to think.

"I'm here to see my father. Savannah hijacked me on the way to his ranch."

There it was again. The way he looked at Savannah with adoration. *I'm an idiot. Just take your girlfriend and go away, please.*

"Nothing like being hijacked by a beautiful woman," Max said in a snarky tone.

Treat's hearty laughter wrapped itself around her heart and squeezed. *Now you're making fun of me?*

"She's beautiful, yes, but she's also my little sister." Treat smiled at Savannah, who crinkled her nose at him in a cute, sisterly way.

"Yeah, he's so not my type." Savannah laughed. "Hey, Max, why don't you join us for coffee?"

"Um..." *I'd rather be shot in the head. Sister?* Suddenly Max remembered that only Treat and one of his brothers had been able to make it to the wedding. Now she really felt stupid. "I have to be available on-site to field any problems, and I have so much to do—" *Like burying my head in the dirt.*

"Go, Max. You deserve the break. She works like a monster sunup till sundown. Max, just keep your earpiece on in case there's a real emergency," Chaz said. "Sorry, guys, but I've gotta run. Max, don't forget to ask Joey about that sign when you have a chance."

She watched Chaz walk away and was quick to bring up the list of excuses she'd already run through in her mind. "I actually have some lighting issues that I need to attend to."

Savannah smiled. "Are you sure? We don't mind." She arched a brow in her brother's direction.

"Max, I would be honored if you'd join us."

Every bit of her body—especially those naughty areas that she was trying so hard to ignore—screamed, *Yes! Yes! Go!* But Max had no desire to get hurt again. "I'm sorry, but I really can't." *Breathe, I can't breathe. There's no way I can sit with you and pretend to sip coffee.*

Treat took her hand and brought it to his lips. She closed her eyes as his sensuous lips warmed her skin.

"May I call you?" Treat asked again.

Still lost in that single kiss, fantasizing about what she'd like him to kiss next, Max had to shake her head to pull herself back to the conversation. She tapped her earpiece, hoping she could pass her momentary digression off as a technical issue. She was acting like those brainless bimbos she hated. *Why does he have that effect on me?* Max couldn't believe he was laying it on so thick in front of his sister, but maybe Savannah was used to seeing this side of Treat. He probably treated all single women this way. Why then was she tearing out a piece of paper from her planner and writing her cell phone number on it? And why was she staring at his ass as he walked away? *Oh God, I'm in so much trouble.*

Chapter Four

HAL BRADEN'S crowded driveway told Treat everything he needed to know. He stepped from the SUV as Savannah caught up to him. Savannah had peppered him with enough questions when they'd had coffee. He'd tried to downplay his feelings about Max and said she'd worked with Scarlet to help organize Blake's wedding. He thought he'd seen a bit of disbelief in Savannah's eyes, but if she didn't trust his answers, she never let on. The last thing he needed was more questions—especially in front of his siblings.

"This was supposed to be a relaxing getaway, not a party," Treat said as Savannah looped her arm around his.

"It's not a party. Everyone's schedule was clear, so we thought..."

Treat sighed at the thought of a busy weekend, but he was glad his brothers would be there. It would be good to see his family all in one place again. They each had built successful careers that had made them very wealthy—but kept them too busy for regular get-togethers.

The smell of home wrapped itself around Treat like a warm embrace: fresh-cut wood, steak on the grill, and too much testosterone for one household filled the entry foyer.

"There's my boy." Hal stood from his favorite leather recliner and hugged Treat. The two men stood eye to eye. Hal's lush black hair was now layered with thick patches of gray around his temples.

"Dad."

"Son. It's good to see you." His father gave him a pat on the back as he moved to hug Savannah. "Sweetie, did you have a nice afternoon with your big brother?"

"Yeah. I always do."

The way Savannah's eyes lit up when they walked out to the backyard to greet their brothers told Treat of her adoration for each of them. He hoped that never changed, but had Savannah known how he'd treated Max at the resort, that adoration would have withered away quickly. The thought shamed him.

Rex was the third-eldest brother in the family and the first to reach him when he arrived. He hesitated for just a second before saying, "Treat, glad to have you back, man." Rex worked on the ranch with his father, and his muscular physique was proof of the hard physical labor he endured. Like their brother Dane, who spent his days trying to save the lives of sharks, Rex sported a year-round tan.

"How's he holding up?" Treat lifted his eyes to his father. His father was sixty-five years old and still strong as an ox, but that didn't keep Treat from worrying about him. He worried about them all, but since his mother died when he was eleven—an age when every kid believes their parents will live forever—he counted every day with his father as a blessing.

"He's good." Rex put his arm around Treat and walked him away from Dane, who was hovering close by. "You okay?" Treat was close to all of his siblings, but each relationship was different. Rex was three years Treat's junior, and as such, the competitiveness Treat felt with Dane, who was just a year and a half younger, had never been present in his relationship with Rex. Although he and Rex often confided in each other when it came to personal matters, Rex carried a chip on his shoulder about the family business.

"Yeah. I needed a break. Got a little burnt out." Treat watched Rex narrow his eyes. He knew his brother wasn't buying his excuse, but he wasn't ready to expose his feelings for Max just yet.

"Yeah? You sure?"

Treat nodded. "Of course. I'm fine. Really."

"Can we have him back now, Rex?" Dane asked with a grin.

Rex feigned a punch to Dane's gut as he walked past.

Dane embraced Treat. He was three inches shorter

than Treat and every bit as dark and handsome, the only difference being Dane's brown eyes always seemed to be dancing with optimism, while Treat's often appeared more serious, contemplative. "You should have seen the girl I banged last night," Dane whispered.

Treat laughed at their running joke. In reality, Dane was more likely to be chasing big fish than bedding women. "I already had her mother," Treat joked, but this time, the joke tasted wrong as it rolled off his tongue. He looked at his father. His dark eyes had harbored the pain of missing his wife for more years than Treat could count, and he once again felt the newfound draw of wanting to experience the love his parents had shared—the draw that he'd begun to recognize when he'd met Max.

Dane pulled away, laughing. "You always were the king."

Treat went to the stone barbeque pit, where Josh was tending to steaks and baked potatoes, and put an arm around his brother's shoulder.

"And how's my famous dress-designing brother?" Josh was the leanest, least aggressive of the Braden crew. With a love of fashion since the day he could pick out his own clothes, Josh was a designer to the stars and owned several high-end fashion boutiques.

"Hey." Josh smiled. "I do more than dresses." Because Josh had a sweet demeanor and had always been tight-lipped about his female conquests, Treat and his brothers had spent many nights of their youth pestering him to kiss and tell. He'd held strong then, even about the heart-quaking crush he'd had on Riley Banks—the one that everyone else knew about but Josh thought he had hidden. No matter how much his brothers prodded him for details, Josh continued to keep his private life just that—private.

"Yeah, yeah. I hear you're wiping Vera Wang off the map." Treat was proud of Josh, and his only hope for Josh was that he was happy.

Josh shook his head. "One day."

"Where's Hugh?" The youngest of the Bradens, Hugh was the biggest risk taker of them all, and his career as a race-car driver was a testament to the way he lived his life—fast cars, and even faster women. He was supremely self-centered, which at times rubbed Treat the wrong way.

Josh shrugged. "Race, maybe? Steaks are ready. Shall we eat?" Josh asked.

"We shall." Treat took off his jacket, watching his father walk to the table with one arm around Savannah, the other around Dane. Boy, he'd missed them.

Treat set the platter of steaks in the center of the long table, alongside the salad, wine, beer, vegetables, and three types of sliced bread—typical Braden fare. There weren't many family gatherings that weren't centered around a barbeque of some sort.

"You started without me?" Hugh barged into the yard with his arms open and a grin on his face. His wind-tossed, thick, wavy hair gave him a playful appearance. "Treat, you've graced us with your presence after all."

"Good to see you too, Hugh." Treat stood and wrapped an arm around him.

"Had a race. Sorry." Hugh sat down and was the first to snag the largest steak off the platter.

Treat shook his head. "So, Dad, are you ever going to let me pay for that stone patio you keep talking about?"

Rex smirked. "He doesn't need your money, Treat. He needs my time."

"I didn't mean anything by it," Treat said.

"We're so busy running the ranch that I haven't had time to get started. But I will," he said with a harsh stare.

He and Rex could get along like two peas in a pod, but it could change on a dime when the family ranch was brought up. "I was just saying that I could help. Bring a crew to help you out," Treat offered.

"Are you the crew?" Rex asked pointedly.

Treat stared him down. Rex was never going to let up about the family ranch, and exactly what his beef was, was never quite clear to Treat.

"Boys, settle down. I need a patio like I need a hole in my head. Tell me about your resorts, Treat. What did you decide about Thailand?" his father asked.

"I'm thinking about it. It's a solid resort and the numbers work. I'm just...Lately I haven't been in an acquiring mood," Treat explained. He'd been negotiating a deal on a resort in Thailand, and when the Justice of the Peace who was supposed to preside over Blake's wedding had fallen ill, Treat had stepped in to officiate and had canceled his trip to Thailand. He and Max had been heading to the island for the wedding when they'd been caught in a storm, and it was then, while they were trapped on the boat and he couldn't ignore the fear and pain in Max's eyes, that he realized it wasn't the raging sea she feared. It was him—and that realization had cut him to his core. That was the moment when Treat had known he'd made the biggest mistake of his life.

Spending that time on the boat with Max had left an imprint on his heart that he couldn't shake. He'd tabled the Thailand deal and had begun to reexamine his motivations and view himself with a whole new perspective.

"He's in Max mode," Savannah added.

Treat glared at her.

"Who's Max?" Josh asked.

"Some hot girl who works at the festival and has Treat all googly-eyed," Savannah said.

"Hmm...Max is a girl?" Josh arched a brow and grinned.

"Yes, she's a woman. No, I'm not in Max mode. Jesus, Savannah." Treat bit into a hunk of steak, wishing Savannah had never seen her. Max's number had been burning a hole in his pocket ever since she'd given it to him, and it was all he could do not to get up and call her right that second.

"Treat, googly-eyed? You gotta be kidding me. The man eats women for breakfast," Hugh said with a deep laugh. He was always quick to throw a barb and just as quick to return to whatever he was doing for himself beforehand—in this instance, he turned his attention back to his plate of food and speared a forkful of salad.

Treat threw his napkin on the table. "Cut the shit, okay?" He knew he was overreacting, and he knew Hugh was only stating what had once been the truth. Bile rose in his throat just thinking of himself in that player role. Yeah, he'd been with a lot of women, but not because he didn't want more. He'd been afraid to fall in love.

Hugh shrugged off his roar. "I won today. First place."

"Good job, son." His father raised his beer bottle. "To Hugh."

"To Huge!" the boys said in unison.

Savannah shook her head. "Idiots," she said with a laugh.

AFTER DINNER Treat, Dane, and Rex cleared the table and did the dishes while Savannah visited with her father, and Josh and Hugh talked about Hugh's racing.

"Something you want to tell us about?" Dane asked once they were safely in the kitchen, away from the others.

"I have no idea what you're talking about." Treat turned his eyes away from Dane and began digging in a drawer for a dish towel.

"Is that Max from Blake's wedding?" Dane asked.

"How would you know Max from Blake's wedding? You never even met her." Treat watched Dane cringe

28

under his scrutiny. "You're seeing Lacy, aren't you?" Lacy was Blake's wife Danica's half sister, and Dane had given Treat a message to pass on to Lacy after he'd had to leave before the wedding.

"Nope." Dane set his mouth in a harsh line and focused on scrubbing a plate dry, much harder than it called for.

Treat wouldn't let Dane get away with cutting him off. "Then how do you know Max?" Treat briefly wondered if Dane had somehow met and hooked up with her. He'd bedded Treat's girlfriend when they were in college, and Treat was still not over it. Dane was known for one thing among his brothers—well, ten inches of one thing. The thought of him anywhere near Max made the hairs on the back of his neck stand on edge and his muscles twitch.

"Dane?" he asked with a fisted hand. He and his brothers had come to blows many times over the years, but it had been forever since he'd felt the urge to punch anyone. Max wasn't even his to protect, but he couldn't stop his protective claws from showing.

"Leave him alone, Treat." Rex planted himself between them.

Treat stared at Dane until he relented.

"I talked to Lacy a few days later, to apologize for not being at the wedding. She told me about Max coordinating the event, and the storm, and..."

Treat clenched his jaw. *Don't say anything about me and Max on the boat or I might have to kill you.*

"Anyway, I know she hooked up with Justin, and I

just assumed..." Dane shrugged.

Savannah breezed into the kitchen just in time to catch Treat as he lifted his hand to grab his brother.

"What are you doing?" She looked from one brother to the other.

"Dude's out of control," Dane said, taking a step back. "I don't think I've seen you this jealous since Mary Jane."

"Dane! Rex, get him out of here," Savannah ordered.

Treat lowered his fist. "Sorry, Dane. I'm sorry. I don't know what got into me," he said as Rex and Dane left the room. He straightened his shirt and calmed his breathing. "Sorry, Savannah."

"Are you all right? Why was he bringing up Mary Jane?" she asked.

Mary Jane had been Treat's girlfriend his second year of college. Dane had come up for a weekend, and Treat had found them in bed together. She had tried to reconcile, but he'd known there was no way he'd ever measure up after she'd been with his brother—nor would he want to. Any girlfriend who would sleep with his brother was not a girlfriend he needed. He'd gone out and slept with the most beautiful girl on campus the next night—right after sending Dane back home.

It had taken months for Dane and Treat to get back on sure footing after the incident with Mary Jane. The frightened look in Savannah's eyes pulled Treat from his jealous rage. Savannah was particularly sensitive to her brothers being at odds, and even though it had been years since they'd fought over a woman, he knew she worried about him and Dane falling right back into that uncomfortable pattern. He bit back his anger and reassured her.

"I'm fine. He was just being an ass," Treat answered.

"Yeah, well, you all can be one at some time or another," Savannah said, fixing his collar.

Dane and Rex came back in carrying more dishes.

"Is it safe?" Rex asked.

Treat locked eyes with Dane in a silent warning not to talk about Max and Justin in the same breath again. Ever.

"Treat, you have to go out with me and Hugh tonight," Savannah said. "There's an event."

"What are we, dog shit?" Rex asked.

Savannah put her hand on his and Dane's shoulders. "You're anything but dog shit. That's the problem. I don't want to spend the evening beating women away with a stick." She turned back to Treat. "Besides, it's the festival after-party. Hugh has a date and two extra tickets, and Max might be there."

Treat shook his head. The mention of Justin and Max had made his blood boil, and he wasn't sure he could even look at Max without feeling it rip right through him again. "I'm beat," he said.

"Yeah, well, wake up. You're going."

Chapter Five

WHY THE HELL had she given him her number? Why hadn't he called? She'd taken out her battery and rebooted the phone—twice—and had been checking her messages like she was obsessive compulsive. As she walked through the gates with Chaz, she kept waiting for him to say something to her about Treat.

"Max?" Chaz lifted his lips into a crooked smile. "You've done it again."

She and Chaz had reviewed the finances from the morning before leaving, and it was obvious that Chaz was still thinking about their overwhelming success. They'd already almost matched the previous year's total festival revenue.

She shook her head. "Not me, boss. We did it. At least the first day went off without a hitch."

"Don't forget, you said you'd do the after-party swing tonight. I can't wait to go home and see Trevor and Lexi. It's been a long day." Chaz and Kaylie had been married for only six months, but their twins were almost three years old.

The after-parties were one of the highlights of the film festival. Intimate gatherings with celebs, where locals and fans could dance the night away and take home expensive swag, to boot. *Crap.* She'd forgotten about the parties. Maybe she could get out of it. "Aren't the kids asleep by now?"

"Yeah, but I like to see them. Besides, they're asleep." He raised his eyebrows. "We're still newlyweds, after all."

HER CLOSET LOOKED more like a teenager's than that of an almost-thirty-year-old woman, with too many T-shirts and jeans to count and not nearly enough grown-up clothes. Max inspected the few dresses she owned. She selected two and hung them on the closet door so that she could visualize herself in them. They were both black and short, standard party attire. One was tight fitting with a plunging neckline, leaving very little to the imagination, while the other was more conservative with a ring neck and slit pockets at the hips.

Her cell phone rang and Max froze. The incoming phone number was restricted. *Treat?* What would she say? What would he say? What if he asked her out? It rang two more times. She stared at it as if she were trying to decide whether or not to touch a land mine; her heart pounded against her rib cage, her body trembled, and her brain was unable to form a coherent thought. When the phone stopped ringing, she dove onto the bed and pushed the green button.

"Hello? Hello?"

Silence.

Max pushed the End button and banged her head against the mattress. She waited for her message light to blink on. When it didn't, she pushed herself to her feet with disgust.

"You're such a fool," she said to her reflection in the mirror. She stripped off her clothes and stepped angrily into the shower. "An idiot, a chicken." She scrubbed her scalp so hard she was sure she was leaving a trail of cuts. "Maybe it's better this way." She rinsed the suds from her hair, soaped and scrubbed her body, and then dried herself off and stood in front of the mirror.

"You're better off without him," she tried to convince herself. She flipped her head upside down and turned on the hair dryer. Her wavy brown hair fluffed into a sultry style that hung almost below her shoulders. "You can do better," she said with a wicked grin.

Max hadn't been on a date since she'd left Nassau. She'd been denying her sexual urges for years—literally—because of a frightening scenario that had unfolded in the bedroom years earlier. Maybe it was time she broke that wretched streak and forgot Treat altogether. It wasn't in her nature to pick up a man, and even the thought of it petrified her. But on another level, maybe having a one-night stand was just what she needed to get over him.

"Maybe that is what I need. A distraction." She hadn't even had a reason to dress like a woman since Nassau, much less feel like one.

She went heavy on the makeup. Swinging her hips to the music on the radio, she stepped into one of the few lace thongs she owned, and then slipped into the skintight dress with the plunging neckline. She spun around as the tunes escalated and slipped her bare feet into her efficient black heels. She stood before the mirror, surveying herself from top to bottom. Her dark eyeliner said, *Take Me*, her body screamed, *Touch me*, and her crimson lips whispered, *Now*, but the total package, including the efficient heels, shouted, *Faker!*

She kicked off her heels and stared at her other footwear options with a frown. Efficient, efficient, efficient. No matter which dress she chose, she'd feel like a fake. *How on earth did I make it this far?* She snagged her phone from the bed and texted Kaylie, who had become one of her closest friends since she and Chaz married.

Can I borrow your high black heels?

Her phone vibrated. *High black heels lol. U mean the fuck-me heels? Lol.*

Max rolled her eyes and texted back. *I guess.*

Kaylie's text came through seconds later. *Who's the guy?*

She texted, *Festival after-party. Yes or no?*

A minute later her phone vibrated. *Yup. Babies R sleeping. Will leave on porch.*

Max spritzed on her sexiest perfume, put on her

flip-flops, grabbed her purse and keys, and headed for Kaylie's.

Twenty minutes later she was walking up Kaylie's front steps. As promised, the black stilettos were on the front porch.

"I can't believe you didn't tell me about Treat!"

Max started. "Kaylie, you scared the crap out of me."

Kaylie came out of the dark garage and into the light of the porch. She wore a nighty that barely covered her underwear—at least Max hoped she was wearing underwear—and fuzzy slippers beneath one of Chaz's winter coats, which hung open and dwarfed her thin frame.

"I'm not seeing Treat. I'm going to the after-party because your husband wanted to spend time with you," Max snapped, trying to get her pulse to settle.

"Chaz said Treat showed up today." Kaylie brushed her blond hair away from her face. "Did he call you? I knew there was something going on at the wedding."

Max heard a faint ringing. "There was nothing going on at the wedding, and he didn't come to see me. He's in Weston to see his dad, and it was just a coincidence that he was at the festival." *I wish he'd been there to see me.*

"There are no coincidences in life. Hey, is that your phone?" Kaylie asked.

"I thought it was the house phone," Max answered.

Kaylie shook her head. "We turn off the ringers when the kids go to bed."

Max ran for her car and tugged the door open. Her phone had already stopped ringing. She checked the missed call log and saw the restricted number had popped up again. She let out a breath and felt the confidence she'd bolstered begin to deflate.

"Sorry, Max. Were you expecting that he might call?" Kaylie asked.

Max turned to her and couldn't hide her disappointment. "Not really. He asked for my number, but you know how that goes." She feigned a smile.

"Oh, Max. Look at you. I didn't even notice how hot you look. Girl, if he is at that after-party, he won't be able to keep his eyes—or his hands—off of you."

"Thanks, but he won't be there." Max shook her head. "I'm not like you, Kaylie. This is all so easy for you. I had to talk myself into dressing like this, and I still feel like I'm playing dress up."

"Well, you sure fooled me. Listen, this is all there is to it. It's all a game. It's them against you, and usually you both have the same agenda—to get the sexiest one into bed."

"Kay—"

"Save it, sister. And trust me, okay? I know what I'm talking about. The next time you see Treat, you act as if you're the sex-starved man, like you can't keep your eyes or hands off of him. That'll knock him off his game, and you'll start to see the real him."

"I don't know if I can do that." *Can I? A sex-starved man?*

"If you want to win him over, then you have to. Then, when he thinks he's gonna get you into bed, you pull back. Remember, you control the strings. Think of

him as a marionette and yourself as the puppet master."
Kaylie looked up at the dark sky. Her blond hair
cascaded down her back, and her blue eyes held a
mixture of innocence and excitement. "Hey, that's good.
I just made that up." She looked at Max with pride.
"Anyway, you're in control. You'll totally knock down
his defenses and it'll be more comfortable—for both of
you."

Max shook her head.

"Listen, Max. At that point, you don't have to do
anything. You pull away and you're the queen of
seduction. You follow through and you're a sexual
tigress. Win-win." Kaylie shrugged.

"What if I want to be with him and he turns me
down?" *Again.*

"Any man who turns you down isn't worth it." She
must have seen Max cringe, because Kaylie quickly
added, "Oh my God. Did he turn you down at the
wedding?"

Max shook her head. Then she nodded. "Sort of. Not
really. I don't know."

"Oh, Maxy." Kaylie pulled her into a hug. "Trust me.
He won't hesitate after you do this. Win-win. You
remember that." She shook her head. "What on earth
was he thinking?"

"Win-win," Max repeated. *Maybe I can do this.*

Chapter Six

HUGH AND HIS date, Nova Bashe, a comically tall, impossibly skinny Swedish swimsuit model, were flanked by photographers as they made their way into the party. Hugh looked back with a shrug and a wave. Treat was glad to be out of the limelight. Max didn't strike him as an after-party type of woman, and the last thing he wanted to do was hang out with drunken celebrities. He planned to hide in the shadows and keep an eye on his sister.

"Thanks for coming with me. I knew I could count on you," Savannah said, looking gorgeous in her gold minidress.

"Why aren't you with Connor Dean?" Treat asked, swirling the liquor in his glass.

"Are you kidding? He'll have a whole entourage. I'm off duty when he's out drinking. I can't be held responsible for his liquored-up state, even if that's when he gets in the most trouble. He gave me tickets, of course, but I gave them to the girls in my office. Now, they're the kind of girls who love this stuff."

"So, why did you want to come then?"

Savannah looked around, and then pointed across the room.

Treat followed the line of her finger and there, in the dim light of the nightclub, stood Max.

"See you later, big brother." Savannah kissed his cheek and disappeared into a crowd of people off to his left.

Treat couldn't take his eyes off of Max. There she was. He'd blown it once, and he wasn't going to blow it again. His heart started that thunderous dance again, and he took a step in her direction just as she lifted her eyes and connected with his.

Damn, she was gorgeous. Her hair looked so full and sexy. He wondered what it would feel like to run his fingers through it. *What does it smell like? What does she smell like? What does she taste—* He stopped himself from taking that thought any further. The muscles in his legs tensed as he crossed the dance floor. He ignored the gyrating bodies, never taking his eyes from hers, afraid that if he did, she might not be there when he looked again.

She held a drink between both hands. She bit her lower lip as he approached, and his body reacted instantly when she released her lip and ran her tongue along the corner of her mouth.

Two more steps and he'd be close enough to touch

her. One more step, and the same rush of perfume she'd worn at the resort assaulted his senses, sending a thrill through his chest.

"Max," he said.

She didn't lower her eyes the way she had at the resort. She narrowed them in a heated stare.

He drank in her revealing dress, the way it hugged her hips and plunged so deeply between her firm breasts that it made him want to lick all the way from her neck to her belly button. *Stop. That's not what you want with her,* he reminded himself.

"Treat." She ran her eyes seductively down his body, then brought her drink to her lips. She took a sip and licked the alcohol from her lips while dropping her eyes to just below his waist, where they lingered.

What happened to the shy girl who couldn't hold my gaze?

"What are you doing here?" Her eyes trailed slowly back up.

His pulse raced and he grasped for words. "Um, I...My brother." He took a drink and then began anew. "My brother had extra tickets. I came with him and Savannah."

She looked around the room.

"She disappeared into the crowd," he explained.

"Who's your brother?"

The last thing he wanted to do was talk about Hugh. Hugh was far closer to her age, a subject Treat had been trying to ignore. Not only did Hugh have the Braden looks and wealth, he also loved the thrill of living on the edge and ran with a fast crowd—and women flocked to him.

"Hugh Braden."

Her eyes lit up. "The race-car driver?"

Damn it. He nodded.

She took a step closer to him and ran her finger down his chest. "I'm glad you're here."

Holy hell, she was killing him. He had to touch her, had to feel that silky skin. He wanted to pull her body against his and kiss her right then and there. Hell, he wanted to do so much more than kiss her, and he had the hard-on to prove it.

She tugged his tie playfully, and Treat swore it had a direct line to his penis from the way his body reacted. She was more than a foot shorter than him, and when she stood that close to him in that delectable dress, the curves of her breasts beckoned him. He wasn't going to make it. He hadn't planned to sleep with her tonight, but his body heated up in a way that he might not be able to cool down. *Damn it.* He wanted to take it slow, get to know her better; and most importantly, to clear the air about what happened in Nassau.

"Max," he said quietly.

The way she looked up, with those innocent eyes, made him want to take her in his arms and take care of her, never let anyone hurt her. He'd never felt such protective urges before toward any female besides Savannah.

"LET'S GO SOMEPLACE." Max couldn't believe what she

was doing—from the seductive glances to the words that expertly slipped off her tongue. She felt like an entirely different person, and she liked it. When she looked at him, those hurt feelings fell away. She'd planned on finding a stranger to take away the memory of him, but now that he was right there before her, she knew a stranger wasn't the answer. There was no forgetting Treat Braden.

The minute their eyes connected, she'd known it was now or never, and she still couldn't believe she was pulling off all the things that Kaylie had suggested. *And they were working!* He was putty in her hands. The problem was, she would be putty in his the minute the tables were turned.

Treat put a hand on the curve of her lower back and guided her toward the exit. That simple touch sent adrenaline soaring through her veins.

Max tried to ignore the jealous stares from women as they passed. Treat was undeniably handsome, and his height alone demanded attention, but taking in the whole picture—gorgeous, thick black hair, smoldering dark eyes, set off by richly tanned skin, a broad chest, and slim waist—made her heat up in all the right places. Her heart swelled with pride to be with him tonight, and for a minute, she took the fantasy even further. What would it feel like to be in his arms, to have his hands on her naked body? She shivered with the thought.

When they stepped through the doors and into the cool night air, Max crossed her arms over her body.

She'd hurried to Kaylie's and had forgotten to bring a sweater. Treat wrapped his arms around her. They felt so safe and strong, and his masculine smell sent her mind reeling.

"Shall I drive?" he asked.

Shit. She hadn't thought this through. *Where are we going? How will I get my car back?* How could efficient Max have forgotten so much? She nodded, hoping she'd figure out the rest on the way.

His Lexus SUV had leather seats, which were cold when she sat down. He started the truck and leaned over the console.

"Let me warm you up."

He reached across her lap and she readied herself for a kiss. And, boy, was she ready. Her eyes were at half-mast; she slowed her breathing and parted her lips.

He pushed a button on the door. "Heated seats," he said, then sat back up.

Max thought her heart might explode in her chest. *Jesus, really? I should have leaned in and taken the kiss. Next time...*

Treat pulled out of the parking lot. "Where to, beautiful?"

Did he need to talk like that? Pulling her in with his seductive words and smooth voice? She could barely think, much less talk.

"Left at the light. I live in Allure."

He nodded and headed out of town. The silence was deafening, and Max felt her confidence slipping away. *What would Kaylie do?* She reached over and turned on the radio, then moved her shoulders slowly to the beat.

Treat put his hand on hers and held on tight. He brought her hand to his lips and kissed it.

"Max, I love the feel of your skin."

Touch me. Pull over the truck and touch me. She tried to keep her hand from trembling against his thigh, where he held it beneath his. What do you say when a man says that to you? She had so little experience with seduction and realized too late that she was way out of her league.

"Thank you?" *Ugh. Shoot me. Please shoot me.*

"Thank you." He glanced over with a serious look, before turning his attention back to the road. "For giving me another chance."

Max knew she didn't have a chance in hell of turning him away. She wanted him more with every word he spoke. She guided him toward her apartment.

As he parked the truck, Max suddenly realized that she was taking Treat Braden to a one-bedroom apartment. The man owned resorts all over the world. She was dying inside, but there was no alternative. She couldn't magically create a glamorous house for her to call her own.

"It's nice here," Treat said. He walked around and opened Max's door for her.

She wished he'd stop being a gentleman already. It was too hard, waiting for the first kiss, the first touch. And now there he was in all his glory, standing beside her open door like a dream. Max swung her legs out and stepped onto the runner. He took her hands to help her down, and instead of stepping down, she leaned forward and settled her lips over his. His hands moved to her waist. *God, he tastes sweet.* His tongue explored her mouth slowly and sensuously. He drew her closer, until her body was against his. Without any thought, Max encircled her arms around his neck and pulled herself up, wrapping her legs around his waist.

He grasped her thighs and kicked the door closed.

She could have kissed him all night, right there under the streetlights, with her dress hiked up around her waist and a set of headlights coming right for them. *Headlights? Headlights!* Max pulled back, and sure enough, there was a car backing into the parking lot across from them.

"Oh gosh. We...I..."

He set her gently on the ground, without so much as a blush, then opened the truck door and grabbed her purse. "Perhaps we should go inside," he said.

She hurried toward her third-floor apartment, hoping to avoid whoever had seen them in the parking lot—and to get back to kissing. At the door, she closed her eyes as she fiddled with the key, praying she could get through the night without making a fool out of herself. Being in a dark room at the party, with all those people, she could almost pretend she was in a movie. But here, about to enter her apartment, she was suddenly scared shitless. She turned her back on the closed door and said, "My apartment is small."

"I like small."

"It's not glamorous. It's...utilitarian."

He put a hand on her waist. "I'm all about efficiency."

The heat beneath his hand made her stop and catch her breath. "There's nothing really fancy about it." She swallowed hard as he put his other hand on her waist and moved in closer. His breath was sweet and warm. She licked her lips, dying to taste him again.

He moved his hand to her face, then lifted her chin and tilted her head back. "Fancy is overrated," he said, covering her lips with his.

She dropped her keys and pulled him closer, thankful his hands were holding her up. Every stroke of his tongue made her melt a little further under his spell. She had never craved kissing anyone so much or enjoyed it for so long. She dug her hands beneath his thick hair and pulled him harder against her. His desire pressed against her middle, and a moan escaped her lips into his mouth.

She drew away, embarrassed. Max had never been a verbal lover. How could she be a verbal kisser? His eyes were so dark, so desirous. She reached for her keys and unlocked the door, feeling his heat behind her, driving her faster into the dark apartment.

Treat closed the door behind them, and she watched him taking in the secrets of her private living space. Surveying the small, tidy living room with one beige couch and an overstuffed chair, then skimming the bar that separated the cozy kitchen from the rest of the apartment.

"It's small, I know, but—"

"It's perfect," he whispered.

Max had had only two males in her apartment before. And she was pretty sure the Cub Scout selling popcorn with his mother didn't count. She had absolutely no idea what to do with a man like Treat in her apartment.

He must have sensed her nervousness, because he went to the bookshelves and brought the candles to the coffee table, and lit them with a silent smile. She didn't think her heart could beat any faster than it was.

"Sit next to me," he said as he took off his jacket and laid it neatly on the chair.

Max breathed a sigh of relief when he took control. She felt his presence like a torch beside her. Her nerves tensed with anticipation.

"Tell me something about yourself," he said.

She had no idea what to say. She was too inexperienced to come up with a quick, sexy answer.

"I'll start," he offered. "My favorite place in the world, besides right here on your couch this very second, is Wellfleet, Massachusetts."

"You travel all over the world and your favorite place is some Podunk town in Massachusetts?" She had to laugh, which, she had to admit, lessened the tightening of her nerves.

"Yeah, it is. I have a little house on the bay. It's quiet, nice."

He put his hand on her leg, stirring those nerves again.

"What gets your juices flowing?" she asked,

immediately realizing she deserved the amorous look he was giving her. "I mean, outside of...this."

"That's easy. My work. I get such a thrill out of taking a resort from flat to finished, making it world-renowned. Even the negotiations are exciting to me. When I walk into a room and I know that the people on the other side of the table want something I'm not willing to give, just being able to turn it around is the biggest high I've found."

"I see it in your eyes. Even now, they're so alive. That's how I feel about my job, too. It's the same. I mean, not on the same scale, but the same thrill."

He ran his finger down her cheek, and her entire body clenched with desire.

"What else?" he asked in a seductive voice.

I want to kiss you right this very second and never stop. "I love sweets. Chocolate mostly. And I hate jelly." *Jelly? I'm so lame. I'll tell you anything—just kiss me already.*

"Okay, no jelly." He smiled, resting his hand on her thigh. "My favorite color is blue," he said.

My favorite color is your hand on my body. "Lavender," she managed. "Favorite smell?" *This is not good. Smell? Kill me. Please just slit my throat and put me out of my misery.*

He cupped the back of her head with his free hand and nuzzled into her neck. She closed her eyes against the shudder his warm breath sent through her.

"Toasted almond ice cream."

"What?" It took her a minute to remember she'd

asked him a question. "Ice cream has a smell?" A hazy, horny fog had enveloped her mind, spurred on by the stirrings between her thighs.

"A delicious one," he said.

The way he said *delicious* made her lick her lips.

"Tell me something you love." He moved so close she could taste his minty breath as he spoke.

She clung to the edge of the couch, sure that if she didn't, she'd pounce on him like a lioness on her prey and devour him in ways that made her blush to think about.

"My favorite flowers are Knock Out roses." She'd never seen them in person, only in pictures.

"Knock Out roses," he whispered.

Chapter Seven

TREAT COULD hardly believe he was sitting beside Max, the woman he'd been thinking about, dreaming about, pining over, for the past six months. Her kisses were sweeter than sugar and so warm they made him ache for her. He'd wanted to take her right there in the parking lot. He had to pull it together. She was *not* a one-night stand, and if his racing heart and flaming nerves were any indication, she was destined to be so much more than any woman he'd ever been with.

He was as nervous as a teenage boy readying to feel up a girl for the first time. What on earth was causing him to lose his edge? Nerves hadn't been a part of his sex life since he was a kid, and all the talking in the world wasn't helping the throbbing reminder in his pants, which only reinforced his nervousness.

"Max." Just sitting beside her, touching her thigh, the way she looked at him with desire and embarrassment, all wrapped up into one, sped up his thrum of desire. "You're so beautiful."

She leaned in to kiss him, and he held her back gently. He needed to talk to her first. He had to apologize. Treat wasn't a man who treated women poorly. The fact that he had hurt her had been weighing heavily on him. She'd blown him off when he'd apologized, and it was a half-ass apology anyway. He hadn't taken the time to really apologize the way she deserved. He wanted—no, he needed—to explain things to her.

"Max, I want to talk to you first."

She froze beneath his touch and closed her eyes. "It's me. You don't want me again, right?"

"What? No." He grabbed her wrist as she pushed herself from the couch. "Max, that's not it at all. You're misinterpreting my hesitation." Why did he always have to sound so damned professional? Why couldn't he pour out his emotions?

Her chest rose and fell with each breath as he watched anger reach her narrowing eyes. Damn it. She was misconstruing his intentions; he could see it. *The hell with it*. He'd explain it to her later. After. When she was too tired to run away or even think.

He pulled her down onto his lap and kissed her— hard—until he felt the tension in her body ease, and she leaned in to him. *God, she feels good*. He brought his hand to her waist, and she lifted her arm around his neck. He cupped her breast, caressing her through the filmy fabric of her dress, feeling her nipple harden beneath his touch. He needed her—all of her. She arched her neck, and he kissed the edge of her jaw, the dip between her chin, then took her neck into his mouth in a long, sensuous suck that felt like it might pull the come right out of him.

She moaned, urging him, pressing her chest into his hand. He pulled her dress to the side and took her breast into his mouth, sucking, licking, as she writhed on his lap, grinding herself into him. He moved to the other side, lapping at the crest of her breast before gently teasing her nipple with the tip of his tongue. She grabbed his hair and pulled his mouth harder around her, then lifted his head away from her delicious breast and looked at him with hunger.

"Bedroom?" she said in a heady voice.

He rose with her in his arms and walked through the open bedroom door. Her bedroom was exactly what he'd envisioned, just like the rest of her organized nest. She had a simple dresser, king-sized bed, and a nightstand, all neat and tidy. The only item out of place was a single black dress hanging at the entrance to her closet. She kept her room just as organized as he did, and that only deepened his attraction to her.

"May I?" he asked before lowering her to the bed.

"Please," she answered.

He set her on the edge of the bed and removed his tie, setting it neatly on the dresser before unbuttoning his shirt.

Max reached for his pants, and he took her hand in his. "Not yet," he whispered. He folded his shirt and set it beside his tie, then brought her to her feet and turned her around. Moonlight streamed through the window, illuminating her body as he unzipped her dress and dropped the straps from her shoulders to her forearms, trapping her arms beneath. He kissed the tender skin on the back of her neck until she tensed beneath his touch. Her skin was smooth and soft beneath his lips as he kissed along the curve of her back, sliding her dress down to her waist. She was more beautiful than any woman Treat had ever been with, and it took all of his resolve to take it slow, pushing past the intoxicated rush of the innocence that softened her sexuality. Her silky stomach arched into his hands as he ran his fingers up from behind and caressed her bare breasts. She gasped as he took her nipples between his index fingers and thumbs, teasing, squeezing, until they stood erect and she moaned in pleasure—and oh, what that moan did to him. He ran his tongue along the side of her slim, delicate neck, sucking gently, licking the tender spots.

He released his hold on her dress, and it dropped to the floor. He pressed his body against hers, chest to back, skin to skin, then ran his hands down her sides and gripped her hips. When she pressed in to him, he wanted nothing more than to taste her—all of her. He kissed his way down her back, to the sensitive skin just above her panties, then ran his finger beneath the strap of her lacy thong and followed it down the front, slipping it over her damp curls. Lightly teasing the hot and sensitive flesh between her legs made him swell with desire. He pressed himself against her at the same moment he slipped his finger inside of her, drawing out another sweet moan of pleasure.

She grabbed his wrist, pushing his hand deeper into her, and he bit in to the crest of her shoulder, cupping her breast with his free hand. God, he wanted to be inside her. She arched her neck against him, and he moved his other hand down between her legs, rubbing the sweet bundle of nerves with one hand while probing her deep and slow with the other. He felt her tightening around his fingers as she gasped in quick breaths. Her body throbbed and pulsed against him as she clenched his arms, rose up on her toes, and called for him in a husky, breathless voice.

"That's it. Come for me," he whispered as she came down from her beautiful orgasm.

He turned her around, her eyes heavy with desire, and he kissed her again, probing, tasting, and devouring her, unable to get enough of her. She reached for his pants and unbuttoned them in one quick effort.

"Good Lord. Let me just look at you," he said in a deep, leg-numbing voice. She was so perfectly feminine, so contradictory to the woman who'd been standing on the car earlier, taking charge of the world before her. How could he have ever done anything to hurt her?

"Treat," she whispered. She wiggled her finger, motioning for him to come even closer; then she dropped to the edge of the bed, wearing nothing but a black lacy thong, and in the space of a second, she'd freed him from his boxer briefs and pulled his hips in close.

"Max," he said. "Let me—"

She shook her head and took him into her mouth.

MAX WAS LOST in a game of pleasure. She'd never been so open with a man before. She hardly knew him at all, but she felt so connected to him that she didn't want to turn away. The way he touched her without rushing, with total focus on pleasuring her. For once, she wanted to follow her heart. As Max took him in her mouth, she felt like she'd known him for years. His skin was salty, sweet...familiar.

He wrapped his fingers in her hair as she drew him in and out of her mouth, licking his tip in slow circles, then drawing him back in again. He groaned and pulled her head back, watching her as he drew himself away from her lips. Looking deep into her eyes, he said only one word, and the intense desire behind that word robbed her of any coherent thoughts.

"Max."

With one hand still wrapped around the width of him, and shivering with the delight of having brought him so much pleasure, Max slid out of her thong.

Treat slipped his hands under her arms and lifted her like she was as light as a feather until her legs were once again wrapped around his waist. She held on to his neck as he reached for the dresser, kissing her while he grabbed the square plastic package he must have set there and tossed it onto the bed.

He laid her on her back, his legs between hers, the

hunger in his eyes mirroring the lust racing through her body. She reached for the package and he stopped her, then covered her breasts with his hands and lowered his mouth to her hip. Max sank back into the bed and closed her eyes as he licked a path from her hip to the top of her thigh, then slid his strong hands down her ribs to her hips again. He was so strong, so masculine, and she felt small within his hands. He squeezed her hips, licking the insides of her thighs, stopping short of the heat that was ready and waiting for him, then kissed a path back up, around her curls, to the delicate skin just above. Every nerve was heightened beneath his moist kisses. Max arched her hips. *Lick me. Touch me.* He splayed his hands on her thighs and squeezed softly.

He spread her legs gently apart and licked the tender skin beside her luscious folds. Max clenched the comforter in her fists. He was drawing every nerve to the surface. She was so close—she shifted her hips, hoping to catch a flick of his tongue, but he held her leg down as he teased her, licking up and down the skin between her thigh and her sex. He rolled her over so that she was lying on her belly and took her ass in his hands, then ran his tongue in the crease above her legs. Every inch of Max's skin was on fire, almost numb. She'd never been loved so completely before, never had anyone touch every inch of her flesh. He ran his hands up the sides of her hips and ribs, then dragged his body along hers until she felt the length of him against her rear. His tongue was hot and wet on the back of her neck; his hands grasped at her hair as he moved in a slow rhythm against her. Every touch of his hands was erotic; every breath against her skin sent her pulse racing. He took her earlobe in her mouth, then whispered, "I never want this evening to end."

The combination of his moist tongue and the passion in his voice had her shuddering beneath him. He kissed down the length of her spine, squeezing her ribs gently, each pulse heightening her arousal. He kissed the flesh of her right cheek, then the backs of her thighs as he drew them apart slowly and slid his two fingers inside her again. Max sucked in a breath, arching her bottom into the air just enough to give him better access. He slid them in and out painfully slowly, lingering over the spot that made her toes curl under and her insides reach for him. In the next breath, Max was writhing beneath him, his powerful arm holding her tightly around her hips as she bucked against his hand.

She mourned the retreat of his fingers, craving more of him as he turned her back over. Max panted, trying to make her brain functional again, but she was so far gone, and he was licking, kissing, caressing her body until she thought she might burst.

"Show me how to love you," he whispered.

Max closed her eyes. She couldn't.

He ascended her body until they were eye to eye. Max could feel his hard shaft against her. God, she wanted him inside of her.

"Make love to me," she whispered.

He smiled. "Show me how you want me to love

you."

Max turned away, feeling the heat of a blush rushing up her cheeks.

He took her hand and drew it down to her center. "Show me," he said.

Max reached for him instead and pulled him close. She wanted to show him—oh, how she wanted to show him the ways she'd learned to touch herself while fantasizing about him late at night, alone in her bedroom—but she couldn't. She wouldn't. She reached for the condom again, and this time he took it from her fingers and opened it with his teeth, then slid it on.

Yes. Take me. Love me.

Max slid down, taking all of him in. His girth sent a shock through her loins. Powerless to hide her surprise, or the smile that tugged on her cheeks, she grinned like a fool in his beautiful arms, moving at a slow, even rhythm. She expected his strength to overpower her, his muscles to squeeze her too tightly as he held on. Instead, his grasp was gentle, his thrusts slow and even.

"Nothing has ever felt so right," he said. He looked directly into her eyes with an intense gaze. "Max, I'm here. I'm not going anywhere. You can trust me."

Fear crept into Max's mind. *Trust me.* This was the same man who'd made her feel dirty and cheap at the resort. *Go away. Stop.* She tried to push the awful thoughts aside. She didn't want the overwhelming sensation of being intimate with him to end. But she couldn't escape the tightening of her nerves or the memories from Nassau that were rushing into her mind, blocking her pleasure, sounding off like warning bells. She looked into his eyes, now so full of desire, but as quickly as she saw his beauty, she remembered the disgusted look cast from those dark, sensuous eyes—the one that confirmed what she'd already been feeling—that she had acted cheap and trampy. She froze beneath him, caught in a web of insatiable desire and fear.

"Max?"

She couldn't speak. She lay beneath him, staring at him. How could he be the same man who had hurt her? And yet...he was. She pushed at his chest and he jumped off her—quickly.

"Max, what is it? Did I hurt you? I tried to go slow—"

Max shook her head, pulling the covers up and covering her body. "This was a mistake." Her voice trembled. "We shouldn't have..." She pulled her knees in to her chest, would disappear if she could. "I'm sorry. I shouldn't have..."

The hurt in his eyes was all-consuming as he stood in all his masculine magnificence and pulled on his clothes, never looking away from her. "Why? What changed?"

Max turned away, her body still shuddering from his touch, her heart unwilling to let him go.

"Max, if this is about what happened at the resort, I tried to talk to you about that before we...before we came together."

Max felt her heart cracking inside her chest. She'd

felt so connected to him, so overwhelmingly happy. She wanted him like she'd never desired another man in her life, and yet he was the man who had hurt her and walked away. Just like…No. She'd promised herself she would never even think of *him* again.

She stood and pulled a T-shirt from her drawer, then went into the bathroom and washed up, hoping he would leave.

When she came back out, he was sitting in the living room, fully dressed, his elbows resting on his knees, his face in his hands. He stood when she came into the room.

"Max, please. Let's talk about this."

"Can you take me to get my car please?" *Damn it.* Why hadn't she driven separately? She'd been too hung up in the moment of being with a man like Treat. What an idiot she was. The last thing she wanted was to be trapped in a truck with him for twenty minutes, but she was expected at the festival early tomorrow morning, and she had no one else to take her. She never should have allowed herself the fantasy of waking up in his arms, or forgetting—even for a moment—how he'd made her feel in Nassau.

She grabbed her keys and purse, and he followed her down to his SUV. She cringed when he opened the door for her, then waited until she stepped in and closed the door gently. She could do with some door slamming, yelling, loud music, anything to release the tension, anger, and loneliness that ate away at her insides.

"Max, can we at least talk?"

Max stared out the window. She didn't want to hear his excuses. She'd heard enough excuses for a lifetime.

"If you won't talk, will you at least listen? Please?"

When she didn't respond, he continued. "When I first saw you at the resort, I felt something. I don't know what it was exactly, but it scared me."

Max laughed under her breath. *Scared you? You expect me to believe that? A man like you?*

"I didn't know what to do with my instant attraction to you. I mean, I've been attracted to women before, but with you it was different. I wanted to take care of you. I wanted to lo—"

Max closed her eyes. There was no way he was going to say *love you*. No. No way possible. Maybe *look into your eyes*, but not *love you*.

"I had never felt anything so powerful. Then, before I had a chance to even process what I was feeling, or why, there you were, in the same clothes as the night before, when you were with…I can't even say his name it makes me so mad."

"You have no right to be mad about anything I do," Max snapped. Though a little piece of her was secretly flattered. She couldn't remember the last time a man had noticed her in that way.

"You're right, and I knew it then." His voice took on a shamed, soft tone. "When I looked at you."

Max winced, feeling the pain all over again from that one degrading look. Thankfully, he pulled into the parking lot and she climbed from the truck, keys in hand.

"Max."

"Listen. All I want to do right now is bury my face in a big chocolate cake and forget tonight ever happened." She took one last long look at him and turned away, trying to keep her splintering heart from shattering.

Chapter Eight

TREAT'S CELL PHONE rang at eight o'clock the next morning. He fumbled with it, hoping it was Max, and answered without looking at the number. "Hello?"

"Since when do you leave your little sister at a party?"

Savannah. "You had Hugh to drive you home."

"Hugh? Hugh! Hugh was too busy with supernova to even think about me. Lucky for you, Connor's driver was free." Savannah was trying to sound annoyed, but Treat knew her better than that. She was really fishing for information.

"Honey, I'm sorry about last night. I just went to sleep a few hours ago. Can I call you later?"

"So? How did it go with Max? I saw you two leaving looking at each other like you couldn't wait to eat each other alive."

"Nice talk from my baby sister," Treat said with a

smile. He draped his arm over his eyes and sighed. "I gotta go, Savannah. Love you." As always, he waited for her to say goodbye. No matter how mad Treat was at any of his siblings, he never hung up on them. His mother's death had been a painful reminder that he never knew just when he'd see or talk to them for the last time.

His bedroom door swung open. "Hey, asshole. You gonna get up and help Dad today or what?" Despite his harsh words, Rex was smiling.

"Rex? What the hell?"

"Just sayin'." Rex left the door open, his obnoxious way of saying, *If I'm not resting, neither are you.*

Treat pulled his exhausted body from the bed and trudged across the room to the bathroom. He'd taken that short walk a million times before, and never had it felt so lonely. He leaned over the sink and looked at himself in the mirror—really looked at himself. The dark eyes, tousled hair, and perfectly golden tan had always served him well with women. Treat knew what he looked like compared to most men. He appreciated the genes he and his siblings had been blessed with, and even though he appreciated it, he acknowledged the fact that he'd abused that gift for a very long time. Now, as he struggled to look past the beautiful exterior, to see what Max had seen, he found that he didn't have to dig very deep. He saw the jealous, scared man who had given her a look of revulsion. He'd been aware of the look even as it settled onto his face like a mask. He'd known the hurt it would cause, and he'd still let it come through.

I'm an asshole.

A prick.

A goddamned chickenshit.

He turned on the shower, waiting until it was steaming hot to step in. The water singed his skin, and he made no effort to cool the temperature. He wasn't a kid anymore. He knew better than to do things that might hurt a person's feelings, and the look he'd given Max in Nassau was hurtful and wrong. He knew what that look had said to her, and yet he'd still cast it in her direction. She'd given him that hurt right back on the boat—and he'd deserved it. *I was an inconsiderate tool. The kind of man I would never spend time with.* No wonder Max didn't want to, either. He was pushing forty, and he understood how doing something like that brought shame on the family, even if they weren't aware of what he'd done. He knew that no matter what, Max would always wonder if the rest of his family possessed the same asshole component that he did.

What had he been thinking last night? He never should have let things get so far without talking to her first. He'd known that, damn it. He'd known it then, but he'd let their desires lead the path. He'd never have done that with his career. You lead with your mind, not anything else. It figured that the one time he got it wrong was the one time that it mattered.

He dried himself off and looked down at his groin. *Troublemaker.* From that moment forward, he was going to do everything he could to right his wrong. He had to make things right. He had to tell Max how his heart had never felt as full as when he was with her. Hell, just looking at her, he knew he was falling in a way he'd never fallen before. How ridiculous was that? And yet it wasn't ridiculous at all. It was the most important thing that had ever happened to him.

HE FOUND REX at the stables, looking over Hope, the horse his father had bought for his mother when she'd first found out she was sick. In recent years, Hope's red hair had faded and white sprouted thickly among the lightened patches.

"The prince walks," Rex teased. He wore a black shirt, stretched tight across his massive chest. Rex wore his hair longer than his brothers, down to his collar, and with his cowboy hat pulled low, accentuating the sharp angles of his jaw and Grecian nose, he was even more striking.

"Good morning to you, too, brother dear." Treat ran his hand along Hope's back. She neighed, nuzzling her nose into his chest. "How is the old girl?"

"She's holding up okay, but she's slowing down," his father said.

Treat hadn't seen his father bending down by a bucket in the stall.

"She's thirty-three next January. I'm just keeping an eye on her. I never like our animals to suffer, and Hope here..."

His father didn't have to finish the sentence—*was your mother's.* Treat and Rex exchanged a sorrowful glance.

"You've done well by her, Dad. Mom would be proud." Treat laid a hand on his father's shoulder.

"I know she is," his father said. His father swore he still felt their mother's presence around the ranch, and though Treat had never felt her—not for a lack of trying—he believed his father did.

He remembered sitting in his room as a child, night after night, praying he'd feel whatever his father had felt, hoping against all hope, making promises with God. *I'll be good. I'll never fight with my brothers again. I'll help Dad forever. I'll do whatever you want, just please, please let me feel Mom one more time.* His prayers had gone unanswered, and now, as he thought of how painful all those early years without his mother had been—and how much he missed Max after just a few hours—he understood how devastated his father must have been.

"Dad, would you mind telling me about when you and Mom met?" Treat watched his father's eyes light up, and he caught that light and held on to it to lift his own spirits.

"Here we go," Rex said. "I'm gonna take Johnny Boy out for a quick ride while you two relive the good old days." Rex headed for Johnny Boy's stall.

Rex always escaped when they talked about their mother, and Treat was glad to have his father to himself. Now he could talk to him man-to-man.

"Your mother was so beautiful, sitting on her daddy's fence, watching the horses, when my father and

I drove up. I swear, Treat, when she turned and looked at me, something inside me fell into place. Even at fourteen, I knew she was the woman I was going to marry. I just didn't know how to convince her of it." He continued, reliving the stories that Treat had heard a hundred times before. His mother's mother was Brazilian, her father a Colorado rancher. His father liked to remind him that his mother had gotten all of the beauty of her mother with the stubbornness of her father. "But her heart..." His father looked up and away, as though he could see her standing in the distance. "Her heart was as sensitive as a newborn bird. The wrong word, the wrong look, and that bullheadedness that had angered you a minute before would wash away as quick as rain makes mud. And just like that, you'd crush her spirit."

Just like Max. "What did you do then?"

His father looked at him for a long time before he responded. Treat fidgeted under his gaze.

"Son, I did everything I could; that's what I did. There was nothing I wouldn't have done for her. My ego didn't exist when it came to your mother, and Lord knows she knew it, too." He laughed under his breath. "I swear that woman used it to her advantage."

Treat was too busy mulling over what his father had said to respond.

His father stood and set a hand on his shoulder. "You wanna talk about her?"

"Mom?"

He shook his head. "The woman who's got my son

so tied up in knots that he's coming to his daddy for relationship advice."

"Dad."

His father shook his head. "Don't deny it, son. I've been there, done that. Ain't no use pretending that noose around your heart doesn't tighten every time you see whoever this woman is."

Family knows no boundaries. Treat was already formulating his plan. Every time he thought of Max, he had that feeling—the same one his father described—and he'd be damned if he was going to ignore it.

Chapter Nine

IT WASN'T UNTIL Max stopped to buy coffee on her way to the festival that she realized she'd left her purse in Treat's vehicle. After she'd gone back to her apartment and changed the sheets, she'd tried to sleep, but every time she closed her eyes, she saw Treat's eyes looking back at her with so much emotion that it sent her running from her bedroom to the couch, where she'd tossed and turned all night.

When she got to the office, Max consumed enough caffeine to hold her through the morning. Now her stomach was growling as loud as could be as she sat across from Chaz going over figures from the day before. The second day of the festival always ran a little smoother than the first. The staff was used to the procedures, and Max wasn't called every ten minutes to handle an issue. She was always amazed at how much more responsibility the staff could handle after a single day of being thrown feetfirst into the fire, and she was thankful for the breathing room.

"Wanna stop for lunch?" Chaz asked.

"No. I'm fine." *All these numbers are blurring together, and I see Treat on every page.*

He closed the ledger and stood. "Nonsense. We've been at it all morning. Come on. We'll go to Kale's and grab a bite."

She pushed herself to her feet with a sigh.

"What's up with you today? I don't think I've ever seen you this tired."

I was this tired the two weeks after your wedding, but you were on your honeymoon. "I just didn't sleep very well last night." *Or at all.*

"Stay too late at the party?" Chaz held the door open for her.

She shrugged, avoiding real communication. They were graced with another warm afternoon, and Max knew that the beauty of the day was lost on her sour mood. She couldn't think past what she'd felt for Treat the night before. She'd never initiated touching a man like she had with him, and oddly, she wasn't embarrassed or ashamed by her actions. She'd *wanted* to do it—and *that* was the only thing that gave her pause. *That* was the buffer of the hurt he'd caused her in Nassau. What exactly *that* was, she couldn't nail down.

At the restaurant, she picked at her salad while Chaz caught her up on all of the new things the twins had been learning.

Max's phone vibrated, and she froze.

"Aren't you going to check that?" Chaz asked.

"No."

"Okay, Max, spill it. You always check your phone. What is it that you always tell me?" He looked up, thinking.

"If someone takes the time to text, you damned well better be kind enough to check it."

"Right," he said. "That's it. I seem to remember you drilling that into my head a few years ago."

"Yeah, well, I didn't do a very good job, considering that I had to remind you about what I'd said."

Chaz's phone vibrated. "Great, it's probably an issue. Maybe our earpieces aren't working?" He checked his text.

She turned on her microphone and spoke to one of the staff members, then turned it off again. "Radio's fine."

"This is from Kaylie, and I'm reading this word for word. *Something must be wrong with Max. Not answering my texts. Check pls.* So, don't tell me I'm reading you wrong."

His cocky smile was too much for Max to try to dissuade. She was too exhausted to argue about if her head was or wasn't on straight today. It wasn't. And she blamed Treat.

"I'm gonna go back to the office. I'm just tired; that's all. Thanks for lunch."

"Okay," he said hesitantly. "Max, is there anything I can do?"

She shook her head and took a step, then turned

back. "Sure. Have them wrap my salad. Maybe I'll eat it for dinner." *Alone, while I sulk.*

She was responding to her text from Kaylie when her earpiece buzzed.

"Yeah?"

"Max, got a guy down here says he's looking for you."

She checked her watch. The deliveries weren't supposed to come for another hour. "Patron, delivery, or sponsor?"

"Hold on."

She heard a muffled conversation that she couldn't make out.

"He says none of the above."

Max stopped walking. *Treat.* "Um, is he really tall?" She held her breath. *Please say no. No, please say yes. Oh God. Don't say anything. Just let him go away.*

"Freakishly."

She closed her eyes as her heart raced, and every nerve in her body pulsed with the memory of his touch.

"Max?"

She touched the earpiece. "Yeah, I'm here. I'm busy. Send him away." Then she remembered her purse. *Damn it.* She needed her purse. "Hey, does he have my purse?" she asked.

"No. Hands are empty."

Confused, she headed for the office. "Send him away." *Where's my damned purse? Why doesn't he have it? What's he doing if he's not here to give me my purse?* She clicked off the earpiece and read Kaylie's text again.

How was hottie?

Didn't end up seeing him, she texted back. Out of sight, out of mind. If she was going to make it through the foreseeable future, that's what she'd have to strive for.

THE AFTERNOON DRAGGED by in slow motion, with each issue taking twice as long as the last. By dinnertime, Max was exhausted, hungry, and in worse mental shape than she could ever remember experiencing. *Is this what liking and hating a man at the same time feels like?*

She tried to eat her leftover salad, but even the sight of it turned her stomach. She guzzled more coffee and decided to duck into a theater for a few minutes. Maybe she could close her eyes and no one would notice. The minute her butt hit the only available seat in the theater, her earpiece buzzed. She hauled herself back out into the cool evening air.

"Yeah?"

"Max? Delivery for you."

"I'm not expecting any deliveries. Who's the vendor?" She walked to the fence at the edge of the property and stared into the rear lot. There were no delivery trucks.

"Forget it, Max. I'll have someone run it up to the office."

"Thanks."

Chaz was texting when Max entered the office. She relaxed into the couch. Her head fell back and she closed her eyes. Chaz's phone buzzed three times in quick succession.

"Text fight?" she asked.

Chaz sighed. "No." He responded to the texts, and his phone continued to buzz several times in a row.

She lifted her head and opened her eyes. "Anything I can do?" she asked.

He finally put the phone down on his desk and looked at her. "Max, we're so slow tonight. Why don't you take off?"

She snapped to attention. "What?"

"You heard me. Just take off early. We've got this covered."

Adrenaline drove her to the edge of his desk. "What's going on? I've never left a festival early, and you know we're anything but slow tonight." Max rubbed her temples. "You know you can't handle it without me, either. So what the hell is going on?"

"You're exhausted," he said.

"Yeah, so? I'm tired, so what? I can still do my job. Look, I'm sorry if I overstepped my boundaries by being so worn out. I take full responsibility, but there's no reason to make me leave early." *Shit. I'd better pull it together.*

When he didn't respond, she said, "I love my job, Chaz. Have I done something wrong?"

"Relax. No. Even when you're tired, you do twice the work of anyone else."

Max felt unexpected tears pushing at her eyes. "Then what is it? Why do you need to get rid of me?"

There was a knock at the door, and Max moved to answer it. "Hi, Mark. What's up?"

Mark was one of the temporary festival staffers. He carried an enormous white box into the office and set it on the table.

"Just got this delivery," he said on his way back out the door.

"Were you expecting something?" Chaz asked.

She shook her head and lifted the lid. The smell itself was enough to send her stomach into a flurry of desire—and not the sexual kind. Chaz hovered over her shoulder.

"Sponsor?" he asked.

"Probably," she said, then dipped her finger into the thick chocolate frosting and licked it off. She removed the card that was taped to the inside of the box and opened it. "Maybe it's from Café Deluxe, that new bakery sponsor. Oh my God, that's delicious."

She arched a brow while she read the card aloud while grinning.

"Max, I hope this helps ease the pain I've caused you. Dive right in..." Max lowered the note, unable to control her slack jaw or the rush of her pulse. *Treat.* She snapped the card shut as a flush warmed her cheeks.

"O-kay, then. Someone did something wrong," Chaz said. "It must have been an awfully bad thing to send you a cake big enough to feed an army."

I said I wanted to bury my face in chocolate cake. Damn it. Why do you have to make this so hard? She closed the top of the box. "Why don't you take it home to Kaylie and the kids?"

"Max." Chaz shook his head. "I think that whoever sent this probably meant for you to have it. That's not a cheap cake."

"It's okay. He can afford it. He eats cake like this for breakfast." *And women like me for dinner.*

Chapter Ten

TREAT HADN'T EATEN all day. He wasn't surprised when Max refused to see him, but he wasn't going to give up on them that easily. If nothing else, if she wouldn't let him into her life, then at least she could let him really talk with her about his feelings and allow him to try and explain himself more effectively.

He hoped the cake might sweeten her up just a little and bring that thick wall she'd erected between them down just long enough for her to listen, and to understand, even if only a little, to what he had to say. After talking with his father today, Treat was even more convinced that what he was feeling for Max was far bigger than like and was bordering on the one thing he'd tried to avoid his whole life.

When he wasn't trying to figure out how to make her listen, he was telling himself that it was okay to get close to her. That if he fell for her, she wouldn't die like his mother had. But even as he repeatedly tried to convince himself that the fear was unfounded, he never really quite believed it.

After all but the last two cars pulled out of the parking lot and the interior festival lights went dark, Treat waited in the cover of night for the back gates to open one last time.

His pulse raced when he saw her walking beneath the glow of the lighted gate beside Chaz. Her shoulders were rounded forward, as though they were too heavy for her sexy little frame to support. Treat had the urge to run and swoop her into his arms, for her head to rest against his chest while he held her, safe and warm. Chaz carried the enormous cake box that Treat had sent, and when Chaz went to his car without giving the cake back to Max, his gut clenched.

Treat went to Max's driver's side door and knocked on the window, startling her into a scream.

Seconds later, Chaz was running for him. Treat held his hands up. "Chaz, it's me, Treat. I didn't mean to startle her."

"Treat? What are you..."

He watched understanding dawn on Chaz, while embarrassment consumed Max and caused her to cover her face with her hands.

"I'm sorry. I'm so sorry. I just wanted to talk to Max, and I didn't want to interrupt her at work," Treat explained.

Chaz looked at Max. "Max?"

"It's fine," she answered.

Chaz turned his back and leaned closer to Treat. "The cake? Impressive. Kaylie asked me to get Max to leave early for you. I tried, but you know Max."

I hope to get to know her even better.

"Thank you. Sorry I had Kaylie try to get her outside for a bit," Treat said, though he wasn't really sorry.

Chaz nodded. "Pretty damned romantic. You realize you're setting the bar pretty high for us normal guys, right?"

Treat smiled. He watched Chaz drive away, and a minute later, Max got out of her car. "You scared the crap out of me," she said.

"I know. I wasn't thinking."

She crossed her arms, and he couldn't help but smile at the way she was so obviously steeling herself against him. Chinking that wall into place.

"Do you have my purse?" Her clipped words and crossed arms contrasted sharply against the hurt in her eyes.

"I do," he said.

When he didn't move, she said, "Well? Can I have it?"

"Oh, yeah, of course." How could he have forgotten? He retrieved the purse, and as she climbed back into her car, Treat gently touched her arm. "Max, all I want to do is talk. Nothing else. Please. I think I owe you that much."

"You owe me that much? Isn't that a little arrogant?" she asked.

"I thought it was better than saying *you* owed me

anything at all, which you don't." He saw her resolve soften. "Please? Just take a walk with me? I'll keep my hands to myself. I won't let us get caught up in any hanky-panky."

She stepped from the car with a reluctant sigh. "Hanky-panky? I haven't heard that since I was twelve."

"Maybe you're hanging out with the wrong crowd?" Relieved that she'd at least stepped from the car, he offered her his arm.

She shoved her hands deep into her pockets. "Where would you like to walk?"

Her refusal of his arm stung. She didn't even want to touch him? At all? That was a very bad sign. But at least they were walking, and that was a start.

WHY HAD SHE agreed to a walk? Now that they were alone, all she could think about was how he smelled like sweet masculinity. Before last night, she'd never smelled the cologne he was wearing, and she knew that if she ever smelled it on someone else, there was no way it would smell as delicious as he did at that moment.

Oh, dear God. Focus. He's still the guy who hurt me.

And sent me a cake.

And waited for me in the dark.

His nervousness infiltrated the silence like another person between them.

"Was Savannah mad that you left last night?" Max asked.

"Not really. But she will be mad now. She called this

morning, and I forgot to call her back. Do you mind if I just send her a quick text?"

Rather than finding fault that he hadn't called her back, she admired his dedication to his family. "No, go ahead."

He did, and as he texted her, his lips rose to a smile.

"You really love your family, don't you?"

"Sure. Don't you?" he asked as he put his phone in his pocket.

"Yeah, I guess. But I don't have any siblings." *Why am I telling you about my family? Focus, Max.*

"I can't even imagine life without them. My mom died when I was eleven, after being sick for years, and afterward, I tried to step into her shoes and take care of them, but I never really pulled it off."

Her resolve chipped away as she imagined him as a little boy, crushed by the death of his mother and trying to be strong for his brothers and sister.

He continued in a solemn voice. "I mean, I protected them, which was easy. I'm big, so people didn't mess with them too much, but I couldn't be Mom." He shook his head. "I couldn't even come close."

They walked along the street that led to town. Goose bumps rose on Max's arms, and she wished she'd grabbed her jacket from the car.

"I'm sure they appreciated all that you were able to do," she offered.

"You know, that's just it. After years of hoping and praying that she'd be okay, I was so broken by her death that I really didn't do much. I think I let them down, and when it was time to go away to college, I was kind of relieved to get out from under all that guilt."

His emotions were so raw, as if he'd just experienced leaving his family yesterday instead of years earlier. Max couldn't stifle the urge to comfort him. He smiled as she wrapped her arm into his.

"I've never told anyone that before."

"No?" *He trusts me. I wish I could trust him.*

He shook his head. "It feels good to tell you. I want to tell you." He looked down at her and she was drawn into the sincere and hopeful way he looked at her.

She felt like metal, and he was the magnet, but as she felt his legs stop walking, it was too much. Her determination was fading, and she needed to hang on to it so that she didn't make the same mistake twice. She drew her eyes back to the sidewalk and broke the connection. Her rapid pulse, however, didn't take the hint.

"Everyone expected me to help Dad run the ranch, and as much as I wanted to help him, it would mean reliving those memories—the memories of what I couldn't do—and that was too much for me."

"I'm sure your family understands," she said.

"No. I never told them. I still haven't. I can't. I'm too ashamed."

There it was again, another crushing blow to her resolve. What man admitted to being ashamed of anything, much less something so intimate?

"I don't think I ever did more than any other older sibling does. I let them crawl into my bed at night. I listened when they cried. I told them everything would be okay. You know, normal stuff."

It was after midnight, and because of the festival, the restaurants and cafés were still open. Max paused, taking in the sparkling lights that glistened through the large windows along the sidewalk and the sound of music that filtered out of the restaurant doors, soaking in the romantic feel of the little town as she listened to Treat.

"I wish I had a brother to listen when I cried when I was younger. I would have done anything to have someone to confide in," she admitted. "I still wish I did."

"You have Kaylie," he said, then winced.

"Yeah, I do." She'd almost forgotten that he'd met Kaylie and the rest of the wedding party in Nassau.

"I have to confess, I called Blake to ask for advice about reaching you, and he gave me Kaylie's number. He said that if anyone could reach you, it would be her. It was Kaylie's idea to try to get you to come outside...for me."

Kaylie? Chaz's texts. Ugh, how embarrassing.

"You called her?" She didn't know if she should be flattered that he'd go to such an extent or angry that he'd put his nose into her personal business.

"I did," he said with a straight face.

When she smiled, he did as well.

"I'm sorry. I just wanted to talk to you," he said honestly.

"How long were you waiting outside the festival?"

"Since you wouldn't see me when I brought the

cake."

"Oh, my God. You've been waiting since dinnertime?" *Flattered. Definitely flattered.*

"Kaylie called and said that Chaz couldn't get you to leave early, so…"

Is there anything he won't do? She had trouble deciding if that was good or bad.

Max's stomach growled.

"Wanna grab a bite?" he asked. "I haven't eaten all day, and you're obviously hungry."

Max was surprised to realize that she no longer felt sick to her stomach. "Yes, I'd like that." *Way to stand your ground.*

They sat in the back of a little Italian restaurant. Max scanned the menu. Although she was hungry, she knew she wouldn't be able to eat a whole meal while butterflies were tap dancing in her stomach, not to mention how late it was. When she'd tried to share a meal with…the guy she refused to think about…he'd called her cheap and gross. She'd never again asked another man to share.

"It's late. Would you like to share a dish instead of getting two whole meals?"

She looked up at him incredulously. *How could he possibly know?*

"I'm sorry. Are you not a sharer? I forget that some people don't like to eat off of other people's plates."

Damn him. Chalk that up to one more thing to like about him. "No. I love to share. I just…Most guys hate to share food. Why don't you choose? I'm no good at making food decisions," she admitted.

"Most women don't like men to order for them, either."

His smile held so much contentedness that Max almost reached for his hand. Instead, she put her hands in her lap. After what happened last night, she wasn't taking any chances. She'd listen to his explanation, thank him for the meal, and then go home to bed. Alone. Really.

TREAT HAD NEVER felt as relaxed during a meal as he did with Max right then. They each had a glass of wine, and they laughed about the size of the cake he'd sent her.

"I have to admit, no one's ever sent me an enormous chocolate cake before," she said.

He knew she was being careful with what she said and how she said it. He couldn't ignore the tension running across her shoulders each time their forks clinked on their shared plate, and she pulled back, as if she'd just realized that they were getting too close. But there was no denying that she was opening up to him, which meant her heart might be receptive, too.

He bided his time as long as he was able, in case she heard what he had to say and decided to bolt. He knew from last night that the possibility was as real as the food they'd just shared. He asked the waiter for two more glasses of wine, but not without first asking Max.

"Yes, thank you," she'd answered with a tentative smile.

"May I?" he asked, moving the candle and the condiments from the center of the table so that the space between them was clear. *The fewer obstacles, the better.*

"I don't want to spoil a wonderful evening, but I have been thinking about you all day. Hell, I've been thinking about you for six months, seven days, and I have no idea how many hours." He watched her eyebrows rise in surprise. "Max, the last thing I want is for you to misread me."

"I don't think I misread you," she said with a shake of her head.

"No, you didn't. I wanted to be the guy you were with, and when I saw you in Nassau and knew you'd spent the night with that other guy, I realized I'd lost my chance. You saw an ugly, jealous, petty side of me that I don't think has ever reared its ugly head." He ran a hand through his thick hair, thinking of the condescending look he'd given her when he'd seen her wearing the same clothes she'd had on the night before, her cheeks flushed, her hair tousled. Just the thought of it made jealousy simmer within him again. "That's not true. There was one time in college when my brother Dane slept with my girlfriend. I probably shared that look then, too."

She didn't respond.

"But I wasn't your boyfriend," he said, knowing he'd read her silence perfectly.

"Exactly." She nodded.

Her walls were going up again, and he had to slip in

before they reached the top. He feared he'd never have another chance.

"I had no claim to you, and I did the wrong thing. I let my pain guide me, and I never should have. I've regretted it ever since the very second I saw the hurt in your eyes. There's no excuse. I was wrong. I didn't know what to do with the magnitude of emotions that I was feeling. Max, I have never been in love before."

She narrowed her eyes.

"I've never been in love," he corrected himself. "So I didn't understand what I felt when I saw you."

"You didn't even know me," she said in almost a whisper.

"No. I didn't."

"I could have been a nasty, awful, devious person."

"Yes, you could have," he admitted.

"I could have been a gold digger and convinced you to spend all sorts of money on me."

He raised his brows and smiled. "I hadn't thought of that, but yes, you could have."

She narrowed her eyes and lowered her voice. "So how can you compare what you felt—lust, desire, whatever—with love?"

The look on her face pained him. Her eyes pleaded, *Love me!* while her contentious tone screamed, *Liar!*

Treat did the one thing he knew was right and the only thing he wanted to do. He told the truth. "I have spent my entire life afraid to fall in love. I assumed that, like with my mother, when you love someone too much, God takes them away. It sounds stupid when I say it aloud, and cognitively, I know that I worry because I was so young when I lost my mother and spent many years watching my father grieve for her. Hell, he's still grieving for her. But, Max, even though I know it sounds irrational, it's true, and now I'm trying to push this fear I've lived with for so long aside, and it's scary and empowering all at the same time."

He waited for her to respond. Every passing second was excruciating. Every passing minute confirmed her disbelief. He didn't know what else to do but to continue.

"Whatever I felt when I saw you, it brought the belief right up to the surface again, and in my head I thought, *Don't get close to her. Something will happen to one of you.*"

Max stared, her mouth slightly parted, her face a blank slate. The pleading and screaming was gone from her eyes.

"Max?"

She finished her wine.

She doesn't believe me. I've lost any chance I had.

"Max, are you gonna say anything?"

The waiter came by with the check, and Treat was thankful for a distraction from the tension of his looming confession. He paid the waiter quickly while his mind ticked off seconds as if they were inches—each one drawing Max further away from him.

"Thank you for telling me."

Chapter Eleven

MAX BANGED HER head on the steering wheel. *Thanks for telling me? What the hell was I thinking?* He'd poured out his heart to her and she'd thrown away his raw emotions like they'd meant nothing. Didn't she believe him? She pondered the thought, replaying the evening in her mind. She'd seen his eyes change in the restaurant, heard the vulnerability in his voice. She hadn't even meant to say *Thank you for telling me.* She didn't know why she'd said it. All she remembered was trying to keep herself from admitting to him how hurt she'd been by...that guy. She didn't want to have to try to explain how someone else had called her names and that she'd stayed with him anyway. Sure, she was much younger then and she should have gotten past it, but the hurt had cut her to the core, and that flash of a look from Treat had come with the same sharp edge.

She'd believed every word he said as he poured his

heart out on the table for her to see. And then she'd broken him. She'd goddamn broken him. She saw it in the way he walked with his arms closer to his body, his pace quicker than on their way into town. She knew it from the silence that separated them like a barrier. And if she had to do it all over again, she might just do it again, because she was broken, too.

She pulled into the apartment complex and her cell phone vibrated with an incoming text. This time she picked it up quickly, hoping it was Treat.

So? Everything okay?

Kaylie. She debated not texting back as she walked toward the stairs, but the words that Chaz had parroted back to her floated into her mind. She stopped walking and texted, *Nope. Couldn't B worse. Going 2 bed. Alone.*

She climbed the steps feeling twice as exhausted as she had ten minutes earlier. Her phone vibrated again. She stopped on the second floor to read the text.

Sorry. Want me 2 come over?

She smiled, wishing she hadn't given away the chocolate cake. A sweets coma might just make her feel better. She texted, *I'm okay. Thx tho.*

A small gift bag hung from her apartment doorknob.

"I was coming to get that."

Max jumped. "Jesus, Treat. You scared the shit out of me again." She put her hand over her heart and leaned against the wall, trying to calm her racing heart.

"I'm truly sorry. I thought I could beat you here." He reached for the bag.

"What's in that?"

"Nothing. It was stupid," he answered.

Standing close to him again brought a different kind of rush through her body. She reached for the bag, brushing his hand. He glanced down, as if longing for the touch, then released the bag to Max.

She peered inside and removed two envelopes. She looked up at him.

"I'm gonna go." He held her gaze and reached out, gently touching her cheek in a way that sent a million naughty thoughts through her mind, chased by one overwhelming feeling that was bigger than anything she'd ever felt.

"Goodbye, Max."

She watched him descend the stairs, and when his footsteps faded into the night, she opened the small envelope marked "1" and read the handwritten note.

Dearest Max,

If I chicken out tonight and do not tell you why I was such an ass in Nassau, just read the other note. If I do tell you, toss the bag away and kiss me.

Yours, Treat

She smiled. He had told her. *Toss the bag away and kiss me.* She looked at the empty stairwell, then quickly tore open the other envelope with trembling hands. *Hurry! Hurry!* Her heart pushed her to move faster.

Dearest Max,

I never believed in love at first sight until I met you, and it scared me so badly that I didn't have a clue about what to do. I'm sorry, Max. I wanted to take care of you, but if I've failed you, I'll leave you alone to heal.

Love, Treat.

She pressed the notes to her heart and opened the door. She thought about chasing after him, but she'd made a mistake once, and her heart wasn't ready. She had to be sure this time. Her mind was dancing with happiness as she read and reread the note over and over during the next two hours as she lay on her bed thinking of the evening and letting the words in his note sink in. Every hour that passed brought more surety. Treat had gone to great lengths, romantic lengths, to let her know how he felt, and she'd been cold. As her heart opened to him, she thought of how she'd apologize for the way she left things. *Thank you for telling me.* Sure, she hadn't handled things well in the restaurant, but wouldn't he understand? Any man who could reveal such personal turmoil would certainly understand being wounded by a past love.

Max fell asleep with the letters in her hands.

Chapter Twelve

SAYING GOODBYE TO his father would be the hardest part of the evening. Even harder than accepting that he would never set eyes on Max again.

"I've been waiting up for you, son," his father said. "Figured you might need to talk."

Treat told his father everything. Every sordid detail, from the way he'd made Max feel that night in Nassau to the intimacy they'd shared and the way they were torn apart by her memory of his hurtful actions. He told his father about the cake, the walk, and the feelings that had taken him off guard and left him floundering—and he told his father about the fear he'd secretly carried his whole life.

Hal Braden wasn't a man who talked just to hear his own voice. He chose his words carefully and rarely doled out unsolicited advice to his children. So when he asked Treat to listen carefully, Treat did just that.

"Treat, I've been waiting for you to figure out what was holding your heart back all these years. For a while, I wasn't sure if it was something I did when you were growing up. I did my best, but being both mother and father had its trying times. Then I worried that maybe you just hadn't met the right woman yet. But when I looked into your eyes earlier today, I saw the fear in them. And I saw the love, too. I knew that what I'd worried about for so long was true. Son, your mama didn't die because of our love for each other. Surely you know that."

Treat felt something on his cheek and wiped it away. *A tear.* He nodded, unable to form a response.

"This life we're given is so short. It'll be gone before you know it and, son, you're a good man. You're a loving, kind, generous man with so much more to give than flashy resorts. Always have been. Just because you allow yourself to love doesn't mean that some higher power will steal that person away from you—or steal you away from her. If you don't allow yourself to love, to fully saturate yourself with someone else's life, someone else's feelings, if you don't allow your ego to disappear and your heart to beat *for* another person, so that every breath you take is taken *for* that person, well, then, I'm afraid you'll be missing out on one of life's only blessings. And besides your family and giving life to children, it's the only blessing that really matters."

His father handed him a small velvet bag. Treat knew what it contained. He could feel the circle within his fingers.

"She wanted you to have this, and somehow, today, she knew it was the right time."

"Dad," Treat said with a tinge of disbelief mixed with pity for his father's constant belief that his mother continued to speak to him even after her death.

"It's yours, son, to do with as you wish. I'm just doing what I'm told."

FOR THE SECOND time in less than a week, Treat tossed aside his worries about flashing his wealth and chartered a small private plane. He wasn't ready to go back to Nassau—not nearly ready. He didn't know if he'd ever be ready. He had to go someplace that didn't remind him of Max, even though he knew that anytime he sat in a restaurant—any restaurant—he'd always see her beautiful face staring back at him. If ever he was to touch another woman—who was he kidding? There would be no other woman for a very, very long time. He wondered how he'd ever gone from one woman's bed to the next like he was changing his socks. The thought sickened him.

As the plane touched down, he reiterated his promise to himself not to get in touch with Max. Why make things any more difficult for her? She deserved a relationship that was right from the get-go, not some guy who screwed up so badly that it hurt her to look at him.

It took some finagling to get a car at that hour, but where there was money, there was always a way. The streets were crowded, which surprised him. October in

New England wasn't exactly high season for tourists. The sun came up as he drove the rental car down a dirt road on a narrow strip that led to the bay. He rounded the last curve slowly, avoiding the enormous rosebush that he continually forgot to ask the gardener to trim back. He stopped the car. *Knock Out roses. Max's favorite flowers.* Sadness tugged at his heart. A second later, the bungalow came into view and Treat let out a long, relieved sigh.

He breathed in the salty air. It had been too long since he'd last been to the Cape. He pulled his bags from his trunk and headed for the front door. Smitty, the caretaker who had been watching over the house since Treat purchased it eight years earlier, had known Treat's mother, and he'd always had an affinity toward Treat. Treat felt guilty for calling him at such a crazy hour to prepare the bungalow for his arrival, but he paid him handsomely for his trouble.

He smiled at the weathered cedar shingles. The Cape had been one of his mother's favorite places. They'd visited a few times, before she was too sick to travel, and each time he arrived at the little cottage, the very things that used to make her smile brought the same joy to him. He'd bought the place from the owners who had rented it to his family each of those times they'd visited.

He could almost hear her sweet voice as he unlocked the door and stepped inside. *Oh, Treaty, look! The shingles have weathered. Don't you just love the graying and the texture of them?* She'd shake her head and tell him how she loved a house where each of the pieces that held it together was different from the rest.

The curtains whipped around the open encasement windows. He could count on Smitty to do just as he'd asked. He stood in the breeze and stared out over the bay. Goose bumps formed on his arms, and he found his father's thick, gray cable-knit sweater right beside the sofa table. *Good old Smitty.* He slipped it on, and a strange feeling came over him, as if he was not alone. He looked around the cozy space, and a shiver ran through him. If he didn't know better, he'd have thought his mother were right there with him in the cottage, smiling about him wearing the sweater she'd knitted for his father. A strand of guilt tugged at his heart for dismissing his father's beliefs so easily.

He shook the wishful thought away and turned his phone off. The last thing he wanted was to be bothered with resort issues. His assistants were capable and efficient. They could deal with any emergencies that came up. That's why he paid them so well. And he definitely didn't want to talk with Savannah, who he was sure would be angry about him leaving without saying goodbye. She'd calm down once she understood the reasons why he'd left. Of course, that would mean owning up to the way he'd made Max feel, and that was just one more thing he couldn't deal with at the moment. He tossed his phone and keys into the pottery bowl on the dining room table, then threw a few logs into the fireplace, remembering how his mother had taught him to build a tepee out of bark. Once the fire caught, he lay down on the large sofa thinking about Max. Why hadn't she come after him when she read the notes? Maybe she hadn't read them. Maybe she never would.

He wondered if his father had bared his soul to his mother, and if so, how his mother might have handled it. But he couldn't wrap his mind around the idea of his parents being in an unhappy situation to begin with. All he envisioned was his mother's smiling eyes, and all he could feel was the warmth of her generous heart. He kicked his feet up on the sofa's arm, hunkered down in his father's sweater, and—with the mixture of cool air flowing through the window and warm air from the fire—he fell asleep to the soothing memories of his mother.

Chapter Thirteen

MAX AWOKE WITH a smile on her lips and Treat's letters beside her. She picked them up and read them again, then turned on the radio. She danced her way into the shower singing along to "My Type of Crazy" by Thompson Square. She was surprised at how much her outlook had changed overnight. The combination of a good night's sleep and everything Treat had done and said gave her the confidence, and the desire, to try to work things out with him. What kind of man sends an enormous cake to a woman when he's hurt her? Or leaves notes professing his love on her doorknob?

Treat. That's who.

It was Sunday, and she was relieved that the festival was over, though she still needed to swing by and go over the final figures with Chaz. She pulled her hair into a ponytail, threw on a pair of jeans, a T-shirt, and a hoodie, slipped on her sneakers, and headed out the door. She'd get her work done quickly; then, when Treat called, as she was sure he would after the notes he'd left, she'd make plans to meet him when she was done.

Just thinking about how happy he'd be, how relieved they'd both be, brought a bounce to her step.

CHAZ WAS ALREADY at the office when she arrived.

"How'd they like the cake?" she asked.

He looked up from the spreadsheets. Hints of the late night shone in the dark circles beneath his eyes. "Chocolate smiles for breakfast," he said with a smile. "Kaylie thanks you, but she said she'll hate you when it lands on her hips."

"Oh, please. That woman gave birth to twins and is still the hottest girl in all of Allure."

"Maybe so. She also said that she'd call you later."

Max sat across from Chaz and began going through the records from the day before. "Hey, Chaz. I'm really sorry that I was so exhausted and in such a petulant mood yesterday."

Chaz set the papers down. "Actually, it was kind of nice to see that you're as normal as the rest of us."

"Is that supposed to be a compliment?" she asked.

"Yeah, actually, it is. You're always so damned on top of things. So yeah, it was nice to see that you have a less neurotic side to you."

"Neurotic?" She arched a brow. "That's not complimentary. I'm a damn good work wife. Just ask your...wife wife."

"My wife wife loves your neurosis, and so do I." He

looked down at the spreadsheets, and after a couple minutes, he sat back and watched Max work.

"Spit it out," she said.

"What?"

"Whatever is causing you to look at me like a big brother who knows something that he shouldn't."

Chaz laughed. "Is that what I look like?"

She studied his face with a serious scowl. "It's either that, or I've grown a third eye in the middle of my head."

"Let's go with me knowing something. It's not hard to figure out after Kaylie was trying to get you to leave early and Treat showed up in the parking lot."

"Okay, let's go with the third eye thing." She buried her nose back in the spreadsheets.

"Max."

"Chaz," she said without raising her eyes.

"Just tell me this. Are you going to fall in love, get married, and move away to a tropical island?"

Max sat back and put her pencil between her teeth. She pushed her glasses up on her nose. "Is that what the stare is for? You're wondering who will do your sponsor coordination if I'm whisked away under the guise of love?"

"Embarrassingly, no, because I know that no matter where you live, I can convince you to still do the coordination and show up for the festival. I just want to know if I'm going to lose my work wife and, more importantly, my friend."

Max looked back down at the spreadsheets,

thinking about how much that meant to her. "You could never lose me. But no one is running off and getting married. We haven't even gotten to the being-able-to-spend-seven-hours-together-without-fighting stage."

"Funny. Treat doesn't seem like the fighting type."

"He's not." She flashed him a mischievous grin.

Two and a half hours later, they set their work aside.

"I'm so glad you closed the office Monday," Max said. For the past three years, Chaz had closed the office the Monday after the festival.

"We work so hard over the weekend, it just makes sense. Go relax. Have some fun," he said.

Max checked her cell phone several times and was surprised not to have heard from Treat. She assumed he was spending time with his family, relaxing after two very stressful nights. She couldn't wait to erase some of that tension.

On her way back to her apartment, she realized that she didn't have Treat's number, which meant she would have to wait for him to call her. Or...

She punched his father's name into her cell phone, followed the links to obtain his address, and then plugged it into her GPS. With a confident smile on her lips, for the first time in days, she headed out of Allure and toward Hal Braden's ranch.

TREAT AWOKE TO a knock at his door. With nothing but embers left in the fireplace, he shivered as he answered it.

"TB!"

His childhood friend, Charley "Chuck" Holtz, stood before him. More gray than brown up top and more belly than muscle in the middle, Chuck beamed with the same vibrancy he'd always possessed.

"Chuck, how are you?" Treat waved him in.

"Smitty told me he opened the old place up for you. Saw the rental parked out front and thought I'd stop by. Haven't seen you in a year. What brings you out?" Chuck had a thick New England accent. The word "parked" came out sounding like "pahked."

"Just needed a break."

"Bonnie's having a bonfire tomorrow night. Wanna join us?"

Treat rolled the idea over in his mind. He had no plans. It might do him good to spend time away from the bungalow, and Chuck and Bonnie were such a nice couple. "Sure."

"Great. I'm heading into town to meet her now. Wanna come along? We're having dinner at the Pearl."

Treat hesitated. Tomorrow night he'd be rested and more able to deal with being civil around company. His mind was still mourning Max. God, he missed her.

"Come on, TB. It'll be fun. Bonnie would be so upset if she didn't get to say hello to you. She tells everyone she knows about you. You know how that goes. Around here you're a big deal, a big fish in a small pond." He winked.

The last thing Treat wanted to deal with was to be

shown off like a trophy. "I'm a little tired. I just got in a few hours ago."

"Come on. I'll make sure we don't stay out too late."

It was hard to ignore Chuck's enthusiasm. "Why not."

"Great. Let's go," Chuck said with a wave.

"Now?" Treat looked down at his clothes. He desperately needed a shower. He touched his chin. *And a shave.*

"You're at the Cape. No one looks at what you're wearing. Up here, jeans and T-shirts are dressing up."

"All right then. Just give me a second to wash my face and brush my teeth." He picked up his bags and went upstairs to the bedroom. "Make yourself at home," he hollered down. He heard the refrigerator open and the clink of beer bottles. *Good old Smitty.*

"I already am," Chuck called up.

Chapter Fourteen

SHOWING UP AT Treat's father's house had seemed like such a good idea when she'd first thought of it, but the sight of the sprawling brick home and several expensive cars around an enormous circular driveway had her second-guessing her plan. She parked behind a black Mercedes SLS and looked down at her clothes. *Sneakers?* What was she thinking? She nearly jumped out of her skin when someone banged on her window. She tried to smile when she saw Savannah waving, but she was too nervous to quite pull it off.

"Max! Hi!"

Left with no choice short of restarting the car and backing out of the driveway, she opened her door.

"Hi. Savannah, right?" *What am I doing here?*

Four of the most gorgeous men she'd ever seen were heading in her direction, each one more striking than the next. Behind them followed an older clone of

Treat. *OhGodOhGodOhGod.*

"Yeah. We met at the festival." Savannah waved at the dark-haired men.

Do they run a modeling agency here? GQ *headquarters?* She caught a glimpse of her reflection in the car window and quickly took her hair out of her ponytail and shook it free.

"What are you doing here?" Before Max could answer, Savannah said to the others, "This is Max. Treat's Max."

One of the men stepped forward. "Hi, Dane," the man said.

Dane? The one who slept with Treat's girlfriend? Max already didn't care for him.

"We're Treat's brothers," he said.

You mean GQ *genes run in the entire family?*

"This is Rex, Hugh, and Josh." Each of the men stepped forward and shook her hand with a ready smile that lit up their handsome faces. Even with their good looks and fine physiques, none of them struck the same fluttery chord in her heart as Treat had. *Where is he?*

The older man stepped forward. "Max, it's a pleasure to meet you, my dear. Welcome to the Braden ranch." He stepped forward and embraced her.

"Oh, um..." She put her arms around him, feeling awkward and strangely comforted at the same time.

"We were just going to barbeque. I hope you'll join us," Hal said.

He put his arm around her and guided her toward the backyard before she could say a word. She didn't miss the coy smiles and nods from the others as she was shuttled away. She wondered where Treat was.

"Thank you, sir. I actually—"

"Hal. There are no sirs on the Braden ranch unless you're here to piss one of us off." He smiled and continued walking toward the backyard, as if Max was an invited guest.

"Thank you. Hal, I actually came to see Treat. Is he here?"

Josh, with his tightly shorn hair and slimmer build, wearing slacks and a polo shirt, tended to the barbeque pit with jeans-clad Dane, whose dark eyes danced with mischief and curiosity as he snuck peeks at Max.

"Treat was called away," Hal said.

"Called away?" she asked. "Do you know when he'll be back? I could come back later."

Hal was already on his way to Josh's side. He slung an arm around his son's shoulder in an easy, comfortable fashion. Max watched Savannah set another plate at the table as Hugh headed back inside and reappeared a minute later with a beer in his hand.

"Did you get one for our guest?" Savannah asked with a nip of irritation.

"No, really—" Max interrupted, but Hugh was already on his way back inside.

He came back with an ice-cold beer. "Here you are, Max."

"Thank you, but I really shouldn't stay," she said.

"Nonsense. You don't have to eat if you're not hungry," Hal said just as her stomach growled. "But then again..."

Why do I keep forgetting to eat?

The family moved so quickly that Max was a little overwhelmed, which was not a feeling she experienced often. She should be helping, organizing, doing something other than standing around with her jaw hanging open; instead she was letting them guide her from one place to the next. Hell, she should be running for her car. She had no business being at Treat's father's house. *Especially without him.*

Before she had a chance to make her feet and mind work in unison and escape the backyard, she had a plate full of food and was laughing at a joke Dane had made.

"How did you and Treat meet?" Josh asked.

"I can answer that," Dane said.

"Let the lady speak," Josh said.

Hugh reached across the table in front of Max. She leaned back, giving him room to retrieve the condiments. It struck her how different each of Treat's brothers were. Treat had impeccable manners, and he'd never sneak peeks at anyone—at least she couldn't imagine him doing so.

Savannah narrowed her eyes at Hugh, and after a moment of confusion, he finally took the hint.

"Excuse me," Hugh said, withdrawing his arm.

Max raised an eyebrow at the way Savannah jumped in just as a mother might have done. She loved watching Treat's family in action. It was so different from her own family's silent meals. "That's okay," she said with a smile.

"Max?" Josh asked again.

She'd been surveying the family so intently that she'd forgotten that Josh had asked her a question. "Oh, sorry. We met at a friend's wedding." *I could just bolt. Not say a word and take off running for my car.*

"Cousin Blake's wedding. Remember? You were all too busy to attend." Dane glared at Hugh.

"What? I had an award ceremony." Hugh lifted his palms toward the air as he explained. He was much more demonstrative than his brothers were. Max watched his eyebrows draw together, as if he didn't understand what the issue was.

"Don't you always?" Dane said.

"Oh, please. You ran off to some shark-infested area and missed it, too." Josh folded his napkin in his lap, crossed one ankle over the other leg, and leaned back in his chair.

"At least I made an appearance first, which is more than I can say for any of you," Dane said with a smirk.

Max enjoyed the playful banter and couldn't help but wonder what it must be like to have that many siblings—that many people who would be there for her. Dane was as quippy as Hugh was clueless to what she was sure his siblings saw as his self-centeredness.

"We were supporting Hugh," Savannah explained.

"Right, for his five minutes of fame that he gets every couple of months. How long has it been since you've seen Blake? You know, he spent a lot of time with us when we were younger, and you get married only once." Dane lifted his chin at Hugh, as if to say, *Top that!*

"As far as I can tell, none of my lovely brothers are walking down the aisle anytime soon. Once, twice, or whatever." Savannah buttered a piece of bread and took a bite.

"Max, have you ever been married?" Hugh asked.

She was about to take a drink and stopped midair, bottle in hand.

"Hugh." All it took was one word and a harsh glare from Hal for everyone at the table to understand that that line of questioning was off-limits—including Max.

"What about you? You're so busy with Connor Dean." Josh said Connor's name in a singsong voice, and Savannah immediately reacted by swatting him on the arms.

Max couldn't help but smile at the ribbing. No wonder Treat enjoyed his family so much. She already felt like one of them. *This can't be good.*

The afternoon meal was comfortable and, Max had to admit, more fun than anything she'd done in a very long time. She kept picturing what it might be like to be there with Treat. How much ribbing would he dole out? What kind of teasing would they thrust upon him? How would he act around her? Would he be openly affectionate, as Blake was with his wife, Danica? Or would he be more reserved in public, like Chaz was toward Kaylie?

What am I doing? I'm not even his girlfriend. Why aren't any of them married? She tried to ignore the red flag that waved like a beacon in her mind.

As she walked to her car with the family in tow— *Did they do everything together?*—she thought about when Treat had said goodbye the night before. Now that she was really thinking about it, something about the way he said it seemed... final. The lingering touch of her cheek, the sadness in his eyes that she'd attributed to her hasty retreat. *Goodbye, Max.* Did he know he was being called away today? What exactly did that mean, *He's been called away?*

Hal embraced her and held her longer than most friends might. He held her like a father might hold his daughter. When he released her, he put his large hands on her shoulders and said, "Treat's out of town. I'm not sure what went on between the two of you, but he was in a hurry."

His eyes searched hers, and she was too numb to speak.

He was in a hurry? Goodbye, Max. *He left on purpose. He wasn't called away. He was saying goodbye for good.*

Hal continued. "I might suggest that you give him some time."

"Oh, Dad." Savannah moved her father's arm from Max's shoulder, and then pulled Max into a hug. "Don't listen to him. If Treat left because something happened between you two, fix it."

"She's giving relationship advice again," Dane said loudly. "Max, Savannah's not exactly the queen of dating. Don't listen to a word she says."

"Look who's talking," Josh joked.

"Boys." Hal put a stop to their taunts.

117

The four men said goodbye to Max, and as she climbed into her car, she was more confused than ever.

Savannah stuck her head into the car's window and said, "Call him. Fix it."

"I don't have his number," Max admitted as Dane dragged Savannah away.

"Leave the girl alone," he said.

Max waited, hoping, praying someone would give her his number, but they were so wrapped up in bickering that she knew she'd get that number only on a hope and a prayer.

As she drove away, watching them in the rearview mirror, she wondered where Treat had gone and why he would have run away without so much as a goodbye. *He did say goodbye. I just didn't know it.* She had to talk to him. She felt his absence like the permanent loss of a loved one, complete with a sinking feeling in the pit of her stomach and a lump in her throat.

She pulled her car over on the side of the road and dialed Treat's assistant's number. Scarlet had been so helpful in planning Chaz's wedding; surely she wouldn't mind tracking him down.

Chapter Fifteen

THE SWEEPING VIEW of Wellfleet Harbor always took Treat's breath away, but tonight, as the cool air blew through the upper deck of the Pearl restaurant and the moon sparkled on the ripples of the bay, thoughts of Max kept him from enjoying its beauty. He was second-guessing his actions with an insurmountable list of what ifs: What if the next morning she reconsidered? What if she did read the notes? What if he'd stayed while she read them? What did she think of them? Did she think they were childish, or romantic and meaningful, as he'd meant for them to be? What if he had tried harder? He could have tried to woo her for another few days with walks, flowers, talks, and kisses—oh, how he wanted to kiss her again.

"Treat?"

Bonnie's voice brought him back to the present. "I'm sorry, Bonnie. Long flight last night. I'm just a little tired. I missed the question."

"I asked how long you were planning on being in town." Bonnie's joyful eyes lit up her plump face when she smiled. His father would have called her a *sturdy woman* or *substantial*, and the fact that she was more confident than most model-skinny women Treat knew made her more beautiful than they could ever hope to be.

"I haven't really decided. A few days? A week? I'm not sure," he answered.

"He lives a hard life. Traveling all over the world to fancy resorts can be exhausting," Chuck teased. He reached for his wife's hand and winked. "Even a man like Treat needs time with normal folks like us."

Treat shook his head and swallowed a gulp of his drink, enjoying the warmth of the bourbon as it slid down his throat. "Bonnie, tell me how things are with you."

"Oh, me? Everything is wonderful. I'm still working at the museum up in P-Town and loving every minute of it. Still reading with the same book club, and helping with community functions. Oh, there's a library book sale on Tuesday. I can't believe that they still wanted to hold it right after the Oyster Fest, but they figured the more people the better. This is the first year they've extended the Oyster Festival to run through Monday. The retailers needed the income boost from the tourists." Bonnie barely slowed down to take a breath. "Anyway, I'm not doing anything too exciting, but I enjoy myself."

"That's what life's all about," Treat said.

"Well, that and enjoying who you're doing it with," Chuck said with another wink.

Bonnie blushed. "Oh, Chuck. Please, not in front of Treat."

"That's okay, Bonnie. Your husband loves you. No need to be embarrassed by it." The tug in Treat's chest had him longing for Max again. No, he couldn't do this to her or to himself. She'd made her feelings clear, and he didn't blame her one bit. The way he'd made her feel was unforgivable, and he had to allow her to move on.

"Do you have someone in your life, Treat?" Bonnie asked.

I wish. "No. No, I don't." He gulped down the rest of his drink and held his hand up to request another.

"Well, you know, Joanie's sister, Amanda, is in town for the Oyster Festival." Bonnie flashed a coy smile.

Treat smiled. "Thank you, Bonnie, but I think I'm out of the game for a while. I just need to relax a bit. I had forgotten about the Oyster Festival. No wonder the streets are jam packed." The thought of trying to make small talk with a woman other than Max increased his longing for her. Talking to her was so easy, and the way she tried so hard to hide her nervousness was adorable. He thought about the weight of her in his arms as he carried her into the bedroom, the way she looked up at him right before taking him into her mouth, tossing aside that girl-next-door image with one blink of her sultry eyes. Women usually flashed a look-what-I-can-do smile at him when they were handling him in that way, showing him that they would do *anything* for him. Not Max. Max looked at him like she was doing something she wanted to do *for herself*—dare he even think it—something that looked a lot like love. A sharp reminder rushed to his groin, and he closed his eyes for a moment to quell his desire.

Surely he was fabricating the feelings that had hovered in her eyes. He was taking himself down a trail he could never follow. He watched the lights of a boat as it drifted away. *Let her go. This is for the best.*

"Well, we'll have a good time at the bonfire tomorrow night."

Treat couldn't imagine anything short of seeing Max picking up his spirits, but he was too polite to dash a friend's efforts. "I'm sure we will, Bonnie."

"Treat." Chuck leaned forward as if he were going to share a secret. "You never know when the right woman will come along," he said with a nod.

"You never know." *She already has.*

THE BUNGALOW WAS cold when Treat returned later that evening. He closed the windows, made a fire, and sat with his laptop open on his lap, his feet up on the coffee table. His e-mail runneth over. He scanned for messages marked "urgent" and tackled each one. Why the staff in Jamaica thought choosing colors for the new lobby furniture was urgent was beyond his comprehension, but he scanned the photos and made quick selections. He clicked on a message from Bill Hayden, the owner of the Thailand resort. He'd been negotiating on a resort in Thailand when he first met Max, and he'd put it on hold after that weekend. These last six months Treat had been anything but on top of his game.

Honoring our verbal agreement of first right of refusal, I've got a solid offer with a closing date in eight weeks. You've got one week to decide. Clock is ticking. Best, Bill.

Never before had he let his personal life interfere with his career, and he was beginning to wonder if his career might be the only thing that would pull him out of the loneliness that had settled heavily inside him. He replied to the e-mail; *Bill, I'll have an offer on your desk in the next seven days. Treat.*

The next e-mail he sent was to his attorney advising him to prepare the offer. Bill was a tough negotiator. Treat expected a few days of back-and-forth before settling on a final figure. Posturing was part of the game. He closed his laptop and clasped his hands behind his head, letting the rush of adrenaline push his mind in a direction other than Max. Focusing on work was just what he needed. He was best when he had a challenge, and Thailand would be just that. Taking over the Thailand resort would consume all of his time and energy for at least three solid months, which was one of the reasons he hadn't pursued it when he'd first met Max six months earlier. When he'd allowed his mind to play with the idea of spending sunny afternoons and sexy nights in Max's arms or rushing around from meeting to meeting to develop relationships with foreign distributors, builders, and the large crew that would be necessary to revamp the Thailand resort, there was no question in his mind which he'd rather do. But now that Max had made her wishes crystal clear, and with his fantasy shot to hell, he forced himself to think, plan, and strategize.

He opened his laptop and pulled up the Thailand reports. Ten minutes later, he was completely immersed in, and distracted by, logistics and finances.

Chapter Sixteen

SCARLET'S CALL came in the next afternoon. "Max, how is my favorite wedding planner?"

"Hi, Scarlet. I hate to bother you, but I was wondering if you might know where I can reach Treat."

"We don't expect him back in Nassau for a few weeks." Scarlet went on to explain that Treat's underlings handled any issues that arose when he wasn't on site.

"I need to speak with him. Would you mind giving me his cell phone number?"

Scarlet was silent for a beat too long.

"Scarlet, he was here in Colorado. I just saw him last night and he asked me to call him. I can't seem to find his number, though." She hated to lie, but she wanted that damned number. Scarlet finally relented after a friendly little plea from Max. Max thanked her profusely before saying goodbye.

Now that Max had it in her hot little hands, she was too scared to use it.

When the phone rang two minutes later, Max's heart nearly leapt from her chest.

"Hi, Kaylie." She heard the disappointment in her own voice.

"Hey, you okay? You sound down."

"Yeah, fine. What's up?"

"I thought you might want to catch up over lunch today."

Max clenched the paper with Treat's number on it in her fist. She felt paralyzed by his disappearance and weak for being one of *those* girls who pined after men. Was she falling right back into the situation she'd sworn she'd never get into again? Was she overlooking red flags that were practically slapping her in the face? Meeting Kaylie for lunch would surely be better than sitting around dissecting her own thoughts.

"Max?"

"Yes, sure." *I've gotta get out of my own head.*

"Great! See you at Felby's at noon."

KAYLIE WAVED from a table near the bar, looking gorgeous as ever in her skinny jeans and off-the-shoulder sweater.

"How come you always look like you've just stepped out of a fashion shoot?" Max asked as she slid into the booth.

Kaylie feigned primping her hair. "Comes naturally, I guess."

They laughed. Max watched the people at the neighboring tables smiling and talking, a little laughter sifting into the air. She let out a sigh, glad to be out of her apartment, where the memory of Treat followed her like a ghost. It was easy to wallow in sadness and confusion when she had no one but her broken heart as a sounding board.

"I ordered us drinks and salads. I hope that's okay," Kaylie said.

"Sure, whatever. You know I don't care. How're Trevor and Lexi? Chaz said they loved the cake."

"Who wouldn't love cake for breakfast? I'm such a bad mom." Kaylie was one of the best moms that Max knew. She spoiled her kids with love and attention rather than gifts, even though they were wealthy enough to buy anything on the planet.

Max listened to Kaylie, but her mind was on the chocolate cake, which brought her back to Treat. She stared at their little booth, and dinner with Treat the evening before came rushing back. Max suddenly, desperately, longed for him.

"What's going on with you? You look like you just lost your best friend, which is really silly because I'm sitting right here with you."

Kaylie had a way of making Max smile. "Ha-ha," Max said with a smirk.

The waitress brought their lunch. Max took a sip and relished the sweetness on her tongue. *Treat's kisses. Don't think about tongues.*

"This" —Kaylie used her fork to draw a big circle in

the air across from Max's face— "is because of Treat, isn't it? You've got it bad. So, catch me up."

Max covered her face with her hand and groaned. "Oh God, it's...it's complicated."

"Listen, I've seen it all and if I haven't seen it, then I've helped someone else through it." Kaylie took a bite of salad.

"It's pretty embarrassing."

"Any good relationship is. I swear, between you and my sister, I worry that I'm the freak when it comes to this stuff, because I don't find anything about sex or relationships embarrassing. It's all just...part of it."

Max looked at her friend's expectant eyes. She wasn't used to talking about dating and men. She didn't have other close female friends, and she'd always drawn a thick line between work and pleasure and was careful to keep the two separate. Max was used to solving things on her own, but this time she felt like she couldn't see the trees beyond the shore. She needed to talk things through with her best friend, even if Kaylie was her boss's wife.

"Okay, start with the basics. The man sent you a cake, and then waited for you in the dark for hours. You don't have to go into details. I mean, it's obvious that something happened and something went very wrong."

"You could say that again." Max leaned across the table and whispered, "We were...you know...and I freaked out and kicked him out." She slid back into her seat, mortified that she'd just admitted it out loud.

"Wait!" Kaylie waved her hands frantically. "You

were in middle of having sex and you told him to leave? Why?"

The people at the neighboring tables looked over. Max shrank down low in the booth and shielded her eyes from them.

Kaylie noticed the stares aimed at Max. She put on a serious face and said to the gawkers, "What? Like you've never done that? Pfft!" She waved a dismissive hand at them and they turned away. She reached across the table and touched Max's hand. "I'm sorry. I didn't mean to embarrass you. Move over." She scooted out of her side of the booth and plopped herself next to Max.

"Okay," she said quietly. "So, what was it? Was his manhood small? Like your pinky? Or was he rude? Did he smell? Was he mean? God, I hate mean guys."

Max cringed. "No, none of those things. He's big."

Kaylie arched a brow.

"Okay, really big." Max smiled. "And he's so romantic. The things he says to me make me swoon like a teenage groupie. Oh, and the way he smells is like...heaven...only better. The way he smells makes me want to climb right into his arms and never leave." Max put her hand over her heart. "He's just...Oh, Kaylie. I sound like an idiot, but when I look into his eyes, there's so much there. It's like, you know how in the movies the guy looks at the girl and her knees go weak and you can just see that she's melting and holding herself back from ripping his clothes off at the same time? That's it. That's me."

Kaylie shook her head. "Wow, Max. I mean, wow.

Then why did you kick him out? Is he all that and a terrible lover? What a shame that would be." Kaylie narrowed her eyes and twisted the end of her hair around her finger. Her blue eyes focused on her glass, and her lips turned down, as if she were mulling over a tragedy.

"No," Max said in a breathy voice. *Since when do I have diarrhea of the mouth—about men?* She couldn't stop herself from talking about Treat. It felt so good to release the feelings that were only getting hotter by the second. "His kisses are sizzling hot, and when he touches me, my whole body wants him to touch me more. And as far as...you know...a-mazing. Really, not that I've been with many men—"

"Yeah, well, I used to wonder if you were gay, because you never even talked about men."

Max made a face.

"Sorry!" Kaylie laughed. "You never even alluded to having a date, so what was I supposed to think?"

"That I was a private person," Max answered.

"Whatever. So, he's hot, well hung, and talented where it counts. So what's the issue? I swear, Max, if you're one of those women with some strange hang-up about feet or something, I'm gonna slap you right upside your head."

Max laughed. "If the rest of him is any indication, his feet could be in footwear modeling ads." Max relaxed back into the corner of the booth and let out a breath. She had to be honest with Kaylie. No—she *wanted* to be honest. How could she figure this out if she wasn't honest with Kaylie and herself?

"Remember when we were in Nassau and you guys saw me in the same clothes I'd worn the night before?" Max closed her eyes against the pain of her impending admission.

"Your walk-of-shame outfit? Of course." Kaylie's eyes opened wide. "Oh my God. You were with Treat?"

"No. That's just it. I wasn't. I was with Justin, just as I told you guys. But we didn't do anything more than kiss good night."

"Max, you're killing me. I still don't get it."

"Well, I never said anything, but when Treat and I first met, there was a connection, or something. I don't know what you would call it, but the second our eyes locked, it was like..."

"We all saw it. Love at first sight. Of course, I said lust at first sight at the time, but you know my sister. She swears by love at first sight ever since she fell in love with Blake."

"I don't know if it was love, but it was something strong." *Love? Do I love him? I can't love him. You don't fall in love overnight. That's a fantasy.* "Something that made me pull away every time I saw him after that first time. And he kept looking at me. It was like everywhere I went, he was there, looking at me like he wanted to devour me, but he never said anything. He didn't ask me out, didn't do anything but stare."

"You are so blind, Max." Kaylie took a sip of her tea. "The man kissed your hand and stared into your eyes. Doesn't that sound like a romance novel to you? He didn't do that to any of us. How could you miss that?"

"I was too busy picking my jaw up from the floor and trying to tamp down the desire to jump him to notice much of anything else." She thought of when they'd first met, and Kaylie was right. He looked right through her with those seductive eyes. "I remember feeling naked. Like he was seeing so much more of me than anyone else could see."

Kaylie let out a dreamy breath. "Isn't that the greatest feeling? That instant when you know someone recognizes that you're something more than what anyone else sees? I remember that with Chaz."

"Hey, we're talking about me here. Focus," Max teased. "Anyway, that afternoon before the rehearsal dinner, I went down to the lobby and basically hung out, hoping I'd see him. When he wasn't anywhere in sight, I went outside and walked around the grounds. Did you know there were three pools, not just one? That place was amazing. Anyway, I ended up on the beach, where I met Justin, and he asked me out." She took a drink, building up her defenses for what she had to tell Kaylie and how it would make her feel to say it aloud. She didn't want pity from her. She needed answers, and relationships weren't like logistics. She could navigate logistics with her eyes closed.

"Treat saw me the next morning. He thought I had slept with Justin, I guess. I didn't really know what he thought at the time, but it was pretty obvious that he thought I was a whore."

"Max!" Kaylie gasped. "No, you're wrong. You have

to be. Everyone has a one-night stand at some point, and I'm sure Treat's had many."

"I never have," she admitted.

"Wait. Never, as in *never*, never?"

Max shook her head. "Not once, and not that night either."

"We'll talk about that after. Wow. Okay, let's figure this out first. So what did Treat say?"

"Nothing."

"Nothing?"

"Nope. It was how he looked at me, like I was dirty." She lowered her voice. "Like I was cheap and slutty. You know how a guy can look down at you and you know just what he's thinking?" Max touched the end of her hair, then dropped her hands to her lap, and finally, crossed her arms to guard her heart from reliving the pain all over again.

"Oh, yeah. I know that look all too well, but unlike you, I give it right back with a quick retort that takes them to their knees."

Max smiled. "Yeah, you would."

"But that's me, not you. Oh, Maxy. I'm so sorry. What did you say? Please tell me you said something to him to straighten him out."

Max shook her head. "I wouldn't even know what to say. I've never been in that situation before. I think I just blushed like a child and looked down at the floor. That's kind of my normal go-to reaction with anything uncomfortable besides work."

"I can't even imagine how you must have felt. I

mean, I've seen you rip people to shreds in a business environment. No offense or anything, but you get shit done and you don't take any flack. You know, I guess this just shows us how multifaceted you are. You're a ballbuster at work, a seductress in the bedroom, and a sensitive kitten at heart." She brushed a strand of hair that had come loose from Max's ponytail from her face. "Max, you must really care about him."

"I think I do," she admitted. "But I don't want to be treated like that by anyone ever again." She'd never told Kaylie about her ex-boyfriend who made her feel worthless every single day for months on end. Until one night when his verbal abuse had taken a turn for the worse and he'd done things to her that she couldn't even think about. He'd grabbed her so roughly that she'd had bruises on her wrist for a week. Max had a good relationship with her mother, but her mother was of the mind-set that women didn't share the trials and tribulations of one's relationships. Because of that, when it came to her boyfriends, Max had never confided in her mother—in good times or in bad. And when Max had answered the phone crying the evening her boyfriend had done those terrible things to her, she'd been unable to put two sentences together, and her mother hadn't even asked what had gone so wrong. With the space that always felt so empty between them, Max hadn't expected her mother to be able to interpret her sobs; yet somehow she had. Her mother had two words for her: *Get out.* That was the night Max packed her bags and drove halfway across the country, leaving that weak persona, and—she'd thought—that broken girl, behind.

Luckily, Kaylie didn't ask whether she'd ever been treated like that before. She assumed that Max had been referring to that one look from Treat.

"And you shouldn't ever have to," Kaylie said, pulling Max into a hug.

Max wiped the tears that had filled the corners of her eyes. "I'm sorry. I didn't mean to be a buzzkill."

"Who're you kidding? You're not a buzzkill. A buzzkill is sending a guy out in the middle of the night mid-you-know-what." She smiled.

"Yeah, about that. That night before we...moved into the bedroom, he was trying to apologize, but I didn't want to hear it. I was afraid I'd just get pissed off and, Kaylie, I wanted him so badly. I've never wanted anyone or anything as much as I wanted to be with him in that way."

"That's love, girl. I mean, there's horny sex and then there's love. Were you thinking about what you wanted to get done after he left?" Kaylie's eyes were serious, contemplative.

"No. I couldn't think past my next breath."

"Were you comparing him to your other lovers?"

"I can count them all on one hand, and no. I seriously couldn't think. I could barely speak." She lowered her voice to a whisper. "And it made me do things that I'd never initiate with anyone else."

"Yup, that's how you know. So, did he ever get to apologize? I mean, what pissed you off so badly that you had to kick him out? I'm still missing something."

Max pulled her shoulders back and said, "I couldn't push the image of that look away. It's stupid, and I know that, but I didn't want to be treated like that in the future, and even though he did all the right things and said things that made my toes curl, I just didn't want to take the chance. So the wall came right back up. Brick and mortar, ten feet high. There was no way he was getting through."

"Girl, you're harsh." Kaylie shook her head. "Did he get pissed?"

Max shook her head. "He was gracious. I think he really wanted to talk, like he was having sex with me because I pushed it, but he'd rather have talked things through first. And then he showed up at work last night, but you know that already."

"That was good, right? I thought it was so romantic."

"Yeah, it was." Max smiled, thinking about their walk and the dinner they'd shared. "He told me stuff that he's never told anyone else."

"If he really and truly did not do one of those..." She lowered her voice an octave. "*Oh yeah, baby, you tell me, I'll tell you* kind of things, where you know they're just trying to get into your pants, then that's a really clear indicator that he's feeling for you what you're feeling for him."

"I know." Max dug into her purse and pulled out the two handwritten notes from Treat. "I was an idiot. I didn't really react to what he told me. I think I was too shocked. When I got home, these were in a bag on my doorknob. He'd put them there before we had dinner, and he showed up to take them after dinner, but I was already there." She shrugged. "And then he said goodbye before I read them. Only I didn't realize he meant *goodbye*, goodbye."

Kaylie read the notes. "Oh, Max. Where is he now?"

"I don't know. He left town in the middle of the night."

"You broke his little heart," Kaylie said. She must have noticed the hurt in Max's eyes about the realization of Treat's hasty departure. "We have to find him. You have to go to him."

Max shook her head. "I don't know. I'm sort of thinking about going away for a few days to figure things out. He told me that his favorite place was Wellfleet in Cape Cod, and I've never been. So I was thinking I'd go there, and…" She shrugged. "Maybe fate will step in, maybe not." *Fate?* Had she really said fate? She had, and the more she thought about fate, the more she wondered about it. Maybe it was fate that had brought them together in the first place, at the gates of the festival, and maybe fate could step in again. Max hadn't even been thinking about going to the Cape until the words left her lips, and now, the more she thought about going, the more right it felt. Even if she didn't see Treat, it would help her to figure out where her heart stood on the whole matter—though now that she knew where she was heading, every bit of her hoped fate would step in and show her the way.

Kaylie groaned. "Has my sister gotten to you? Danica is all about fate and destiny." She rolled her eyes. "I believe in lusty love and creating your life. Listen, you have to make this happen. Find out where he is first and then go see him. Don't chance it, counting on fate. Otherwise, you'll never know what could have happened. He'll always be the one who got away."

Max wasn't listening. She'd already moved on to the romantic notion of the Cape. "Do you think Chaz will give me the week off?"

"What? You're seriously considering this? Are you going to call him?"

She'd almost forgotten that she had his number. "Nope. Something tells me that I need to do this on my own. If fate doesn't step in, then it doesn't, but at least this time I'll be following my heart without anything holding me back."

"Who are you and what have you done with my Max?" Kaylie asked.

Max's eyes grew wide. "Do you think Chaz would mind? It's only four workdays, since we're closed today. I haven't taken a sick day in...well, I've taken three in the eight years I've worked there, and I never take vacation, except a few days here and there to visit my parents." Her mind spun with hope.

"Who are you kidding? Chaz is a romantic. If I tell him why you're going, he'll drive you there himself. In fact, here." Kaylie dug her wallet out of her purse and handed Max her airline frequent-flyer card. "Use our account and you can fly practically free with Chaz's frequent-flyer miles."

Max's eyes lit up. "Are you sure?"

"Yeah, of course. We have too many to ever use anyway. Just log into our account, and make sure when you book it that the actual ticket is in your name. If they need me to call and confirm the purchase, just let me know."

Max hugged her. "You're a saint! Thank you! I'll call Chaz as soon as we leave here, just so he also hears it from me. I need to ask him, even if he tells you it's okay, right?" She didn't wait for Kaylie to answer. "Of course I do. It's the right thing to do." *Just like going to Wellfleet. It feels right.*

They paid the bill and headed out of the restaurant.

"Kaylie, do you think I'm being stupid? I mean, the guy owns a zillion resorts. He could be anywhere in the world."

"Yes, I think you are one hundred percent wacked out of your mind, but if I were Danica, I'd be gushing and telling you how you are doing the right thing and that the spirit gods are all on your side!" She shook her head. "Or some crazy shit like that."

AFTER CHAZ APPROVED her time off, confirming Kaylie's suspicion that he would do anything for love, Max had a hell of a time finding connecting flights into Hyannis, Massachusetts. She booked her flight for the ungodly hour of three in the morning and packed her bags. *This trip is about fate and love and nothing more.* There would be no planning or scheming. No worrying about what others thought or pretending to be something she wasn't. She turned off her cell phone and tucked it into her purse. Three days. She'd give herself three days to figure things out without any disruptions, including phone calls. Treat hadn't called her since he left, and she didn't need the added stress of wondering if he ever would. For the next few days, her phone—and Max herself—were on hiatus. If fate didn't step in, then it wasn't meant to be. With that decided, she spent the rest of the afternoon napping and reading and trying not to think about the romantic fantasy she was wrapping herself up in like a security blanket.

Chapter Seventeen

TREAT HAD THOUGHT about calling Max at least a million times since he'd woken up Monday morning, but he'd promised himself that he wouldn't pressure her into a relationship, and he was sticking to his guns, no matter how hard it was proving to be.

He ate breakfast on the deck and called Savannah as he drank his coffee.

"I've left you at least a dozen messages," she said when she answered the phone.

"Fifteen, to be exact," he said with a smile. "I'm sorry I didn't call right away."

"Sure you are."

"Vanny, I just needed some time." He hadn't called his sister by her nickname since she was a kid, and he had no idea why it had come out of his mouth right then.

"Are you okay? Where are you?" she asked.

"Yeah, I'm okay." He heard the lie in his own voice. "I'm at the Cape."

"Did you listen to my messages?"

He hadn't listened to them because he wasn't in the mood to hear her begging him to call her, but he didn't want to hurt her feelings. "Yeah."

"You're a liar." Her tone was matter-of-fact, not angry. "Wanna know how I know?"

"Because you know me better than I know myself sometimes?"

"Oh, Treat. You sound so...empty."

More than you know.

"I know you didn't listen to my messages because if you had, you'd have been on the first plane back here."

What is she up to now? Treat had a startling thought. "What happened? Is it Dad?"

"No, it's not Dad, you idiot. If something happened to Dad, I would have tracked you down instead of sleeping at night. It's Max."

Treat sprang to his feet. "Something happened to Max?" *No. Please tell me no.* He'd never forgive himself for leaving the way he had if something had happened to her.

"No, relax. Jesus, you really are on edge, aren't you?"

"Just tell me what happened to Max, Savannah."

"She came to Dad's looking for you."

"She what? When? What did she say?" He cringed at what he was about to ask, but couldn't stop himself. "Was Dane there?" He hated the competitive feeling he had toward Dane, but the idea of Dane flirting with Max for even a second sent fire through his veins.

"We were all here, and she came to see you, so I'm not sure what she really wanted to say to you, but you know Dad. He took her under his wing and had her stay for lunch."

The thought of Max alone with his family sent conflicting emotions coursing through him. He pictured her sweet face as she might have watched them act like fools, teasing one another and flirting with her. He wondered if she thought any of his brothers were better looking or nicer than he was. *Oh no, nicer. Damn it. Of course she thinks they're nicer. Why did I have to give her that one look, and how can that one look have led to all of this?*

"Are you still there?"

"Yeah, I'm here," he answered. "Just tell me this: Do you think I should stop thinking about her now? Did one of those lugs hit on her?"

"You're such a softie, Treat. She was like a deer caught in headlights. She's really sweet, you know. The boys were, well, they were who they always are, but Dad wouldn't let them ask too many questions or pry too much."

"Thanks, Savannah. But what did she want? She didn't even have Dad's address."

"Didn't she call you?"

"No. My number's restricted, and we never exchanged numbers. Well, she gave me hers, but I never gave her mine." *I'm an idiot.*

"Given that, then my guess is that she wanted to see you and did the only thing she could think to do. Treat, if you're just messing with her, I think you should back off. I mean, she had that look about her."

Not for the first time, Treat wished he understood women a little better than he did. "What look is that?"

"Like she was inching toward love."

Treat didn't hear anything else she said. "If she comes by again, give her my number and tell her...Never mind. I'm gonna call her right now. Love you, Savannah. And thank you."

Inching toward love. How could Savannah know that? And what if she'd read it wrong? Treat had thought he saw that same look in Max's eyes when they were together, but then her response when he bared his soul to her was so cold. *Thanks for telling me.*

Every muscle in his body tensed as her cell phone rang and voice mail picked up. "Max, hi. It's Treat. I'm, um. Listen, Savannah called and said you went to my dad's ranch." *That's not what I want to say.* "Max, I'm rambling. Call me, please. I'd like to talk. I'd like to see you." He left his phone number, then ended the call and paced. He should have apologized again, ten times, twenty, whatever it took.

Treat contemplated going back to Allure right that second, but he might miss her call when he was on the plane, and what if Savannah had completely misread her intent? Why was this so complicated? *I did this to her.* He had to take his mind off of waiting for her to call. Either she would or she wouldn't. The crowded Oyster

Festival seemed like the perfect place for a distraction. Treat grabbed his keys and headed into town.

MAX STARED AT her phone. The temptation to turn it on was burning a hole in her hand. "Ugh!" She shoved it into the glove compartment of the rental car so that she wouldn't be tempted to make any foolish calls; then she followed the GPS from Hyannis toward Wellfleet. It was a straight shot up the Mid-Cape Highway. She was glad she'd slept on the plane, and the cool New England air gave her renewed energy. She'd forgotten to book a room, but how hard could it be to find a room during the off-season? Traffic came to a grinding halt right after the traffic circle in Orleans. Max consulted her GPS, and with less than twelve miles to go, she'd be into Wellfleet in no time.

Twenty minutes later, she was still stuck in traffic. She'd entered Eastham, a quaint little town with cottages and a few shops off the main drag. She looked for a hotel, and as she inched down the narrow highway, all she saw were cottages with signs out front that read, NO VACANCY. Finally, after sitting in traffic for another fifteen minutes, she pulled into the parking lot of a Four Points Sheraton despite the NO VACANCY sign. How could such a small town be so busy in the middle of October?

She squeezed between a large man and a petite blond woman. The expansive lobby was packed tight with people milling around the registration desk.

"Excuse me. Is this a line?" she asked a middle-aged

man.

"No, hon. We're waiting for the rest of our club. You can squeeze right between those two women."

Max looked at the two plump women who were deep in conversation, standing so close together that there was no way she'd get through; then she looked back at him and arched a brow.

"Harriet, Kelly, please let this young woman through," he said in a friendly tone.

The women parted, never pausing their conversation, and Max slipped through, then wove around two children and another couple and finally reached the desk.

"I'd like to rent a room for tonight," Max said with a smile.

A white-haired woman with leathery skin stood behind the desk looking at Max as if she'd lost her mind. "Honey, you aren't gonna find a place to rent this weekend. This is the Oyster Fest weekend. They extended it an extra day this year. We've been booked for months."

"Do you think any of the hotels near Wellfleet would have a room?" Max asked.

"We're the only hotel on the lower Cape. All the motels, B&Bs, and cottages are booked for miles around. I'm sure of it. We see about twenty-five thousand people here over the festival weekend."

A heavyset woman squeezed in beside Max and asked the woman about transportation to the festival.

"Are you kidding? Nothing?" A deep hole formed in

the pit of Max's stomach. *Where the hell is fate?*

"Honey, we don't kid about things like this," the woman said.

A man pushed his way in front of Max, and Max stepped back, wondering what in the hell she was going to do now. She grabbed a flyer about the festival and a Cape Cod map from a table in the lobby, then went back out to her car and stared at the unrelenting traffic.

"Not exactly the romantic weekend I had in mind," she said as she stood beside her car. She wasn't going to let this bring her mood down. She'd find a place to sleep, even if she had to sleep in her car. She felt like this was where she needed to be, and she'd be damned if she'd give it up.

She climbed into her car and studied the map on the festival flyer, then flipped it over and scanned the event information. It was obvious that she would never get her car anywhere near the festival, but according to the flyer, she was only a few miles from White Crest Beach, where she could catch a shuttle to the events. *Might as well enjoy it.*

AN HOUR LATER, Max climbed out of the shuttle in front of the Wellfleet Town Center. The narrow street and sidewalks were filled with crowds of people moving between stores and vendors. Without even realizing what she was doing, she began studying every dark head of hair that rose above the crowd. She knew the chances of actually seeing Treat were about as slim as winning the lottery, but her heart urged her on.

Large white tents lined the parking lot across the street. Max's eyes lit up at the mass of people, packed in as tight as a school of fish, and leaving barely enough room to step between. Laughter and conversations carried through the beautiful sunny day. *If I'm setting myself up for a major disappointment, I might as well have fun while I'm at it.* She moved with the crowd across the street and into the first tent, where handmade baskets and driftwood painted with beach scenes, boats, and gulls lined long tables.

Max weaved through the crowds from one tent to the next, tasting oysters made fifty different ways, while local artisans smiled and chatted easily with her about their crafts and the festival, and soon looking for Treat fell by the wayside.

"Shuck this!" a man yelled, handing Max an oyster shell.

"Thank you, but I've eaten so many that I think I might explode."

He leaned over the table and said, "That's what your husband is counting on." A wink and a nod later, Max finally got the joke—and it brought her mind right back to Treat.

She already felt like one big, uncontrollable hormone when she was with him. She needed help like she needed a hole in her head. *My hormones are already on speed.* She grinned at the thought as she moved to the next tent.

The afternoon passed swiftly and, as the sun began to set, Max made her way back toward the shuttle bus.

She had to find a hotel, and as the day wore on, the disappointment of not seeing Treat settled in, putting her hopeful energy through a sharp reality check. She was sure her heart had been right, and now she was feeling more and more like one of those bumbling idiot girls who lived their lives in dream states. Not to mention what kept rolling through her mind—if fate *didn't* step in, she'd have taken off work and left Chaz hanging this week for nothing. *And I'll end up back in Allure with a shattered heart that may never heal.*

TREAT COULDN'T BELIEVE his eyes. He had to be dreaming. He stood in front of Abiyoyo, a gift shop on Main Street, among what must have been thousands of people. Down the street, a woman in jeans was crossing the road—from the side, she looked just like Max. It had to be her; the way she walked with her shoulders back, the familiar shift of her slim hips. His pulse raced, but his feet were rooted to the ground as he watched the woman's ponytail swing as she stepped up onto the curb. *Please turn around. Please turn around. Please—*

She shifted. He couldn't quite see her clearly, but he clung to the hope that swelled within him. *Max.* He'd recognize those curves and that graceful neck anywhere. His head finally kicked his feet into motion. He weaved through the crowd, hardly able to breathe. *God, she's beautiful.* She was really there. Right there, in his favorite place on earth.

A shuttle pulled up to the curb, blocking his view. He picked up his pace and jogged toward Town Hall.

"Treat? Treat!"

Bonnie. He spun around. Bonnie hurried toward him with a tall blond woman by her side. Treat's heart pulled him toward Max, while his mind told him that there was no way it could have been her. He looked down the street again just as the shuttle pulled away from the curb.

"Treat, this is Amanda. Amanda, *this* is Treat."

The attractive blonde leaned in and kissed his cheek just as the shuttle passed. He glanced up, and his heart skipped a beat. *Max.* She was there, on the shuttle. It had to be her. His elation was immediately tethered by Amanda's voice in his ear.

"You are everything Bonnie said you'd be," she whispered.

Chapter Eighteen

NO. NO, NO, NO. There was absolutely no way that she'd just seen Treat mid-kiss with some blond woman. No way. Life could not be that cruel. Max took another look out the window, and the confidence she'd bolstered over the last twelve hours took a nosedive.

I'm an idiot. A moron. A fool. She sank down into her seat and tried her best to hold back the sobs that were blooming in her chest. She pressed the sleeve of her sweatshirt to her eyes. *Don't cry. Don't cry. Don't cry. He isn't mine to cry over.*

"Are you okay?" the older man sitting next to her asked in a sympathetic voice.

Max nodded, hoping he wouldn't notice her trembling chin.

"Are you sure? Because you look mighty upset."

Why was he being nice to her? She wasn't asking for help, and when she looked into his old gray eyes, she felt like crying even more.

"I am a little upset," she admitted.

"I thought you might be. You're too pretty of a gal to let anything make you so upset. Wanna talk about it?"

Max smiled. "No, thank you. It's a little embarrassing."

The old man scratched his head. "Alrighty then. Did you enjoy the festival?"

"Yes, it was nice," she answered as the shuttle ambled along the busy road.

"Are you from around here?" he asked. "Wait. Don't answer that. Just say this for me. Park the car in the Harvard yard and party hearty." Every "ar" came out as "ah."

Max laughed. "I know this one." She feigned a New England accent. "Pahk the cah in the Hahvahd yahd and pahty hahty."

"So, you *are* from around here," he teased.

"Colorado, actually. Well, that's where I live now."

He told her the history of the festival and about how it had changed through the years, but Max was too lost in her own sorrow to hear any of the details. She listened instead to the calming cadence of his voice. By the time the shuttle stopped at White Crest Beach, Max's tears were no longer falling. She shook the nice old man's hand and thanked him for making her feel better.

"If you just got in today, you probably don't have any dinner plans," he said. "You're welcome to have dinner with me and the missus, if you'd like. I'm sure

Vicky would enjoy having company. And I promise you, no oysters."

Max thought about her options. With the crowds she'd spent the day maneuvering through, she was sure she'd never get a dinner reservation, and she hadn't passed a single fast food restaurant as she drove up the highway. She wasn't hungry anyway, after the all the oysters she'd eaten, and she still needed to find a place to stay.

"There she is now," he said as a woman pulled up in an old pickup truck.

"Chris, are you bothering that young lady?"

"No, he's been really sweet," Max said. The woman wore her long gray hair pulled back in a ponytail much like Max's, and her wide smile brightened her friendly blue eyes.

"She just got into town today, and I was inviting her to have dinner with us," he answered.

"Why, sure! I have plenty of salmon and chicken, corn on the cob, and I know we have enough Jell-O for desert," the woman said. "By the way, I'm Vicky Smith, Chris's better half. His manners could use a good overhaul."

"I don't know," Max said. The responsible side of her wondered if she was getting herself into an unsafe situation. They seemed nice enough, but...Just then a car pulled up with another older couple in it.

"Hey, Vicky. Y'all coming to the bonfire tonight?" a man asked out the window.

"Oh yeah, we'll be there," Vicky answered. "Hey,

Marge." She waved to a woman walking by. "You coming to the bonfire?"

"I'll be there!" The woman continued on her way.

Max watched the interactions, and unless she had entered some alternate Stephen King universe where the entire town was involved in hacking up tourists, she found them very kind and welcoming. Why shouldn't she go spend some time with them? After all, it didn't look like she'd be able to rent a room anyway, but even if she could, what would she do in a hotel room by herself? Listen to her heart break a little more every time she thought of Treat?

MAX HELPED Vicky with the dishes while Chris gathered blankets and chairs for the bonfire. Max had been hungrier than she'd thought she was, and the meal was delicious. She was glad she'd accepted their generous invitation. But now that the conversation had stalled, thoughts of Treat came rushing back, and sadness wrapped itself around her heavy heart.

"Did you come out just for the festival this weekend?" Vicky asked as she scrubbed a plate, and then handed it to Max to dry. She reminded Max of her own grandmother, who had died ten years earlier. She had the same generous spirit and made the same type of quippy remarks to Chris as her grandmother had made to her grandfather.

"No." *I came searching for a man I didn't really think was here, but he is, with another woman.*

"Work?" Vicky pressed.

"No, not work." Max dried another dish and placed it on the counter.

"Love?"

Max didn't respond.

Vicky set down the dish she was scrubbing. "I'm gonna tell you what my mama told me many years ago. She said, 'Men are like weeds. Some will strangle you until you can't breathe, and some will strangle you once, see you can't breathe, and till your soil for the rest of their lives to make sure you're never strangled again.' Then she would wink at me and say, 'If he strangles you again, get your ass right back here. If he tills your soil, make me some grandbabies.' And that was that. I've never looked back. You just need to find your tiller, Max."

"Is she telling stories again?" Chris came into the kitchen with his coat on.

"Are you ready? Truck packed?" Vicky asked, drying her hands on a dish towel.

"All set. You gals ready?"

"Ready as we'll ever be," Vicky answered.

"Max, did you bring a coat? It gets cold, even with the bonfire. Chris, grab one of my coats."

"Are we going near where my car is parked?"

"Yup."

"I have one in my car. I'll be fine," Max said, suddenly glad that she was tagging along. The weight of her stupid notion of fate stepping in had already begun to lighten with the distraction of dinner. Now, if she could only get the image of Treat and that woman out of her head, maybe she could move her feet to follow them toward the truck.

Chapter Nineteen

TREAT PULLED ON a heavy sweater and cursed beneath his breath when he checked his voicemail and there were no messages from Max. He'd called Max several times that afternoon, and each call went straight to voicemail. He'd driven to where the shuttle had last dropped off, but she wasn't anywhere in sight. He was so damned sure it had been her on that shuttle bus, but it made no sense at all. *What the hell would she be doing in Wellfleet?* He had to be wrong. His eyes were just playing tricks on him. If only Bonnie hadn't called to him. If it had been Max, she'd be in his arms instead of on the shuttle, watching Amanda kiss him.

Amanda was nothing like any woman he'd ever want to date. Sure, she was smart as a whip—a real estate attorney, in fact—but she was pushy in a way that made him feel dirty—and not the good kind of dirty. What kind of woman whispered something so suggestive the first time she met a guy? Bonnie had been her normal peppy self and was completely oblivious to the way Amanda's eyes undressed him. He knew damn well what a woman like that was after. She looked at Treat and saw eye candy and dollar signs, while Max looked right past all of the meaningless facade to the man he was inside. *She also saw the shadow of the mistake I made.* His muscles tensed against the thought.

He'd committed to the damned bonfire, and he would honor the commitment, if for no other reason than to tell Chuck to ask his wife to refrain from setting him up with any other women—ever.

He tried calling Max one more time before driving over to White Crest.

THE WIND PICKED up, turning Treat's thick hair into a mass of dark waves. He stood at the top of the dune looking down at the beach. The town of Wellfleet distributed four bonfire permits per beach, and as he counted the flaming pits, he realized that he had no way of knowing where Chuck and Bonnie's bonfire was. There were enormous groups of people around each bonfire, and for a minute Treat considered going back to the bungalow. Maybe Chuck and Bonnie wouldn't even notice his absence.

Can this day get any worse?

Chuck and Bonnie had been good friends to him for more years than he cared to remember, and as he kicked off his loafers and descended the steep sandy ramp to the beach below, he was glad that he'd made the effort to come out and meet them. The deep, cold sand covered his bare feet with each determined step. Before approaching the gathering of people around each bonfire to find Bonnie and Chuck, he took a moment to listen to the waves as they broke against the shore. The moon hovered over the water like a beacon in the clear dark sky. Laughter filtered up from his right, where children were tossing a ball and diving into the sand to retrieve it.

The feel of the salty sea air on his cheeks had always been one of his favorite sensations. It reminded him of playing along the water's edge when he was younger, while his mother and father watched from the dry sand. He bent down and rolled up the legs of his gray linen pants. From his crouched position, he watched a group of teenagers drawing pictures in the air with sparklers, just as he and his siblings had done. He sank into the sand, remembering his mother's sweet laughter as she teased him, chasing squeals from his lungs as she'd swoop him from the sand and tickle his belly before she'd been too weak to even lift her own chin. He didn't allow himself to visit those memories too often. But now, while he was missing Max and feeling a bit uncomfortable in his own skin, he needed the warmth of them.

"Go ahead. I'll catch up!" Treat heard someone yell. He blinked away the memory, rose to his feet, and headed down the beach toward the first bonfire. *Might as well get this over with.*

A few minutes later he heard his name from behind.

He turned, expecting to see Chuck. Smitty stood where he'd just been sitting, carrying an armful of blankets. He walked back through the dense sand and took the blankets from Smitty's arms.

"Smitty!" Treat embraced his old friend. "I didn't know you'd be here."

"Oh, you know Vicky. Any excuse for a party." Smitty's white hair looked almost gray in the moonlight. "Are you with our bonfire tonight?"

"I don't know. I'm looking for Chuck and Bonnie Holtz."

Smitty shook his head. "They're not with our group." He scanned the people closest to them. "Isn't that them right there?" He pointed to a couple roasting marshmallows around the nearest bonfire.

"Your eyes are better than mine. I think you might be right."

"Treat!"

Amanda. Treat groaned. How was he ever going to make it through the evening?

"Looks like you have a lady friend waiting for you. Here. Give me the blankets and you go join your party." Smitty reached for the blankets.

"That's okay. I'll bring them to your bonfire." *Anything to avoid Amanda.*

Smitty yanked the blankets from his arms, eyeing the woman who was heading their way with a determined look on her face. "That one's not taking no for an answer. We're the last bonfire down on the left.

Stop by later, and bring your friend if you'd like."

Chapter Twenty

MAX PULLED THE top layer of a roasted marshmallow off and put it in her mouth, then licked the sticky sweetness from her fingers. It had been ages since she'd roasted marshmallows, and she was having a wonderful time talking with Vicky and her friends. This was just what she needed. A little time to de-stress and pull herself together. *And to get over Treat's newest girlfriend.*

"Guess who I ran into?" Chris asked when he joined the group.

"God himself?" Vicky teased.

"Sort of. Treat Braden."

Max choked on her marshmallow. *Treat? Did he say Treat Braden? Of course he did. How many other names sound like Treat Braden?*

Vicky patted her on the back. "Get her a drink, quick, Chris."

Chris handed her a bottle of wine, which Max chugged, and when she stopped choking, she chugged some more, until she'd downed half the bottle.

"Max? A little thirsty?" Vicky said with a coy smile.

"Sorry. Thank you, Chris. Do you mind?" She pointed to the bottle. *Treat. Jesus, he's everywhere.*

"Go for it."

Before he finished answering, Max was already guzzling more wine. She lowered it from her lips with a loud, "Ahh." She couldn't drink fast enough. She sucked down another gulp and wiped a drip from her chin.

"Did you say Treat Braden?" she asked.

"Yeah, you know him?" Chris asked.

"Yeah, I know him." Max looked down the beach as she sucked down more wine. "Tall guy, handsome as the day is long?" *Long as the day is handsome!* She finished the bottle of wine and plopped into a beach chair with a loud sigh. *Shoot me now...No...give me another bottle of wine first.* The alcohol warmed the ache and anger that had turned her flesh to ice.

"He's got a place right in Wellfleet. I've known his family for years." Chris laughed. "He still calls me Smitty, like his pop did. It was a nickname I had as a younger man."

"A much younger man," Vicky teased.

"Did you meet Treat here?" Chris asked.

Max shook her head. *I made out with him a few times, and I'm in love with him. Oh, and he keeps breaking my heart.*

Vicky planted herself in the chair beside Max. "I've

been around a long time."

Max stared at the fire, feeling the alcohol chipping away at her defenses and washing away her inhibitions.

"If I didn't know better, and if I'm reading that empty bottle of wine correctly, I'd think that Treat might be the reason you're here."

Max looked at her without answering, then pushed herself to her feet, swaying from side to side until Vicky grabbed her arm and she found her footing. "I'm just gonna go to the bathroom. It's in the parking lot, right?"

"I'll go with you," Vicky said.

"No, I can manage. Thank you, though." She started for the dunes, then turned back. "Vicky, you're a really nice friend."

Max stumbled toward the dunes, mumbling beneath her breath about blond women and tall men. She stumbled up the sandy ramp to the parking lot and found the small cinder-block bathroom. Inside, she flicked on the light and stood in front of the mirror, staring at her drunken, glassy eyes. *Why did I do this to myself? Fly halfway across the country in search of a man who doesn't even want me?*

She removed the elastic from her hair and fluffed her long tresses over her shoulders, surveying herself in the mirror. She turned her face one way, then the other, narrowed her eyes, and then opened them wide again. *I'm a pretty girl. Pretty girls are supposed to have happily-ever-afters. Kaylie got hers. Danica got hers. So why is the blonde getting mine?*

She went to the bathroom, washed up, and headed

back toward the beach. From the top of the dune, she scanned the beach for Treat. She spotted his height first, and her hand flew to her heart. *Look at him.* She bit her lower lip at the tug in her chest. The blonde stood beside him, and she kept touching his shoulder. "Don't touch him," Max said aloud.

She started down the steep incline and fell to her butt on the hard, packed sand of the ramp. She looked at Chris and Vicky's bonfire, where all those nice people were smiling and laughing; then she looked up toward the bonfire where Treat was. *More goddamned happy people.* Max couldn't take it anymore. She'd finally given herself up to a man—and she couldn't even do that right. Here she was, alone, cold, and sitting on a hard sandy ramp. She gave in to the tears that had been begging to be set free for two full days. She didn't wipe them away or cover her face. She didn't care who saw her. She honored her sadness, allowing herself to feel the pain, like her heart had been beaten and tossed away only to be gnawed on by a mangy dog and walked all over again.

Chapter Twenty-One

TREAT HAD TO get away from Amanda. She was clingy and vile, offering to do all sorts of dirty things to him and refusing to accept his gentlemanly denials. She was so persistent that he half expected to hear, *All that for a cool five hundred dollars.* He was on the verge of telling her flat out, *I will not sleep with you—ever.* He'd never had to go that far before. Then again, he'd never been so in love with one woman that he'd turn down another.

Max. He had to find her. Even the thought of Max seeing him with Amanda standing this close to him turned his stomach. His only hope was that it really hadn't been Max, and that she was safe at home in Colorado.

"I'll tell you what," Amanda said as she guzzled another beer. "If you'll take a walk with me—one walk." She leaned in closer, her breath warming his ear, and whispered, "I promise you, I'll rock your world. I'll be *your* treat."

Treat closed his eyes against his boiling anger. It would be so easy to take her—down the beach, at his bungalow, where didn't matter. He could have a string of nameless, faceless women if he wanted them. *That part of my life is over, and I'm never going back to it.* Not now that he knew what it was like to feel more than lust, to look into someone's eyes and want so much more than sexual gratification. To want a lifetime of smiles and handholding, breakfasts, and yes, saucy, sumptuous, scorching hot nights of making love. When he opened his eyes, his decision was easy. Enough was enough. He spotted Chuck and Bonnie by the dunes.

"Excuse me," he said.

"Chuck, I had a great time. Thank you for the invitation, but I really have to run. I'm still catching up on my sleep."

Chuck winked. "Taking Amanda with you?"

"No and, Bonnie, you know I think the world of you, but I'd never give a woman like that a second thought. I'm sorry, but she's a bit aggressive."

Bonnie flushed. "I know. I'm sorry. I guess I thought that a guy like you was used to women throwing themselves at him and that she'd just fit right in."

It surprised him that she would think of him like that, or rather, that she'd think he might act on it if they had. "Yes, but have you ever seen me with any women since you've known me?"

"Well, no," she admitted.

He put his hand on her shoulder and kissed her

cheek. "Then please don't underestimate me." He patted Chuck on the arm. "Thanks, buddy. We'll catch up soon."

"Are you leaving town again?" Chuck asked.

"Thinking about a trip to Colorado." Treat headed down the beach toward Smitty's bonfire, thinking about Max. If it hadn't been her on that shuttle, then he'd make damn sure that if she'd give him another chance, he'd never be in a situation where his actions could be misconstrued again. Hell, he never wanted to be away from her again.

"Treat!"

Treat stopped in his tracks, reminding himself not to lose his cool, as Amanda ran to his side. Up ahead, Vicky was heading toward the parking lot. She plopped herself down next to someone who had her knees pulled up to her chest and her head buried in her arms. *Is everyone having a shitty night?*

Amanda touched his shoulder. "I didn't get to give you a kiss goodbye." She leaned in as he pulled back, catching sight of Vicky helping someone to her feet. *Max.* In the split second she looked over, Amanda planted a kiss right on his cheek—and Max ran up the ramp.

"Max, wait!" Vicky yelled.

Max. Max! "Max!" he yelled.

"Treat!" Amanda ran after him.

Treat spun around. "I'm sure you're a wonderful woman, but I am not—nor will I ever be—interested in you." He didn't realize he had yelled it until he was halfway up the ramp and passing Vicky.

"Way to go, Treat. That woman's got a fairly loose reputation," Vicky said. "Get the one that matters!"

Max fumbled with her keys by a little white car.

"Max!" he hollered.

She turned her back to him.

"Max." He spoke softly as he approached. "Max, it's not what you think."

"Like it's not what I thought when you gave me that look? God, you gave me that look and made me feel like shit, and look at you. One minute you're professing your love to me and the next you're making out with a blonde on the streets of Wellfleet. No wonder this is your favorite place. You probably have a woman at every port." She unlocked her car door, unsteady on her feet. "I should have known."

"Max?" Vicky said.

Max turned, her face flushed as she looked between them.

"Max, I've known Treat since he was a boy," Vicky said.

"I can't believe you know Chris and Vicky," Max spat at Treat.

"Chris? Oh, you mean Smitty." Treat's eyes darted between Max and Vicky.

"Yes, Smitty," Vicky clarified. "Max, we see Treat when he's in town. We know his whole family, and he isn't who you think he is," Vicky said.

"See? Even she knows what you're like," Max spat at him.

"What? No, Max," Treat couldn't let her go—not this

time. Not ever again.

"No, Max, he's not the person *you* think he is. It's none of my business, and I'll leave you two alone to hash this out in a second, but first..." She turned to Treat. "Do not let her drive. She's the sweetest, kindest woman I have met in a long time."

"I promise," Treat said quietly.

"Max," Vicky continued, "Treat has women after him all the time. Of course he does. Just look at him. It's a wonder he can go anywhere looking like that. But he's a gentleman. He doesn't have a girl in this port. I've never seen him bring a woman here, or even date a woman here, and he's no spring chicken. That's a lot of years without a steady woman on his arm." She took Max's hand and slipped her keys from it. "Max, he's your tiller." She nodded. "Trust me, Max. Trust me."

Vicky handed the keys to Treat, kissed his cheek, and then whispered in his ear, "Hurt her and I'll kill you. And I want a front seat at the wedding."

Treat was too shocked to move. His heart was swimming in gratitude for what Vicky had said about him. He wanted to make her proud, and he knew he would. There was no woman alive more important to him than Max, except perhaps Savannah, but at that moment, even Savannah was pushed to the back burner. He stepped forward and looked down into Max's sad eyes. He touched her arm and felt her trembling.

"You're cold."

MAX WAS INTOXICATED, confused, and sad, but she'd had too much wine to feel cold. "I'm not," she managed.

"It was you on the shuttle, wasn't it?" he asked.

She nodded, the kiss she'd witnessed burning a hole right through her stomach.

"Max," he whispered, "I didn't kiss her. Not once. I don't even know her. She's a friend of Bonnie's—a friend of a friend."

"I heard what you said to her. I think the whole beach did." Max looked into his eyes, and despite the internal walls she'd constructed, the hurt in his eyes weaseled its way around them.

"I don't want anyone but you, Max. Just you. Always."

Max looked away, breaking the spell that was holding her together. Damn the sincerity in his voice. She'd come to Wellfleet because she felt herself falling in love with him, and she heard him turn away that beautiful blonde, and still she was angry—angry at herself for being so weak as to fall for a fantasy and angry at Vicky's words, which were picking away at that anger. *He's your tiller.*

Her chest tightened. At first the tears came slow and quiet; then her breathing quickened and sobs shuddered through her. She buried her face in her hands and leaned against the car.

"Why?" she yelled. "Why do you want me, of all people?"

"Because, Max, you are kind and generous; you're loving and beautiful. Because the moment I saw you, my heart tumbled and it has yet to recover. I'm sorry, Max, for any pain I've caused you, but *you* are the woman I want to be with." The honesty in his voice was deafening. She turned away from it—from him.

He wrapped his arms around her. She thrashed from side to side, trying to get free from his too-tight grasp. His body was so warm, so strong as she struggled against him. His heart thundered against her cheek, a tangible rhythm to her sobs. He held her until her body stopped shaking and her sobs turned to silent, streaming tears.

She felt his arm slip down to the crook behind her knee; then she was in his strong arms, and he was carrying her, kissing her forehead. Red flags waved in her mind, but despite them, she felt safe. She closed her eyes against the warning bells. She had to deal with this one way or another, drunk or not. They needed to put closure to whatever it was that was going on between them or find a way to get through it. *He's your tiller.*

"I'll drive you to your hotel," he said as he buckled her into his car and reclined the passenger seat.

"I don't have one," she admitted.

"Cottage?"

She shook her head.

"Where are you staying?"

Sobs found her once again, and she forced her words out between them. "I came here...hoping...hoping to find you. I forgot...reservations. Every place is booked." She turned away from him.

"Efficient Max forgot to book a hotel reservation?"

She didn't have to see his face to hear his grin. "It's not funny!" she snapped.

"No, it's not. Some might say it's fate."

Fate. Fate?

"You know what that means, don't you?"

Max shook her head. *I'm too confused to know anything right now. You're so damned wonderful to me every single time we're together, and I'm too fucked up to accept it.*

"You were thinking with your heart."

Chapter Twenty-Two

HE CARRIED HER into his bungalow and laid her on the couch. He slipped off her shoes and covered her with the softest blanket Max had ever felt, and then he went to work making a fire. She was too emotionally exhausted to do anything but lie there and watch him.

She looked around the room, which was not much bigger than her apartment, but much nicer, with a stone fireplace that went up two stories and a cathedral ceiling. Besides the couch, the room boasted only a coffee table and bookshelves to match, both intricately carved from wood and painted white. She was glad to see the bookshelves not only full of books, but also decorated with knickknacks and candles, much like her own. Beyond the door there was a quaint kitchen and a table for four tucked into a nook. Encasement windows lined the back of the house and a set of French doors led to a deck. A staircase ran between the kitchen and the living room, and she assumed his bedroom was up those stairs.

She couldn't stop her mind from traveling to that bedroom, remembering what it had been like to be touched by him, to be beneath him. She closed her eyes and a moment later felt the side of the couch dip down.

"Are you warm enough?" he asked.

She nodded.

"I'm going to run a bath for you."

Just the thought of being submerged beneath the warm water eased her tension. They needed to talk and figure things out, but that could wait. She also didn't want to end up masking her concerns with sex, like she had the first time they were together—even if she allowed herself to admit the truth, that she'd been hungry for him since he'd walked away from her apartment.

She touched his hand, and even that sent a shiver of desire through her. "Thank you," she said.

He set his other hand on top of hers and cast a mischievous grin her way. "I don't want you to worry. I'm not going to try to woo you with my sexual prowess." His eyes grew serious, and his voice deepened. "I just want to take care of you. I won't try anything and, Max, I know we can talk after you've had some rest, but I have to say it now or I'll never forgive myself. I'm sorry isn't enough to repair the hurt I have caused, but I will live with that regret for the rest of my life, and it'll serve as a reminder of the pain I never, ever want to cause you again."

The lump in Max's throat kept her from speaking, and when he reached up and brushed a hair from her cheek, tucking it gently behind her ear, she closed her eyes, memorizing the whisper of his intimate touch.

Treat went upstairs, and Max closed her eyes. *I'm an idiot. I keep running from him, and he's so good to me.*

He came downstairs a few minutes later and scooped her up again. Although it went against every fiber of her being to be seen as anything even close to a damsel in distress, she cuddled against him, allowing herself to relish in his warmth and generosity.

The smell of warm vanilla filled the spacious candle-lit bathroom. Treat set her down on the ceramic floor, and she longed to be back in his arms, against his warmth. The idea of a warm bath had seemed wonderfully decadent when she was downstairs, when it was just a thought, like an intangible dream, but now, as she stood in the bathroom alone with Treat and her body was reacting to his generous and incredibly romantic gesture in ways that were making it hard for her to think straight, her nerves began to tingle. She looked in the mirror, and Treat's intimate gaze sent a sobering dose of reality through her. He looked at her like the thought of living without her would be too painful to endure—reflecting the very feelings she'd been trying to deny. She had to tell him the truth, to come clean with all that she'd been holding back. It wasn't fair that he'd revealed his fears to her and she'd hidden behind her own.

"I'll be right outside the door if you need anything,

sweetness." He turned away.

Sweetness. The endearment sent shivers through her. "Don't go," she whispered.

He turned, and in that breath, she saw relief in the lowering of his shoulders and the slight curl of his lips.

"Are you sure? I don't want to make you feel uncomfortable. I only want to help you feel better, even if that means you need a life without me in it. I'll understand."

She knew he would, too, from the honesty in his voice. She opened her mouth to tell him about her secret, then shook her head instead. She couldn't risk ruining the safety she felt. "I want you here. With me." How could one man make her feel so safe after the roller coaster of emotions she'd experienced over the past forty-eight hours? When she looked into his eyes, the very worries that had sent her reeling in anger now seemed far, far away.

"Please?"

"Anything for you, sweetness. Anything at all."

She took a step toward him and splayed her hands on the hard muscles of his stomach, then rested her cheek on his chest and closed her eyes.

"I'm here," was all he said as he rested his head on hers. And it was all she needed to hear.

Treat slipped her sweatshirt from her shoulders and laid it neatly on the counter next to a basket of soaps and lotions. Max loved his propensity for organization. *Just like me.*

She lifted her arms as he took off her shirt.

"You're even more beautiful in the candlelight," he whispered, then unbuttoned his own shirt and stepped from his pants.

Max had to close her eyes against the primal urges that gathered in her belly and spread through her like wildfire. She felt his fingers adeptly removing her pants, lifting each of her calves with his gentle touch.

She opened her eyes and met his tender and steady gaze.

Treat took her glasses off and set them on the counter. "Max," he whispered.

She felt the tension in his palm as he cupped her face; at the same time, her eyes lowered. His obvious desire sent tantalizing thrills through her. She wanted to feel his body against her. Before she could reach for him, he was guiding her to the tub and lowering her down. Then he stepped in behind her and settled her against him. She closed her eyes as he washed her arms sensually with a warm, soapy cloth and gathered her hair in his hand, moving it over one of her shoulders. Max had never felt so cherished as he slid the cloth along her shoulder and neck, slowly, lovingly. She moaned at the gentle caress.

He took her hands in his and washed each of her fingers, her palms, her wrists.

"Relax," he whispered as she leaned forward. He gently brought her back against his chest.

"Rest," he said, reaching under the water to wash her legs.

The cloth moved slowly up her thighs to the bend of

her hip, then slowly back down to the crest of her knee. He slid his hands along her lower belly, caressing her rib cage, her hips, and along her inner thighs. Max closed her eyes and let her legs fall open against his; his thighs held her as a willing captive, and his thick, muscular, arms reached around her, creating a loving cocoon that made her feel small and feminine—and very, very desirous.

He wrapped his arms around her middle, leaning his cheek against hers. His breath warmed her damp shoulders, and Max wanted to stay right there, with his heart beating against her back, forever.

Chapter Twenty-Three

NOTHING IN HIS life had ever given Treat the ceaseless feeling of happiness as taking care of Max for the last hour had. He could feel her tension releasing in every breath she took, in the way her eyes rode at half-mast, and the slow waning of her anger, replaced with a contented haze. Everything about Max was sublime, and as much as his body cried out for her, sex wasn't what he craved. This closeness was enough. If they did nothing else tonight, he would be sated.

The bubbles dissipated and the water cooled. Max moved closer to him, stealing his warmth, and as much as he hated to move, he wanted her warm and safe in his bed.

"Let me dry you off, sweetness."

She moved as if she were half asleep, her slender arms reaching for him as she stood. Treat helped her step from the tub and wrapped her in a thick towel, then took another towel and gently patted her dry. He moved from her neck and shoulders to her arms, remembering the way his heart ached the first time he'd set eyes on her and how the unfamiliar emotion had frightened him. Now he understood the emotion, and the only fear he had was of not being the man Max wanted him to be—the man she deserved. In order to do that, he needed to learn about her insecurities, her dreams.

Treat was every bit an alpha male, from his height and strength to his desire to protect, but never had anyone incited his protective reflexes as strongly as his family had—until he met Max. When that first emotion had hit him, it had shaken him to his core, and he hadn't known how to handle the impulses. Now, as he knelt before Max, wiping the water from her body, he knew just what to do. He embraced those impulses. He would protect Max's heart with simple acts of kindness and love. The only nagging doubt of allowing himself to fully open up and love her, and to let her love him in return, was the worry caused by his mother's death, and he was working on that. He kept his father's words close to remind him to let those fears go. *Your mama didn't die because of our love for each other.*

He was surprised when Max reached for his neck, wanting him to carry her to the bedroom. He knew the first time he'd carried her from the car that she might fight him. She was strong and self-sufficient, and she was proud of that. The woman he was carrying to his bed never failed to surprise him—even the way she went from intense sexuality to full-on fear showed her strength. Most women would have continued making love, rationalized their minds out of ending the intimacy. In his experience, most women feared losing the men in their lives. Max wasn't anything like most women.

He drew back the covers with one hand and laid her on the clean sheets, then grabbed one of his clean T-shirts from his dresser.

"I'm just going to put this on you, sweetness." He slid the shirt over her head and smoothed it down almost to her knees. Damn, she looked adorable and sexy all at once.

Treat slipped into a pair of boxer briefs, then brought the candles from the bathroom and placed them on the slate in front of the fireplace in the master bedroom. He lay beside Max, leaning on one elbow so he could take care of whatever she needed.

"Why are you so good to me?" Max asked.

"Because you deserve it."

"I'm pretty drunk," she admitted.

"That's okay. I'm not. I won't let you take advantage of me." He rubbed his fingers lightly across her forehead, and she closed her eyes.

"Mmm. That feels so good."

"Good," he whispered. The last thing he wanted to do was break the trusting mood of his bedroom. He'd thought about what she'd look like in his bed too many times to count, and he knew bringing up the hurt of when he'd left Allure so quickly might cause her to run again, but he couldn't take the chance of not talking things through—because of how badly that had backfired last time.

"Sweetness, can we talk?"

"Tired," she said.

"I know. I just don't want to wake up at two a.m. and find you angry with me again. We should deal with all of this, figure out where we stand."

She curled in to the curve of his arm. "I don't want to stand. I want to stay right here. Forever."

Forever. Forever was just what he wanted, but not without a clear conscience. He had to clear the air.

"Max, the reason I left town was to let you live your life without me in it. I didn't want you to feel the pressure of my presence." *Or the hurt.* "I promised myself I wouldn't contact you. I'd let you be."

She wrapped her arm around his belly and snuggled in closer. So much emotion welled within him that he had to close his eyes, swallowing past the love in his heart, to gain the courage to continue.

"Then, when I saw you on the street, I knew in that moment that I couldn't do it."

"Treat," she whispered.

"Yes?"

"I followed you. Doesn't that tell you something? I didn't know you'd be here, but you said it was your favorite place on earth, and I hoped against everything in my world that you'd be here. I couldn't walk away either."

She looked up at him, her green eyes glistening in

the candlelight. Treat felt the thrum of desire building again.

"I believe you." She ran her finger across the waistband of his skivvies. "I heard what you said to the blonde," she repeated. "I heard what you said to me, the night we had dinner, and I read your notes a hundred times." She leaned up and touched his cheek, sending a shiver through him. "I know that night at my apartment, before we...when we were in the living room...I know you wanted to tell me you were sorry then. I saw it in your eyes. But I wasn't ready to hear it." She laid her head back on his chest and sighed.

He pulled her closer. *She knows.* The tension in his chest lessened a little.

"There's something I haven't told you."

"Shh, you don't have to." He stroked her hair.

"No, I want to be completely honest with you. There's something about me that you need to know." She leaned on her elbow and looked at him.

"Whatever it is, please, share it only if you feel like you really want to. I'm not a possessive person by nature. What came over me at Nassau was new to me. I did it out of fear, sweetness, so please, you don't need—"

She put her finger over his lips. "Shh. I'm telling you because I think we both know that whatever this is between us is bigger than both of us have ever experienced before, and you need to know why it's just as hard for me as it is for you. I should have told you that night when you told me about your mom, but I couldn't. I was too afraid to open up and let you in."

Treat sat up against the headboard, taking in how cute she looked, dwarfed by his T-shirt, and the stark contrast to the serious look on her face. "Okay. I'm listening."

She took his hand, and a sinking feeling settled into his stomach.

"Before I tell you, what exactly am I wearing? What does PASG stand for?" She pulled the bottom of the T-shirt away from her body and looked down at it. "Is that some strange sexual reference?"

He knew she was stalling, grasping for levity instead of revealing whatever it was she felt she had to say. Treat wanted her to be comfortable, and as he watched her lips trying to form a smile and her eyes trying to climb out from the shadow of whatever was haunting her, he soaked in her effort. With each passing moment, each minuscule change in her eyes or her facial expressions, he learned more about her. Treat knew he'd make every effort to remember it all, so if there was a next time that she had something so troubling to deal with, he'd know how to comfort her.

He smiled. "No. Provincetown AIDS Support Group. It's a local group that I support."

"Oh, that's really nice. As long as you're not making me look silly."

"You could never look silly. Please, tell me what you wanted to tell me. I want to know."

Her eyes darkened again, and he squeezed her hand. "When I was a senior in college, I dated this guy.

He was handsome and smart and funny, the kind of guy that everyone loved. Things were fine for a long time, but as we got closer to graduation, we moved in together, and over the next few months, he changed. I've never understood what caused him to change, but he did. He became verbally abusive, withdrawn."

Treat's protective juices were flowing, and he did his best to rein them in. "Go on," he said. *If he hurt you, I'll kill him.*

"It became, I don't know, a way of life, I suppose. He called me names and told me I was worthless, and in all honesty, I was weak." She searched his eyes. "You look like you're ready to explode. Maybe I shouldn't say anything else."

"No. Continue, please." The thought of someone being verbally abusive to Max pushed every button in his body. The anger coursing through him was stronger than any fury he'd ever felt.

"Anyway, as I said, I was weak. My parents are great—they really are—but Mom and I have never really talked about relationships." Max shook her head. "Before my grandmother died, she told me that the secret to a lasting relationship was to always speak your mind. But my mother had already convinced me that was the wrong road to take and that I shouldn't complain or try to change things." She furrowed her brow. "I think my grandmother told me that because of how my mom's relationship was. She was so submissive. Not that my father was ever abusive, but Mom never really spoke her mind." Max sighed. "It's no wonder that Mom and I never talked about relationships."

Treat put his arm around her waist and slid her protectively against him.

"Anyway, he'd grabbed my arm and—Treat, you're trembling."

He unclenched his jaw just long enough to say, "I don't want to scare you, but I'd like to kill this asshole."

"There's more, but I'll stop—"

"I'm not an evil person. I'm not going to track him down like an animal and hurt him, Max." *Though I want nothing more.* "But I'd be lying if I told you I wasn't mad enough to *want* to do those things, and I promised myself I'd always be honest with you." An intense heat of worry soared through Treat. He took a deep breath, trying to understand the reaction that bore a hole in his gut. It could only be driven by his love for Max.

She touched his chest, and that simple skin-to-skin contact brought his anger down a notch. *She's here. She's safe.*

"That was the only time he'd ever grabbed me, and I lost it. After he went to bed, I was still crying. That night, my mom happened to call, and I didn't even have to say anything. I couldn't say anything. That was the one and only time she ever said anything to me about a specific relationship. She said one thing to me, and that one thing changed everything in my life. She said, 'Get out.'"

"So you left?"

"I did. I packed my car and drove all the way to

Colorado and I never looked back. But the thing you need to know is what that did to me. In college, I wasn't the woman who worked for Chaz and could run a festival of over thirty thousand with her eyes closed. I was weak, submissive. I guess I'd patterned myself after my mother without even realizing it, but then, after he grabbed me and I found the courage to leave, I knew I could never be that woman again. I read everything I could about relationships, and I built walls around my heart. Big, giant, thick, impenetrable walls."

"Oh, Max. I'm so sorry."

"Don't be. I've grown up, and I *am* strong and self-sufficient and all the things I strived to be. But after dealing with Scarlet over the phone for all those months, and wondering about you—fantasizing about you—when I finally met you, a part of me let down those defenses. I became a bumbling idiot. I couldn't talk or think, and I was thrown right back into that bedroom again."

"You're none of those things. You're the strongest woman I know, besides Savannah, but she's a whole other story. She was softer before our mom died, too."

Max put her hand on her heart. "I can't imagine what your family has been through. But for me, the feelings that came rumbling back scared me. A lot. I felt myself falling back into that role of a submissive girl again, and I wanted to run, but my legs wouldn't obey my mind. I suddenly felt that softer side of me reemerging, the side that screamed for me to pull down the defenses that I'd worked so hard to create. I *wanted* you to take care of me—and that, more than anything, scared the daylights out of me. I didn't want to be hurt again. I mean, how can you possibly know you want a man to take care of you in that way after one kiss on the hand?

"My heart was controlling everything in me, and my heart wanted you. It was you I was looking for that afternoon when I met Justin. I didn't sleep with him. We shared one good-night kiss, but I never slept with him or even let him touch me. He was a filler, Treat. He filled the gap that you created."

Treat pulled her to him and held her tight. He was relieved that she hadn't slept with Justin. Even the thought of their bodies tangled together made him sick. But he was more relieved by what she'd just said. *He filled the gap that you created.*

Max pulled away. "I want to finish telling you before I lose my courage." She took a deep breath. "This is the hardest part to explain. When you looked at me the way you did, it was just one look, and I know that it's been blown way out of proportion."

"No. I never should have done it."

"Agreed." She smiled. "But it was just a look between two strangers. We weren't lovers or really even friends at that point. I mean, we'd spoken on the phone once or twice, but really I was dealing so much with Scarlet that you were just this elusive name and image in my mind. And I'd be lying if I said that I hadn't fantasized about what you'd look like and how I'd feel when I finally met the intelligent, generous man behind the deep voice, but we had only just met. So I did blow it out of proportion. When you gave me that dirty stare, I was afraid that if I went out with you, I'd be in the same trap as I was in college, and I can never go back there again."

"I'd never do that to you."

"I know that now. That's what I'm trying to tell you. You've already shown me that you will never do that to me. It's not who you are, but you need to know that my defenses go up when my feathers are ruffled, and I'm stubborn and I can be savagely strong when I need to be. So I need to know that if that happens, if I get scared and those walls go up, you'll love me through it."

"I'll love you through anything, Max." He sat up straighter, until they were eye to eye. "I will love you through the good and the bad, the fights and the..." He slipped his arm under her T-shirt and wrapped his arm around her waist. "The spirited, frisky nights. I want you to be strong and tell me I'm full of shit when I am. I want you to call me on anything I do that's hurtful or uncalled for. Max, I'm thirty-seven years old, brought up by a man's man who was also the most gentlemanly man I know. I don't want to be any less than he is."

Max blushed. "I met him."

He brushed her hair from her shoulder. "I know." Treat didn't want to ask, but he couldn't help it. "Did Da—"

Max laughed. "Shh. He was very respectful. Besides, none of those brothers of yours are half the man you are."

She lifted her chin and kissed him lightly on his lips. He pulled her closer and felt her body relaxing, her heart opening up to him. He slid his tongue into her mouth, and she tasted so sweet that he never wanted to stop kissing her. She leaned into him, pushing him down into the mattress, and it took all his strength to pull away.

"Not like this, Max."

"I'm going to try really hard to believe that you mean that in some other way than that you don't want me, because right now, it feels a lot like rejection."

He ran the back of his hand down her cheek. "Oh, I want every piece of you, but not tonight, not after all we've gone through. Sleep on it, and if you still feel the same tomorrow, then I'll unleash the lust that's been building for the past six months, but I don't want to take the chance of you changing your mind. It will hurt too much if I've just made love to you."

She drew her brows together and cocked the right side of her mouth up. "You're a guy. Aren't you always supposed to want sex?"

"I'm a man, and there is no sex that equates to making love to you." He wrapped her in his arms and closed his eyes, willing his hands not to wander to all the dark places that they begged to go.

Chapter Twenty-Four

MAX AWOKE TO the smell of coffee. She went into the bathroom and was surprised to find all of her toiletries laid out in a basket beside the sink. Her shampoo and conditioner were already in the shower. Treat was so thoughtful. She wondered if she'd had an incredible dream, or if last night had really happened.

After she brushed her teeth, she followed a sweet aroma downstairs, where the table was set for two with warm croissants, fresh fruit, and hard-boiled eggs, complete with two different types of jams and butter. In the center of the table sat an enormous vase of pink Knock Out roses. Max's hand covered her heart. She turned toward Treat and saw another vase on the counter, bursting with her favorite flowers.

"Treat?"

"Good morning, sweetness." Treat was already showered and dressed.

God, he looked handsome in his jeans and T-shirt, with a thick, comfy cable-knit sweater thrown over his shoulder. She followed the floral aroma into the cozy living room, where an antique metal bucket overflowed with more Knock Out roses. *You are the most thoughtful man on earth.*

"You did all this?" Max asked as he handed her a deliciously sweet-smelling cup of coffee.

"It wasn't much, but I figured you'd be hungry. Vicky called. She said that she wanted to make sure you were okay, but I think she really wanted to make sure that I had been nice to you."

Drawn in by his smile, Max went to him. "Thank you." She stood on her tiptoes and kissed him. "The roses...they're gorgeous."

"They line the curve of the driveway. Fate?" he asked with a shrug.

Fate indeed. She sat at the table, appreciating his generosity and smelling the sweet aroma of the flowers, and then looked out the windows at the bay below. The sky was a powdery blue with no clouds in sight, and Max couldn't help but feel as though the sky mirrored how she felt, like the fog that had hung over her and Treat had evaporated and all that was left was the beauty between them.

"Thanks for bringing my things in for me," she said.

"I put your clothes in the dresser drawers."

"Treat, I'm not moving in." Why did she feel compelled to define that line?

He sat beside her and kissed her cheek. "Not yet,

anyway," he said. "See? That's why I didn't want to get too close last night. Women are fickle," he teased. She hit him with a napkin.

"If you don't have plans, I'd really like to show you around."

"How can we go anywhere with the crowds?" She popped a piece of the croissant into her mouth.

"They'll all be gone by eleven. In fact, they'll be gone until next May. The festival is like the last hurrah of the season."

"What time is it?"

"Ten thirty."

"Ten thirty? Why didn't you wake me up?" She covered her face. "I'm so embarrassed."

He lowered her hand. "You were tired. Besides, part of loving someone unconditionally means letting their body do whatever it needs to do. And your body needed to sleep."

Max let her mind wander. *What would it be like to be married to you? To wake up beside you every morning, and go to sleep in your arms each night.* She'd slept better last night than she had any other night that she could remember.

Vicky's words came tumbling back to her. *You just need to find your tiller, Max.* And then later, *He's your tiller, Max. Trust me.*

He's your tiller.

MAX WAS GORGEOUS wearing only his T-shirt and her panties. Her hair was still mussed from sleep, and her eyelids were heavy with desire. Treat lowered his lips to hers, closing his eyes and reveling in the feel of her tender kiss. *God I've missed you.* She pressed her hips against him, heightening his desire. He pulled back and took her face between his large, strong hands. The love and lust he felt for Max coalesced as he looked into her wanting eyes, and he didn't know what to do with it as it sent his urges rushing forward. A voice in the back of his mind told him to go slow.

"Max," he whispered.

Max's lips parted, but nothing came out.

"I don't know how to love without you, Max," he said. He narrowed his eyes as he searched hers for any hint of hesitation. She'd been through so much over the previous few days, and the last thing he wanted was to force himself on her—even if every ounce of him craved her love. In her eyes he saw need and want—and something that resembled love, spurring him on. He told himself to go slow, but watching her breasts heave beneath the thin cotton shirt, her taut nipples teasing him, he had to grit his teeth against the urge to throw her on the kitchen table and make love to her until she forgot her own name.

Max slipped her hands beneath his shirt and ran her fingers over his abs, sending a tug of anticipation to his groin. She touched the button of his jeans and stood on her tiptoes—no match for the foot difference between them. He closed the distance between them and settled his lips over hers again. *Damn you taste sweet.* Her tongue flicked his, then swept his mouth in fast, deep strokes. He lifted her into his arms and she wrapped her legs around his waist. Her hair fell like a curtain around their faces as she pressed her body into him and settled her lips over his. She smelled like freshly washed linens and her body felt so damn good against him. Her kisses were rough and hungry. The confusion of the days before came rushing back. The pain of his walking away from her pierced his heart. He had to bury it. Had to get that burn out of his body. Max ran her hands down the sleek lines of his biceps and grabbed hold of his bulbous muscles. Her fingers strained against the girth of them as he placed her on the table and pushed his hips between her legs, at the same time he pulled her forward. His erection strained against his zipper, hard against the thin veil of cotton that separated them.

"Do you still want this?" Treat asked through heavy breaths.

"Yes. God yes, Treat." Her words came out in a rush of hot breath as she reached for his shirt. He lifted her shirt over her head. Her breasts were so perfect, round and firm. He reached behind him and in one swift move he yanked his own T-shirt off, exposing his massive chest and broad shoulders, before taking her in another rough kiss, blinding him with electric shocks, and before she could catch her breath he was stealing her oxygen again. She moaned into his mouth, and that sexy little noise sent his mind reeling. The need to make love to her clutched him like a wicked hand, tightening every muscle in his body. His teeth grazed her lips, her chin, her neck, while his hands groped her ribcage, brushing the underside of her breasts.

"Yes," she whispered.

His tongue stroked her skin, trailing its way down the arc of her breasts. He took one breast greedily into his mouth. She gasped and buried her hands in his hair, pulling his mouth harder against her. She arched into him, gasping as he moved from one breast to the other, exposing her to the cool morning air. She reached for his jeans and fumbled with the button, before giving up and stroking him through the harsh material of his jeans. Treat grabbed her hand and held it in his. He had to have her—more of her. His love for her grew by the second, and every passionate kiss and every sensual caress drove his need deeper. He had to claim her. He took a step back, pinning Max to the table with a hot and hungry stare, and leaving her panting, wearing nothing but her thong, her legs open, her body eager. Jesus she was beautiful. He wished they were upstairs, on the couch, anywhere more respectful, but he was too far gone. He'd never make it another minute. In the next breath his body took over. *Fuck it.* He laid her back on the table and dragged his hands down her breasts, her ribs, to her hips, and slid her to the edge of the table. He rubbed her through the tiny damp swatch of her panties. The need in him burned ruthlessly through his veins. He slipped his finger beneath the material and touched her silky, wet skin. Her eagerness sent a thrill thrumming through his body. Max closed her eyes, arching her hips against his hand as he bent and kissed the tender skin at the top of her thigh, probing her with his fingers before slipping her thong over her slim hips and down her legs. The first flick of his tongue made her shiver beneath his hands. He stroked her sensitive folds with his tongue, and it wasn't enough. She was too sweet for just a taste. He strengthened his licks, finding her sensitive nub with his finger and teasing her until it was swollen and she squirmed on the hard, wooden table. He settled his mouth around her sex, raking his teeth over her clit.

"Yes. Please, Treat," Max cried. She dug her hands in his hair again and arched against his mouth as he pleasured her with faster, more urgent strokes of his tongue. She gasped sexy, fast, little breaths. He felt the tension mounting in the muscles of her thighs and in the force of her hands in his hair. He was determined to give her what she wanted—to love her the way she deserved. He licked faster, probing her with his finger. Max shook her head from side to side. She released his hair and clawed at the table as her body pulsed around the tip of his tongue and she cried out again—a loud indiscernible plea.

He put his hands flat on her belly, licking as the pulses continued in fast succession, then slowly eased, before finally coming to rest, her body raising with each deep breath. Treat ripped open his fly and stepped from his pants, setting his formidable erection free. He grabbed his wallet from the counter and ripped open a condom with his teeth, then sheathed his eager length. In the next breath he pulled her hips forward and thrust into her. Max gasped at the deep penetration, and there was no quelling his primal urges. She grabbed at his shoulders as he took her breast into his mouth and buried himself deeper, thrusting over and over again, before wrapping his powerful arm around her and pulling her to the edge of the table so he could push harder. Every nerve was on fire. Every thrust against her hips left him wanting more, a stronger connection. His thoughts became fragmented. He was blinded by the mounting tension within him.

"Max," Treat said through gritted teeth. He grabbed her cheeks and stared into her eyes. She looked at him through a sexual haze, unfocused and unguarded.

Max shook her head free and grazed his pec muscles with her teeth, then found his nipple and did the same. Treat sucked in a loud, sharp breath as he grabbed her waist, forcing her to match the efforts of his frenetic rhythm. She arched back, her lips fell open, and her eyes fluttered closed as another orgasm shuddered through her, pulsating and tightening around him just as he climbed to the peak of his own glorious release. He rested his head between her breasts, feeling her heart beat against his cheek, and for a moment, he closed his eyes. He pulled Max to him and picked her up in his arms. Treat knew, as he carried her up the stairs for the second time in twenty-four hours, that loving Max completed him in ways that nothing else ever could, and he wondered, as he turned on the shower in the bathroom his mother had used so many years before, how a heart could feel so full.

Chapter Twenty-Five

TREAT WAS RIGHT. The streets of Wellfleet appeared deserted compared to the day before. After picking up her rental car and dropping it off at the bungalow, they headed back into town. They walked hand in hand through the shops, and Max picked out toys for Trevor and Lexi at Abiyoyo. It had been so long since she'd held a man's hand that she found herself studying the way her hand fit snugly into his. His palm engulfed hers. When he found a scarf that he said set off her eyes, he squeezed her hand like it was the most natural reaction in the world, and Max relished in those little things between them that confirmed that somehow, overnight, they'd become a couple.

They walked around the corner and had lunch at a little restaurant called the Juice, where they shared a bowl of New England Clam Chowder and a sandwich. Max felt her heart opening to him even more than it already had. The simple act of sharing another meal together felt natural—like they'd been doing it forever—and new, all at the same time. Treat didn't rush her through the meal, or make her feel hurried as they meandered through an entire street of art galleries. He showed her pieces he loved and took interest in the ones that she swooned over.

When they reached the end of the row of galleries, a little fear tiptoed through Max. They hadn't had enough time together yet. *Would there ever be enough time?* She didn't want to go back to real life. She didn't even know where or what he called home.

"Sweetness, I have a great idea." Treat took both of her hands in his. The excitement in his eyes made her smile. "If you're not too tired, I'd love to go to Provincetown, grab some dinner, and maybe see a show? Or we could just go back to the bungalow and watch a movie and relax. Whatever you want."

I have to know. "Treat."

"Oh, no. What's that look? Did I assume too much? Did you want to find a hotel and have some alone time?" He rubbed his hand along his forehead. "I'm an idiot. I didn't even take into consideration when you might have to be back at work."

She laughed at his dramatic flair. He was always so calm, and she'd clearly rattled him. "No. I'm just curious. Where do you live?"

He laughed, a deep, hearty laugh that turned her heart to mush.

"Live, live? Like, where do I keep all my stuff?"

"Yeah. You know. Where do you call home?"

He took her face in his hands and said, "It doesn't matter, because the moment you tell me it's okay, my home will be wherever you are." He kissed her, and the sheer delight of it brought her to her toes. His silky lips on hers, the way he smelled musky and sweet all at once, everything about him made her crave his touch.

When they finally pulled apart, she said, "Wow."

"Wow?"

"I just love to kiss you."

He put his hands on her waist, and she could see in his eyes that he was thinking the same thing she was—that it would be so great to make out, right there on the street. Just to throw her arms around his neck and have him lift her up into his arms so she could wrap her legs around him and they could just kiss each other senseless. *Oh, wait. Maybe he isn't thinking that.* Why was he covering his mouth and looking away?

"Did I say something wrong?" Max asked tentatively.

He shook his head. "No. You just had my mind racing in ways that it shouldn't be." He looked down, and the problem was evident by the tent in his pants.

She couldn't hide her laugh.

"You're laughing? You're laughing at this? This is not good, Max. I'm not a twenty-something kid. I'm a grown man. I should be able to kiss you without the world knowing that I can barely think past wanting to"—he lowered his voice to a whisper— "be inside of you."

Max grabbed her side and bent over in a fit of laughter.

"You are incorrigible!" He swept her into his arms and spun her around, so his back was to the road. "This is so unfair." He took her hand and walked her behind two enormous hydrangea bushes, then kissed her until her legs turned to spaghetti and her laughter was forgotten. They sank to the ground, where he kissed her deeper, slipping his hand under her hoodie and caressing her breast through her lacy bra. She arched her hips into his, and he kissed her chin, her neck, and down the open V of her shirt to the crest of her breasts.

"Treat," she moaned.

He rubbed her nipple with the pad of his thumb until they were taut and she was clutching his head, bringing his lips back to hers. Every molecule in her body ached for him. She shoved his hand down between her legs, and he rubbed her through her jeans, heightening her arousal.

"Max," he whispered.

Her brain couldn't force her mouth to respond. She lay beside him panting, wanting, craving more of him than his tongue as he licked the dip above her collarbone. *What're you doing? Where are you going?* She opened her eyes as he rose to his feet beside where she lay on the grass, with a big, cocky grin on his face.

"Get over here," she managed, smacking the grass beside her.

Treat crossed his arms. "Two can play at this game."

Max groaned. "You are so unfair!" She held a hand

up for him to help her up.

He pulled so hard she fell against him, and he kissed her again, probing her mouth with such delicate care that it only made her crave him more. She moaned before she could quell the urge, and that was all he needed to pull away with a victorious smile.

"Provincetown?" he asked.

PROVINCETOWN WAS AN artsy community with eclectic shops and street performers along a beautiful coastline. They caught a comedy show, and Max doubled over with laughter in her chair, tears of joy streaming down her cheeks. Watching her laugh had become one of Treat's biggest delights, and as he watched the spark that had returned to her eyes, he swore he'd do everything he could to keep her just as happy as she was right then.

As they made their way out of the club, the evening was cool and the lights from the shops shone in the open doorways.

"Treat! Hey, buddy. How's the hottest guy around?" A man in drag, complete with high heels and thick makeup kissed Treat on each cheek.

"Marcus!" Treat's eyes lit up at the sight of his old friend.

"Maxine tonight," the man said with a flirtatious wink.

"You look beautiful, Maxine." He emphasized *Maxine*. "This is..." Treat didn't know how to label Max—friend, girlfriend?

Max stepped forward and extended a hand. "I'm Max, Treat's weekend plaything." She laughed.

"Uh-uh, honey. My man Treat doesn't do weekend playthings. You must be someone special if you're up here with him." He leaned closer and said, "And I can see why. You are gorgeous. I absolutely love your red frames...and your name!"

"Thank you," she said, touching her glasses.

Weekend plaything? "Everything going well? How's Howie?"

"Oh, sugar, he's just as painful as ever. The man has more mood swings than a pack of PMSing women. But you know I adore him."

Treat put his arm around Maxine and lowered his voice. "And his cancer?"

Maxine's excitement waned for a second, and then she righted the smile on her lips again. "He's hanging in there. He really appreciated—we really appreciated—you pulling those strings with the hospital." Her eyes welled with tears, and she wiped them away and fanned the air. "Whew. I can't go there right now, sugar. I have to perform tonight."

Treat pulled her into a long embrace. "I'm here, okay? If you need me, call me anytime. You know that. Give Howie my love, please."

"Will do, Treat." Maxine reached for Max and hugged her, whispering in her ear, "The man is a saint."

Treat could feel a million unasked questions from Max as they passed a man who looked as though he'd been dunked in thick gold paint standing still as a statue while a few of the remaining tourists threw money into a hat at his feet and took pictures beside him. He waited for her to ask about Howie and Marcus, and when she didn't, he fed her unspoken curiosity.

"Howie lost his insurance a while ago, so I paid cash for his treatments and made a deal with the hospital that when he needed to be there, they'd bill me directly." He shrugged, and then it was his turn to get an answer to the question that was burning his tongue. "You're my weekend plaything?" he asked as they walked into Shop Therapy, a small store that specialized in retro clothing.

"I could tell that you didn't know what to call me." She shrugged.

She fingered through a rack of retro clothes, and Treat turned her around to face her with a serious gaze. "You do know that you are anything but a plaything to me, right?"

She did know, but just hearing it made her smile. "Who is Marcus...Maxine?"

"He's a friend. I've spent so much time up here that I've gotten to know many of the people who live here year-round."

"So many people would have trouble with embracing a man in drag, and you had no hesitation."

"Would you?" he asked Max.

"No, but some guys are really weird about that stuff. I don't know. I guess I'm wrong."

"I'm not most guys."

"Yeah, I know. I actually fell for you a little more

when I saw you hug him," she admitted.

"I'll have to remember that," he teased. They walked toward the back of the shop, and Treat said, "You know, dressing in drag isn't who he is. It's what he does for a living."

"Oh. No, I didn't know. I guess I assumed that drag was a way of life."

"No, at least not for him. He's a fantastic performer. If you'd like, I'll take you to a show sometime." They picked through a rack of T-shirts.

She slipped into the space between the clothing rack and his body. "I would really like that. Life is too short not to let people love whomever they want to love. Love is beautiful, and it should be praised, not picked apart." She touched his stomach and pressed her hips into his.

"See, the more I learn about you, the more I love you." *Love* slipped so easily from his lips, and he liked the way it felt. He searched her eyes for a reaction, waiting for her to pull away. When she didn't, he lowered his lips to hers, intending a sweet, loving kiss, but once he tasted her, he didn't want to pull away. The way Max was pressing her body into his in all the right places made him want to lay her down right there on the floor of the store. He made himself pull away, and for a moment he just watched her lick her lips, and he knew if he didn't move away from her hips and breasts, which were teasing every nerve in his body, he'd be walking around with a hard-on all day. He ran his hand through his hair and took a step back. Max laced her fingers into his and flashed a crooked smile.

"Wanna go upstairs?" he asked.

"What's upstairs?"

He looked around, then whispered, "Adult toys." He watched Max's smile change to a worried frown, and she shrank away from him. He quickly said, "We don't have to."

"Um…"

Treat watched her eyes dart around the store, like she was looking for an escape. "Come on." He took her hand and walked straight out of the store, down the street, and through an alley.

"Where are we going?" Max hurried to keep up.

A minute later they were staring at a sandy beach and a long pier. Treat walked off the edge of the street onto the sand and held his hand up for Max as she jumped down to the beach.

"Treat? Where are you taking me?"

"Right here." He dragged her under the pier. Without the lights and noise from the shops, it was dark and quiet. Only the swishing of the water against the shore cut through the night. He brushed an area of sand. "Sit," he said.

She sank to the sand. He sat next to her and took her hand in his.

"Why are we here?" Max asked. "Are we making out under the boardwalk?" Her eyes weren't dancing with the thought, and the unease in her voice pulled at Treat's heart.

"It's safe and dark, and I figured that since we can't

see each other very well, when we're here, you can tell me anything at all, and I promise I won't say anything about it outside of this safe, dark place. Ever."

She laid her head on his shoulder. "You're too much."

"I saw your face in there, Max. You looked appalled and frightened." He pulled her close. Whatever he saw, he needed to understand. He didn't need sex toys, and he hadn't been intent on buying any, but that didn't mean that he wouldn't have if she were into that sort of thing. He'd do damn near anything if it would please Max. But he wanted to understand what triggered her reaction so that he could be sure he'd tread carefully around it in the future.

"I don't have a lot of experience with men, Treat."

Besides the relief of the statement, he knew there was a *but* coming.

She fiddled with the pocket of her hoodie. "Remember the guy I told you about?"

"Yes." *The one I'd like to beat the shit out of?*

"Are you sure you want to hear this? I mean, it's gonna piss you off even more."

"Look at me, Max." He took her face in his hands and drew her close, until he was sure he had her full attention. "I want to understand whatever it was that flashed through your mind in there. You don't have to tell me, but it might help me to understand how to make you feel safe and secure in our relationship."

She took a deep breath. "It's not easy to say..."

"It might not be, but most things that are

meaningful are not easy." Treat also took a deep breath, preparing himself for her confession. Putting together the idea of adult toys and the fear in her eyes, he drew all sorts of maddening conclusions, and he promised himself not to overreact. He clenched his jaw as she began to explain.

"While we were together, he asked me to try...one of *those*." She blushed and looked away.

"It's okay. I'm not going to judge you, Max," he assured her.

She swallowed hard, then continued. "I was young, and I had the guy everyone wanted, so I thought..." She shrugged. "It can't be that bad. Okay."

He didn't want to hear what that asshole had done to her, but he wanted Max to heal from whatever hurt she was carrying around her neck like a noose. Just talking with his father had helped him so much that he was sure it would help Max to unload her worries, too.

She closed her eyes and spoke in a flat, even tone. "It was the night he grabbed me. We were in the bedroom, and he had undressed me, but he still had his pants on."

He felt her body shaking in his arms. "I'm here, and I'm not going anywhere. You don't have to continue if you don't want to, Max."

"I want to." She opened her eyes and looked into his. "He used...*it*, and at first it wasn't bad, you know? He was just kind of being gentle." She shrugged. "And then I don't know what happened. His eyes changed, almost like a different person took over inside of him, you know?"

A tear slipped down her cheek.

Treat wiped it away with his thumb, trying to keep his own twitching nerves in check, for the pain and anguish he saw in her eyes and what she was likely to have endured.

Max continued with an icy tone. "He was suddenly shoving it into me so hard and saying horrible, nasty things. Cursing at me and calling me names, and somehow...somehow I was able to crawl away from him and grab my clothes. I ran for the door, and that's when he grabbed my arm." She shook her head. Tears were streaming endlessly down her cheeks.

Treat pulled her against his chest. "Shh." He rubbed her back, stifling his mounting rage and his desire to get every detail on the asshole and rip him to shreds.

She pushed away angrily. "There's more. When I looked down, there was blood dripping down my legs. Bright red blood. I don't remember much after that except that my arm hurt like hell and he drank a lot of beer and then passed out in the bedroom. That's when my mom called. That's when I left."

"Max, he had no right to touch you like that." Treat's entire body pulsed with rage, but more important than the desire to hammer the hell out of that asshole was the desire—the visceral need—to help Max heal. "Baby, come here." He held her trembling body against him while she cried. "Let it out. Let all of it out until there's nothing left to tear you up. None of that was your fault, sweetness, and I'll never let anything like that happen to you again."

They remained in that position for a long time, until the footsteps on the pier above them silenced and the moon shone bright on the rippling water.

On the drive back to the bungalow, Max stared out the window, and Treat couldn't stop thinking about the image of Max, scared and bleeding. *What kind of animal would do that to her?* He remembered the way Max had touched him, the way she had craved him in her apartment—and he now understood how much courage it must have taken for her to open up to him in such an intimate way and take him with her mouth—and he also understood how the look he'd given her in Nassau would translate in her mind to a precursor for a hidden aggression. That understanding made him wonder if she'd done things with him out of some sort of fear.

"Sweetness, when you were with me, when you took me beside your bed, why did you do it? You don't have to do those things with me, Max. Ever. I can live our entire lives with nothing but kissing you and touching you. I never want you to feel like you owe me something or you have to live up to what you think other women might do or what other men might want. I'm not them, and you're sure as hell not like any other woman."

She turned to face him, and her eyes told her answer before he heard the words. "I wanted to. I've only been with two other men, Treat. The man I told you about and one other during my senior year of high school. I thought I loved him and that we'd be together forever, but you know how that goes. What do you know at eighteen? We went to separate colleges, and I got the inevitable Dear Jane letter a month later."

"I wish I'd known you then. I'd have loved you forever," he said, and he meant it so much that his heart ached.

"No, you wouldn't have. I told you, I was weak. I wasn't the same person. It's better that we're together now. Besides, I don't think I could have taken all those girls vying for your attention all the time. I was never that strong."

"There weren't actually that many," he said as he parked the car.

"Pfft. Everywhere we go, you are the center of attention, and that's okay. That's good. It makes me proud to be on your arm. But that doesn't mean it's easy. I'm not that strong, Treat. I have insecurities, and your looks stir the pot with every one of them. It's something I'll have to learn to overcome."

He came around the car and opened her door for her, offering his hand when she stepped out.

"I can promise you that I will never act on any advances by any women, and I sure as hell wouldn't ever think of hurting you in any way—and certainly not in a sexual way. Can't you tell how much I adore you, Max? I didn't think I'd ever feel as strongly about anyone as I do about my own family, and my feelings for you put them all to shame."

Chapter Twenty-Six

THEY SAT ON the couch in front of the fire, Max's legs across Treat's lap. He massaged her feet, pressing his thumbs deeply into the arch of her foot.

"You can't even begin to understand how good that feels." Max closed her eyes, enjoying his touch.

"Oh, I think I can."

She opened one eye. "Yeah?"

"It's touch, and touch is good," he said in a husky voice.

Why does your voice turn my entire body on? She pulled her feet from his lap and sat up, tucking them beneath her body.

"Let me do you," she said.

"Why, Max, what kind of man do you think I am?"

She playfully smacked his chest. "Not like that. Let me rub you and make you feel good."

He wiggled his eyebrows. "You naughty girl, you."

He went to a closet that Max hadn't noticed earlier and withdrew a comforter, then spread it out on the floor in front of the fireplace. When he pulled his shirt over his head with one hand, all of her breath rushed from her lungs at the perfectly sculpted physique on the man she loved with every ounce of her soul.

He stepped out of his pants and lay down in his boxer briefs.

"This might be more dangerous than I had anticipated." She was only half teasing. Did he really expect her to touch him without wanting to devour him?

He opened his hand and handed her a small bottle of oil.

"You just happen to keep this in the secret closet with the blanket? How much do you pay everyone to say that you don't bring women up here?" Something told Max that she'd been had.

He turned over and pulled her down beside him. "I don't lie, Max. I've never had anyone but Savannah here with me, and I slept on the couch, which is why the blanket is down here. The oil was something she left here."

Kneeling beside him, she wished she could ignore the jealousy that was creeping into her body. "I'm supposed to buy the old *only-my-sister* routine?"

In the next second, Treat was on his feet and heading for the kitchen, where he retrieved his phone. He pushed a button and a few seconds later said, "Vanny, talk to Max."

Max jumped up. "Oh my God. No way." *What is he doing?* Mortified didn't begin to describe the embarrassment she felt.

He held the phone out toward her with a wide grin. "Go ahead. I'll never have anything to hide from you, and I want you to know it and believe it." He pushed his hand with the phone in it toward her again.

She took it. "H-hello?" Her voice was thin and tethered with embarrassment.

"Max! Hey, girl! You found him! Did he call you?"

Max was surprised by Savannah's enthusiasm. "No, I came to Wellfleet. He'd said it was his favorite place, so I took a chance, and he was here."

"That's fate for you!" Savannah laughed. "The last time I was there, he had to sleep on the couch. Hey, ask him if he ever found my apricot stuff."

"Apricot stuff?"

"Yeah, he'll know what it is. Apricot Kernel Oil." *This cannot really be happening.* Max drew her eyebrows together and lowered the phone. "Savannah wants to know if you found her Apricot Kernel Oil that she left here?"

He grinned, twisting the bottle between his index finger and thumb.

Max stuck her tongue out at him, then covered her eyes.

"Yeah, he has it."

"Oh, good. It's great for aromatherapy. You guys should use it. It's awesome, and it won't leave your skin oily."

When Max didn't respond, Savannah filled the silence.

"That's a little presumptuous of me, right? Max, I just figured that any girl who would track down a guy's father to see him must be crazy for him, and I know he's crazy for you, so…"

"Thanks, Savannah. I'm sure we'll put it to good use." She watched Treat lower himself to the floor with another victorious smile.

"What did you want to talk to me about?" Savannah asked.

Oh, crap! Thinking fast, she said, "Um, oh, I wanted to know what Treat's favorite dessert was. He won't tell me and he said you knew."

"He's such a doofus. Tiramisu. Hey, I gotta run. I'm with Connor."

"Connor Dean? You're working this late?" Max watched Treat lay back down in front of the fireplace.

"Well, sort of. Glad you're with my brother. He's the best man on the planet. And I mean it, Max. Good to the very core. Love you guys; gotta run!"

The phone went dead, and Max followed the line of crow back to Treat's side. She didn't think it was possible that she could feel any stupider than she did at that moment.

"You can ask me anything, Max, and I'll always give you an honest answer. And I'll never blame you for not believing me, because I know people lie, but I'll stand behind everything I ever say."

What could she possibly say to that? He'd been true

to his word with everything he'd ever said to her. *He called his sister!* She dripped oil onto his back and finally said, "I'm sorry for not believing you. But you have to admit, it did sound fishy." She loved the feel of his slippery body beneath her hands.

"How do you know I didn't have this preplanned with Savannah?"

Max's hands stopped moving as she considered his question. She cracked a smile and said, "Because she'd never go along with it. She likes me."

"How about because I like you, and I'd never go along with it?"

Swoon! She bent down and kissed his cheek. "That works, too."

Max slid her hands along the sides of his spine, and then worked the tension outward, toward the sides of his body. She moved slowly, careful to cover every inch of his skin, to touch every muscle, and his appreciative moans urged her on. The more she touched him, the more she wanted to touch him. She followed the lines of his muscles up to the curve of his arm, kneading with a slow and steady rhythm, caressing her way up to his shoulders. She slid her hands over the crest of his muscles; then she slid her fingers forward, to the gentle dip on the other side.

He moaned in pleasure, spurring her on to the other side, where she allowed her hands to linger as she kneaded his shoulder and upper arm. The scent of the warm oil filled the room and heightened her arousal. His skin warmed beneath her hands, and she felt the familiar quickening of her pulse. Between his moan and the sweet aroma, she wished she weren't wearing any clothes so she could slither her naked body alongside of him.

Wait. Wait. Wait. She closed her eyes just long enough to regain control; then she oiled his thighs and kneaded the tension from the massive muscles that twitched beneath her hands.

"Your touch is magical," he said softly.

Max was concentrating on not feeling the pulsating sensation between her legs.

"Mm-hmm." She slid her hands between his thighs and stroked them slow and hard. He opened his legs, and she moved in between them so she could work each leg with both hands.

Her chest constricted at the intimacy. *How can he expect me to look at him lying there for the taking and not do more?* She shot a quick look at Treat's face. His eyes were closed, as if he were almost asleep. She closed her eyes and began kneading first the right cheek, then the left, through the thin cotton of his boxer briefs. She bit her lower lip. Every erotic touch made her hungrier for more. She was already damp, ready for him, and he hadn't even laid a hand on her. To think she'd gone her whole life without ever touching or being touched in such a glorious way.

There was no thought to what Max did next. Removing her clothes and folding them neatly before setting them on the table seemed natural. The fire warmed her skin as she lowered herself to the floor and inched the waistband of his briefs down, then licked along the edge of the sensitive skin, just as he'd done to her at her apartment.

Treat's responsive groan drew her up his body, her breasts grazing his slippery flesh.

"Max," he whispered.

"Shh." She kissed the back of his neck, allowing her tongue to linger on his salty flesh, before kissing his shoulder, and finally settling on the spot just beneath his ear.

He groaned again, drawing her in to deepen the kiss and suck harder. She slid her fingers around his biceps, pressing her hips against his. He tensed beneath her, and she slithered back down and straddled him, facing his feet. Goose bumps rushed up her legs to the edge of her panties as he flipped over beneath her and grasped her hips. She closed her eyes, trying to focus on giving him pleasure rather than wanting him to pleasure her. She leaned forward, using both hands to knead the tension from his calves, ankles, and eventually, his feet, which were just as gorgeous as she'd anticipated.

He pulled her back with one quick movement and licked her through her panties. Max sucked in a breath through clenched teeth, silencing a moan as he used his fingers to move the lace to the side, then lapped her sensitive, wet folds. She closed her eyes and pushed up, arching above him as he pulled her deeper against his mouth, then slid two fingers inside of her.

She couldn't think, could barely breathe, as she tightened around his fingers and pulsed against his incredible tongue. His touch was too much to bear. She shuddered against him, panting, riding the wave of her climax as he lapped and probed her, sending her higher than she'd ever been.

Without a word—she couldn't have spoken if she wanted to—she moved to his side. The fire, and the ecstasy she'd just experienced, drew a flush to her cheeks. He reached for her and she shook her head, her eyes feasting on the heat trapped beneath his briefs. She didn't question her newfound strength or the lack of embarrassment she felt. She felt herself owning the hasty desire that came over her, and she wanted to feed the feeling by teasing and taunting him.

"Max." He reached for her again, and she moved away.

She rubbed the sensitive area just beside his hips. He sucked in air between clenched teeth, letting a sexy groan slip through. Max ran her hands hard and slow up his chest, then leaned down and circled his nipple with her tongue.

He grabbed her head with both hands.

"Uh-uh," she whispered, peeling his hands away. "My terms," she said.

He groaned again, and she kissed his neck. The sensation of her breasts grazing the curls on his chest sent them both reeling. Treat's hungry groan mixed with her quiet moan as she licked his lower lip. "You like?" she asked.

She pressed her body against his. He reached for her, and this time she didn't stop him as he pulled her onto him and kissed her until the taste of her disappeared and his whiskers scratched the sensitive area beside her lips.

"You're driving me crazy," he said.

"All touch is good, remember?" she teased.

The need in his eyes was tangible as he took her head in his hands and kissed her urgently, then eased to a softer, teasing kiss.

His slow, decadent kiss made her writhe with desire.

"Max, I couldn't love you more."

"That's a shame. I was sort of counting on you loving me more each day."

EVERY NERVE ENDING was on fire, and the throbbing between his legs had stolen the blood from his brain. He ran his hand along her hip; then the thought of how she'd been hurt stopped him cold. He pulled her tight against his body, feeling her precious heart beating against his own—the heart he wanted to protect and love.

She pressed her hips against him, and when he pulled back, just inches from her lovely face, he drew the hair from her forehead and kissed her above each eye. The longing in her eyes was undeniable, but their lust had rekindled the overwhelming feelings he'd felt for her the very first time he'd seen her. And now, reconciling the sweet, loving, provocative woman in his arms with the image of her torment, blood dripping down her legs, abused by some bastard he wished he could slaughter, stole that lust and replaced it with a desire to heal her heart—completely.

"Treat." Max reached up and wiped the dampness from his eye. "What's wrong?"

He buried his head in her neck, breathing in the scent of her arousal and feeling her sweet, tender skin against his. He had to pull himself together. Grown men weren't supposed to get as emotional as he was over something that happened so long ago. But damn it, he wanted to heal her more than he wanted to satisfy his urge to make love to her.

"The thought of you, hurt down there..." He shook his head.

"That was a long time ago," she said, running her fingers through his hair.

That intimate touch stimulated his heart to beat a little faster.

"Max, I don't want to ever hurt you. Tonight wasn't supposed to be about sex."

"It's not," she said with innocence. "It's about love. I know that. I want to be with you."

"I want to heal you," he said.

"You will. You've already begun to. Just being able to accept and trust you in my life is a healing step for me. Just like I know it is for you."

He kissed her cheek and laid his head against her shoulder.

"I listened when you told me about how you were afraid to love. This. Us. Being together. It's as much a healing process for you as it is for me," she said.

She kissed him softly, then pulled off her panties, and in one swift move she was beneath him. She arched her hips and he slid inside of her. She closed her eyes, and the sensuous smile that lifted her lips nearly punctured his heart. He moved slow and gently. Every stroke of her slick heat sizzled through him. He grit his teeth against the mounting sensation, holding her shoulders so every thrust filled her completely, and he felt her tightening around him as she grasped at his back for more. She bent her knees and he drove in deeper, then pulled out hastily. *Shit.*

Max's eyes flew open. "What?"

"Condom." Treat jumped to his feet. "I'm sorry," he said as he bolted upstairs.

"Hurry," she called after him.

He took the stairs two at a time, snagged the condom from his nightstand, then hurried back down. He came down on his knees between her legs, ripped open the package, and slid the latex on.

Max stifled a giggle. "Sorry. It was just so funny, watching you run upstairs naked."

"You're not doing anything for my manhood here," he teased.

She laughed again, and she was so damned cute, naked and laughing, that he had to laugh, too.

Suddenly she stopped laughing and reached down to cup his balls—catching him totally off guard. She ran her fingers lightly over them until he thought he might burst. She came up to meet him.

"Love me," she said.

He took her then with a hungry groan. She felt so good. He could feel her heat through the thin protective sheath.

"Faster," she begged, meeting each of his hard thrusts with a tilt of her hips.

"Yes, yes...Oh, God," she cried out. Her insides pulsed as she called out his name, matching his peak thrust for thrust until they both could barely breathe and their bodies shuddered and rocked against each other. They fell asleep in each other's arms, and when the fire went out, the heat they generated kept them warm.

Chapter Twenty-Seven

TREAT WAS ON his phone on the back deck when Max came down from the shower. A warm mug of coffee was on the counter next to a plate of waffles, complete with strawberries around the edges. Max sat beside the open window and watched the tide roll out. She loved his little bungalow, and the more time she spent there, the more comfortable she became.

She didn't mean to eavesdrop on Treat's conversation, but she couldn't miss the frustration in his voice.

"I know I said I was sending an offer, but it's off. I can't move forward with it right now."

She realized that the answer he'd given her about where he lived hadn't really answered the question at all. She wondered if he had a place that he called home, or if the life he led really was one of traveling all the time. It sure seemed that way to her. She started when he pushed to his feet, sending his chair skidding across the deck.

"Cut it off. I'm done. No more acquisitions."

Max froze, now intent on listening to every word.

"I've got enough goddamned money to last me two lifetimes. I don't care. I'm done with it." He paced. "It's one property. Yes, I know it's only three months, but I can't spare three months right now." He paused, obviously listening to whoever was on the phone. "I don't give a damn who won't want to do business with me after this."

Whatever was going on had him tied in knots, and Max was certain that whatever it was, her showing up had spoiled his plans.

"Understood," Treat continued. "I know it's Thailand. Yes, I know what this will mean for my international business."

Max shot a glance at him. *Thailand?* He'd been working on that deal when she first met him in Nassau, and he'd missed his flight because of her then. *Oh, no.* She couldn't ruin his chance at something he'd worked so hard to obtain.

He ran his hand through his hair, pacing again.

"I'm changing things, starting now. No more constant traveling. No more acquisitions that consume all of my attention."

As much as Max knew she should be flattered by what she was hearing, she was too conflicted to enjoy it. There was no forgetting the look in Treat's eyes when he told her how his work provided the biggest thrill he'd ever experienced. She braced herself as he came inside.

"Hey, sweetness. You're up." He kissed her cheek, refilled his coffee cup, and sat at the table as though the tense phone conversation had never happened.

Max saw a shadow of worry behind his eyes. "Everything okay?"

"Fine, why?"

"Nothing, I just thought...Never mind." More worries burrowed into the pit of her stomach. She *was* eavesdropping. She couldn't come out and ask him about the conversation that now made her question the path her heart was taking her down.

He reached across the table and took her hand. "How much time do we have together? When does Chaz need you back at work?"

Don't change your life for me. Change your life for me. Max bit back the conflicting thoughts and tried to remember what day it was. *Wednesday.* "I have to be back by Sunday afternoon, so four days. Treat, if you have to do something for work, I totally understand. Don't let me hold you up. I can catch an earlier flight."

He shook his head. "I just wanted to know how much time we had together."

Max swore there was something hidden behind his smile, and she wrestled with letting him off the hook and making up an excuse to leave early. As much as it would hurt not to be with him, she knew that couples who gave up too much for each other only ended up resenting each other. In the back of her mind, she'd always wondered if that had been the thing that changed her ex-boyfriend. Since he was studying hotel management and could likely find a job anywhere, he'd agreed to move wherever she found a job in her field of marketing. He'd been prepared to relinquish any ideals he'd been dreaming of for his career in order for Max to follow her dreams. *And then he ended up hating me for it.*

By midafternoon temperatures had risen, and they took a walk along the beach.

"I've never been a hand holder," Treat said, holding up their interlaced fingers.

Max smiled. "I guess we've got a world of firsts between us then, because I've never been a masseuse or ever in my entire life had anyone give me a foot massage."

"Really? You've never had a foot massage? Well, sweetness, I'll be sure to take care of that from now on."

They came to a short jetty of rocks. The tide was beginning to come in and they walked to the end and watched as it rolled in, rising along the edge of the enormous rocks.

Treat looked out over the water with his brows drawn together. Max had been watching his face go from placid to contemplative throughout the morning, and she was dying to ask about Thailand, but she knew that if she brought it up, he'd tell her that he would change his life for her without ever looking back. She knew in her heart that he'd canceled the Thailand deal because of their relationship, and the thought of him giving up the aspects of his career that brought him such joy scared her to death. She couldn't shake the prickly reminder that being the impetus for such a major change was not a good thing. *He'll eventually get bored and blame me for everything he never had a chance to accomplish.*

The thought weighed heavily on Max's mind all afternoon. They ate dinner at the Bookstore Restaurant by the harbor, and despite the cozy atmosphere and the beautiful evening, Max was too sidetracked to eat.

"Are you all right?" Treat asked.

"Just tired." She feigned a smile.

"That would be my fault for keeping you up so late the last two nights. I'll let you sleep tonight."

Why did he continually have to be so generous? She reached for his hand and opened her mouth to ask him about the call, but before she could say a word, he spoke.

"Max, I thought maybe we should talk about what we want to do after this week is up."

She swallowed hard against the dull pain in the pit of her stomach. Now was her chance to let him off the hook. She clenched her napkin in her fists beneath the table. "I'll be swamped at work, and I'm sure you will be, too."

"Never too swamped to spend time with you," he said.

She'd finally let herself love him, and now she was realizing that it had been the wrong thing to do. He'd never be happy in one place with a girl like her. He needed the excitement of chasing down resorts and handling tough negotiations. He was a mover and a shaker, while she was a homebody. Maybe she could go with him? Follow his career? Chaz had already said she could telecommute. But would she resent him if she did? Would she be happy traveling all over the world?

"Max? What am I feeling here?"

Aren't guys supposed to hate talking about their feelings? Figures that I'd get the one who is just freaking perfect.

"Nothing, just tired," she lied.

Treat paid the bill and they drove back to the bungalow. Max was silent even though Treat kept looking at her like a sad puppy wanting to know what he'd done wrong.

They sat together under thick blankets on the back deck, watching the night sky bloom above the bay. Max wished she could freeze the evening right then and there and never have to make another decision.

"Are you ready to talk to me yet?" Treat asked.

Max's head rested against his chest, and she desperately wanted to tell him no, she didn't want to talk about it at all. They'd go back to their normal lives and either it would work out between them or it wouldn't. She wanted to tell him to go through with the acquisition of the Thailand resort, not to put his life on hold for her—but she wanted to hold on to him for dear life and never let him go, equally as much. Instead, she said, "There isn't much to talk about."

"Did I do something today that made you sad?"

She touched his cheek. "No. You're so good to me."

He looked out at the water, his dark eyes stuck in a serious gaze. "Are you worried that when we're apart something will happen? That I'll do something?"

"Nope. Not at all." And she wasn't. Max had no worries about Treat being with other women. He'd had a chance for a guaranteed tryst with the beautiful blonde, and he'd turned her down flat. Women were the least of her worries. Lack of trust would have been easier to deal with than what was looming over her like a waiting storm. Being the reason he gave up what he loved versus holding on to him forever was a tug-of-war that had no winner.

He pulled her close, and she closed her eyes, allowing herself once again to play with thoughts of spending every night with him, or being there for him when he returned from work. *Work*. What did someone like him do, anyway?

"Tell me something about what you do. I know you own resorts, but what does that really mean?"

"I don't want to bore you," he answered. "It sounds more glamorous than it is."

She sat up. "I'm serious. I don't really know what you do. I would like to understand it."

He let out a sigh and then smiled. That flicker of excitement she'd seen back at her apartment appeared in his eyes again. "Well, I don't have a set of things that I do on any given day. I have staff that take care of the resorts, and I have managers who oversee the staff, so I spend most of my time working on what comes next."

"What comes next?"

"New acquisitions, mergers, researching areas, distributors, running business valuations. I plan, scheme, analyze." He leaned forward with a burst of enthusiasm. "I've been doing this for twelve years and I swear it never gets old. There's always something new to think about—and then there are renovations, social events. I have to keep a pretty heavy social calendar to maintain the relationships. It's a crazy, fantastic life. It's been a dream, really, a very good dream."

He looked at Max and must have read the worry in her eyes, because when he sat back, the excitement dissipated. "It's been fun, and I'm set for life now. I don't need to keep doing more. This is what I did before I found you, Max." His voice turned serious. "You have to remember, I was filling my days with work and my nights with whatever I could that held no chance for permanence. I was running from my life, Max, not living it." He put his hand on her leg and squeezed. "What I do has always been exciting and fulfilling, but now that I'm ready to really live my life, now that I do have you by my side, I want more. I want the house, you as my wife, and maybe even children one day. I want the dream that I've spent so many years running from."

Max didn't hear anything after *It's a crazy, fantastic life. It's been a dream, really, a very good dream.* Max knew what she had to do.

SOMETHING HAD BEEN off with Max all day. Treat had known it the moment he'd seen her sitting at the kitchen table, fidgeting with her food rather than eating, and the frown she tried so hard to hide made her look like her life was crumbling around her. She hadn't shaken the darkness that lay behind her eyes all day. And now he could feel the tension in her body as she leaned against him. Every breath she took was short, riddled with stress.

He felt the change in her when she'd asked about his work. He'd been afraid to give her a truthful answer. He knew his enthusiasm for his work was intimidating, and yet he'd promised to always be honest, so he was. And now Max looked even more conflicted than she had before.

Treat wanted to take her in his arms and promise her the world that he knew he could give her, but something told him that she also saw his own turmoil. He had no concerns about Max, but Thailand was riding his nerves. He'd worked so hard for that acquisition, and truth be told, he would give up everything to be with Max, but one last foray into negotiations would be a sweet sendoff. It was the three months of international travel to corner the market that caused him concern. There was no way he could expect Max to pick up her life and go with him. He'd never ask her to—because if she did, she might hate him for it later. It was an unfair request.

As he sat with her now, he wrestled with the decision. He'd only just gotten her back in his life, and these last few days were not enough. He wanted a lifetime with her. He wanted everything he'd told her that he wanted, and if giving up acquisitions were what it would take, he'd do it.

"What do you want, Max?"

Max fidgeted with the edge of his sweater.

"Max? How about you? Do you want all those things?"

She shrugged, and that little movement tugged his heartstrings as hard as the day he'd seen her wearing the same outfit she'd had on the night before, when he thought she'd been with Justin.

"Max?" His chest tightened, and his hurt was slowly turning toward something else that he tried to suppress. If she didn't want all those things, then what were they doing together? Why had they revealed their souls to each other?

She looked up at him, and he asked her again, "What is it that you want? With me, where do you envision this going?"

Max pulled away. "I guess maybe we're moving a little fast."

Her words sent a swift kick to his gut. "A little fast? I thought you felt the same connection that I did. I thought you wanted this just as much as I do."

"I...I do, but—"

"But? Max, we can move slower. I never meant to push you. Just tell me what you want and I'll follow your lead." *This can't be happening.* Could he be such a fool to have fallen in love with someone who couldn't love him back? That couldn't be. He felt her love for him in everything she did and said up until that very second.

And still, even now, her eyes told a different story than her words.

"It's cold. Do you mind if we go inside?" Max picked up a blanket and escaped into the bungalow.

I'M DOING THE right thing. I am. I have to do this. The pain of the reality of what she had to do felt like she was peeling her skin back with a paring knife, then slowly tearing it away from her bones.

Treat followed her inside and she knew he was mad. Of course he was. She hated her goddamned self. How could he not? She was breaking both their hearts in order to save his happiness.

"Talk to me sweetness, please. Don't shut me out like this."

I feel like I'm bipolar, taking both of us on a roller coaster ride to hell. "What we have is great, better than great, but we don't even know each other." *Just tell him the truth!*

"I know everything I need to know about you, and what I don't know, I'll learn."

"Treat, you're a smart man. You know there's more to a relationship than what we have."

"You're right. I am smart. I know that love like ours is a once-in-a-lifetime thing, and that even if we have to take it slow, even if we can't move to the next step until ten years from now, that's enough for me."

The anguish and anger in his eyes almost broke her resolve. She had to be strong. He'd give up everything for her, and no matter how much she loved him, her love would never make up for the release of the things that really got his juices flowing. That was like a death sentence for a relationship.

"What're you worried about, Max? Just tell me. Whatever it is, I can fix it. We can fix it. We can work on it. I'll do whatever it takes."

"I know you will, and that's the problem." Max collapsed onto the couch and crossed her arms to keep them from trembling.

Treat sat beside her with a sigh. He put his hand on her leg and tenderly touched her cheek. She froze beneath his touch, desperately trying to rebuild those walls that had kept her safe for so long. *Damn it. Why is it so hard?*

"Are you saying I give too much? I don't understand. Am I smothering you?"

Max shook her head. If she opened her mouth, a flood of tears would follow.

"Sweetness," he whispered. "I can stop giving. I can turn into a mean bastard if you want."

His joke made her smile despite the way her heart was twisting and turning, like two giant hands were wringing it dry.

"You can't give up everything for me. I don't want you to." She closed her eyes with her admission.

"Max, look at me. Please."

She opened her eyes, and he touched her cheek again. She leaned into it, craving his caress. Why had she said anything at all? Why hadn't she left well enough alone? Just let him go back to work—wherever that was—and her go back to Colorado, and just let life unfold? Why did she need to define everything and put it into its place?

"If we—" He turned away.

Max had never met anyone like Treat. His eyes were damp again, like they'd been the night before, when he'd thought about how that man had hurt her. He was more empathetic and loving than any man she'd ever met.

"I can't even say *if*," he continued. "When we're together, neither of us has to give up everything. My businesses can run without me on site all the time, and if you want to continue working, I'll live—we'll live— wherever you want to live. We can have several houses, if that's what you want, anywhere in the world that you want."

Max pushed away from his kindness and paced in front of the fireplace. "I don't want you to buy me stuff. I'm not materialistic."

"I know you're not. That's not what I'm saying."

"I just don't want you to give up everything for me. You'll hate me for it."

He came to her side and pulled her close. Max tried to pull away, but he held her too tight. Leaning against him again, with his arms around her, refusing to let her go, she could almost believe that she should let her worries go.

"Family knows no boundaries, Max. That's something my father ingrained in my head. I hope that you will be my family one day. I could never hate you, and I'd do anything for you," he said as he stroked her hair.

Oh God. His family would never forgive me! I can't take their successful real estate mogul brother and make him a one-house, one-family man.

Max didn't have the energy to fight anymore. She wanted nothing more than to close her eyes and erase the anxious evening that had found them. So she was relieved when he took her hand and led her upstairs.

Treat didn't try to make love to her. He ran a warm bath for her so that she could relax, while he read in the bedroom. Twenty minutes later, she curled up beside him and within minutes he was asleep.

Max's heart wouldn't settle down. Every time she closed her eyes she saw his, dancing with excitement when he told her about how much he loved his work. The look in his eyes when he told her he wanted to live a simple family life was filled with happiness—but how long would it be before he realized he'd made a mistake? She'd missed the signs back in college. The way her boyfriend had suddenly started drinking more, going out to bars more. He'd lost interest in talking with her. She'd never miss those signs again, but she didn't want to recognize them in Treat and know she was the cause of them.

What she was contemplating would break his heart, just like he'd broken hers when he'd left town after the film festival, but what choice did she have? Could she risk his happiness just so she could be with the man she loved? If she got up from the bed. *Oh God, leave Treat?* If she packed her things and drove to the airport. Tears filled her eyes just thinking about it. If she left a note explaining why she'd left. *What would I say?* Would she really be saving him from a lifetime of resentment or would she crush his heart beyond repair?

Max stepped quietly from the bed. She went to the window and stared into the reflection of the moon on the water. She needed a guidebook, or a mother who could tell her the *right* way to handle this. Since she didn't have either, she had to make a choice. Was she selfish if she wanted nothing more than to be with him? No matter what he had to give up?

Max felt like a thief as she gathered her belongings and went silently into the night.

Chapter Twenty-Eight

TREAT'S ARM FELL on an empty sheet. He opened his eyes and listened for Max. The house was too silent. He went to the window and looked down on the empty deck, then went into the bathroom, wondering if she'd gone for a walk. As he took the toothpaste from the basket beside the sink, he realized her things were gone.

"Max?" he called into the empty house. He ran down the stairs, his heart thundering in his chest. He tried to deny the wrenching in his gut. *She can't be gone. She wouldn't do that to me—to us.* He tore open the door and raced to the empty spot in the driveway where her car had been.

"No!" he yelled into the crisp morning air.

Treat stumbled back into the house. *She can't be gone.*

He reached for his phone, and a handwritten note

stopped his heart. He picked it up with a trembling hand.

Dear Treat,

When I read your letters back at my apartment, I knew how much you loved me, and how much I loved you became crystal clear. Being here with you these past few days has only solidified that in my heart and in my mind. But I've been where we are now, where one person has to give up something big to make the relationship work, and in the end, the very love that drives people together can turn to resentment. Once the honeymoon stage runs out and real life comes in with deadlines and pressures and late nights when all you want to do is be left alone, you can't help but lose the feelings that drove you together. And then the resentment creeps in.

I didn't mean to listen to you on the phone, but I overheard you saying you were giving up acquisitions— the very thing that gets your juices flowing. I can't be the one to cause that, and I'm not sure I can travel the world like you do. I like to travel, and I love you, but not having a home and moving around so much would make my need for organization go overboard. And I'm sure it would eventually drive you crazy.

I love you, Treat, but I can't let our very different lives tear apart what we have. If I leave now, we'll always have these past few days. It won't be enough, and I know that, but it's better than waking up one day as strangers who feel trapped in a relationship. I can't go through that again. I'm sorry, but I guess I'm still too weak—even with your love giving me strength.

There's more, and I never thought I'd admit it to anyone, but I may never love anyone the way I love you, so I will share it with you now. Someone once told me that you can't have an honest, happy relationship with a partner until you have an honest, happy relationship with yourself. There are still a few demons lurking in my head, and I think I have to deal with them before I can be a fair partner to anyone, especially you. You deserve so much more.

I know how much you want Thailand. You deserve it, Treat. Go. Do what you are so very good at and what you love. I'll always love you, and I know you'll always love me.

My heart will always belong to you, but please don't follow me. Let us go so you can thrive.

Your sweetness at heart, Max

The lump in his throat didn't change the anger that roared in his chest.

"No." He slammed the letter on the table. "No. I'm not losing you again." His phone rang and he snagged it from the table without looking at the number.

"Max?"

"Uh, no. It's Savannah."

"Sorry." Treat's mind was reeling. He had to call Max and talk her out of what was sure to be the biggest mistake of their lives.

"I thought Max was with you."

He closed his eyes against the urge to snap at her.

"She was."

"Trouble in Loveland?"

"Savannah, not now. What do you need?" He calculated how much time it would take him to get to the airport, drive to Max's apartment, and set things right.

"Sorry. It's Dad. He's sick, and I'm really worried about him."

"I just saw him. He was as strong as an ox." *I'll have to convince Max that acquisitions aren't all that important to me. How can I do that? I'll hire someone to do them. I'll pay the attorney double if I have to.* Treat had built his empire based on his keen negotiating skills and his belief in personally being involved with every transaction. He'd entrenched himself so deeply that there was never a need to look outside of his own abilities, partnered with his legal and financial advisers, when it came to the acquisitions. Now he was seeing another side to what he'd always done. He'd been hiding—from life, from commitment, from love. For the first time in his life, he realized, he cared about someone enough to want to stop hiding. *There's got to be a way.*

"Treat, are you even listening to me?"

The edge in Savannah's voice pulled him back to the call. "Sorry. Tell me again."

"Treat. You have to come home."

"I'm on my way." He hung up and called his travel agent, who had him booked on a flight out of Provincetown forty-five minutes later.

He called Max on the way to the airport, and as the phone went to voice mail, he realized that Max hadn't checked her phone once the whole time they'd been together. In fact, he didn't remember even seeing her phone, which made him wonder if she'd even get his message—but he had to try. "Max, please don't do this. I love you, and we can figure this out. My dad's sick. I'm headed there now. I'll call you once I know what's going on."

BY THE TIME Max arrived at home it was almost noon, and she was exhausted. She'd cried so much on the plane, the stewardess asked her if she needed medical help. *Not unless they can fix a broken heart.* She dropped her bags on the floor and fell into bed.

Nine hours later, Max woke up feeling like a wet dishrag. The headache that thumped and squeezed was only a minor discomfort compared to the ache in her heart, but she'd done the right thing. You can't take an aggressive, successful man and steal him out of his element for good—that would be like caging a bear. Eventually the bear would recognize the bars for what they were and tear them down—even if it meant hurting the person who had been nurturing him, tending to his needs, loving him, for years.

She wandered into her living room feeling dazed and hungover. She eyed the couch, but the memory of Treat sitting beside her on it was too much to bear. *You did this to yourself. He begged you to make a life with him.* The emptiness was like nothing she'd ever known.

She went to the refrigerator and swung open the door. *Blech.* Nothing looked good. She needed something, but she couldn't pinpoint anything that would fill the void.

After wandering aimlessly around the apartment, she finally grabbed a book and went back to bed. Within the first page, she was sucked back into sleep.

THE NEXT MORNING, Max lay in bed stewing over what she'd done. She had no energy to get up from her comfortable bed. She wasn't hungry, and though she knew she should get up and go to work, her motivation had slipped away somewhere in the night. She closed her eyes and faded in and out of sleep until late in the afternoon.

She hauled herself out of bed and went to the little balcony off the living room, where she pressed her hands against the cool glass, thinking of Treat. If she closed her eyes, she could feel the bay breeze against her face and smell the salty air. She could feel Treat's hand on her leg. She opened her eyes with a start.

"You're pathetic," she said to her reflection in the glass. "You did this. You turned him away. This is your fault, and now you have to suck it up." She turned away with tears in her eyes. *Great. Now I've turned into a crazy person who sleeps all day and talks to herself.*

That was enough to send Max into a warm shower. As the water rained over her, she thought of Treat, how much she missed him already and how she'd freaked out when they were first in bed together at her apartment, which brought her mind to her ex-boyfriend and how much he'd messed up her head. God, she hated him. *What the hell have I done? How could that one relationship in college fuck me up so badly?* She turned the water hotter until steam filled the glass doors and she couldn't see out, until the memories of her ex-boyfriend separated from those of Treat, and until the tears that she didn't realize were falling melted into the rain from the faucet.

An hour later, with her hair dry and pinned up into a ponytail, having donned clean jeans and a fresh T-shirt, she headed out to her car. She stood in the parking lot remembering her legs wrapped around Treat's waist just feet from where she now stood. *Ugh! I can't keep doing this to myself. I chose to leave. It's for the best.*

She drove circles around town just to avoid being alone in her apartment and wallowing in memories that made her skin burn with regret. She drove toward the office, but when she entered the dark parking lot, she realized that she was too tired, and it was too late, to do any real work. She drove into the Village, where the familiar lights in the trees brought a smile to her lips. *Treat would love it here.* She forced the thought from her mind.

Max followed the sidewalk past all the stores, around a corner, and down an alley, then disappeared down a few steps. She pulled the heavy door to Taylor's Cove open and waved to the bartender and owner, Joe Taylor.

"What'll ya have, Max?"

Joe's grandfather had opened the pub years earlier, and when Joe had taken it over, he'd encouraged the hard reputation the pub had of catering to bikers and blue-collar workers. Joe might serve a rougher crowd, but he ran a tight ship. He didn't allow any trouble, and the result was a quieter pub where there was little conversation and an abundance of solitude.

As she climbed up on a stool at the empty bar, she waved her hand. "Whatever. Something strong and yummy."

"You look beat, Max. You okay?"

"Yeah, just flew halfway across the United States. I'm tired, but I'm fine." She took the glass without asking what it was and sucked down the pungently sweet liquor, licking her lips as she slammed down the empty glass.

"Wow, that was good!"

"You know my rule, Max." Joe wiped the bar with a towel and removed her empty glass.

Max rolled her eyes. "Yeah, yeah, no refill for a full minute." Max was already feeling the effects of the drink. The tension in her shoulders and neck loosened as she touched her right ear to her shoulder, then the left. *Treat would rub that pain away. Oh my God! Shut up!* "Has it been sixty seconds yet?"

"Almost." Joe leaned on the bar.

She looked around the small tavern and tried to focus on the television, but it didn't hold her attention. There were two older men sitting at a table in the corner, and a younger man was sitting at a table just to her right. *What am I doing here?*

Max dug through her purse for her cell phone. She must have left it at home. *Damn it.* She tried to remember when she'd last used it but couldn't think beyond her desire for another drink. Luckily, Joe was placing one in front of her as she looked up.

"Thank you," she said with a smile. She nursed her drink. The more she drank, the less sure she was about what she'd done. Maybe she shouldn't have taken the onus off of him to realize that giving up the things he loved to be with her was the wrong thing to do. The thought of Treat waking up to find her note no longer seemed the kindest way to have set him free. Maybe she should have stayed put and fought it out with him. She finished her second drink and held up her glass.

"Five minutes, Max."

"Whatever," she said, then went right back to focusing on Treat. Hadn't she told him to love her through her insecurities? This was his fault. It had to be. He should have never let her go. He should have declared his love for her. Wait. Did he? Oh yeah. He had.

Max slid off of her stool to go to the ladies' room, which seemed very far away. Why was the floor wobbling like that?

When she came back to the bar and asked for another drink, Joe shook his head.

"Joe, I'm almost thirty. I'm pretty sure I'm allowed to drink." Joe had always watched over her, ever since she'd first walked in as a twenty-two-year-old, doe-eyed girl.

"Yeah, you are, but when you first came in here you said you weren't a drinker. I've seen you only a handful of times since then, but you never drank like you are tonight, which tells me two things." He leaned over the bar, and Max leaned closer.

Between her exhaustion and the alcohol, she had a hard time remaining still.

"You're either getting over some man, or you've been fired, and since I spoke to Chaz and he assured me that you're still an employee, I'm thinking it's the first."

"You called Chaz?"

He ignored her question. "And because I'm thinking it's the first, and I can't have some guy coming down here with a baseball bat to have at me for allowing you to drink so much that you end up in the hospital, or dead on the side of the road, I'm pulling rank."

Max had to smile. He was right. He had been at this a long time.

"Mind if I join you?" Kaylie slid onto the stool beside Max.

"Oh my God." Max covered her face and groaned. "I'm sorry he called you, Kaylie." She glared at Joe, who shrugged with a caring smile.

"Thanks, Joe," Kaylie said. "Wanna talk about it?" she asked Max.

"God, no," she said, feeling the effects of the alcohol. Maybe it was a good thing she hadn't gotten that third drink.

"So, you went to Mass and he wasn't there. So what? I told you fate was a load of donkey doo."

On second thought. "Joe, now that I have a driver, may I please have another drink?"

Joe brought her half a glass.

"Thanks, Dad," Max teased. She slammed her head back and gulped it down. "Ahh. Okay, now I can talk."

"I can tell this is gonna be good." Kaylie rubbed her hands together.

"Don't get too excited. Long story short, he was there. Fate did step in."

Kaylie touched her arm. "No way. And?"

"And I'm here and he's there, and..."

"And?" Kaylie asked.

Max held her palm up toward the ceiling. "He's wonderful. He's...Oh God, where do I start?"

"I want the good stuff, so start with that."

Max leaned in close so she and Kaylie were head to head, and she whispered, "He's loving and romantic and, Kaylie, oh my God, I never thought I could feel the way I did when I was with him."

Kaylie put her hand on Max's shoulder. "Max, you told me all of this before you saw him. So...what are we really talking about here?"

At the same time that Kaylie said, "Multiple orgasms?" Max said, "It's definitely love."

"Wait, what?" Kaylie said.

Max blushed. "And that other thing," she whispered. "Max!"

Max shot a glance at Joe and saw a wicked grin on his lips. She covered her face. "Great, now I'm the town tramp."

"Oh, stop it. Joe knows you better than that." Kaylie winked at Joe. "You were the town tramp before Treat; now you're also the Wellfleet tramp," she teased.

Max slapped her arm.

Joe sauntered over and leaned in close again. "Maxy, I've never even seen you with a guy besides this one's husband." He nodded at Kaylie. "I think you're a lady, no matter what she says."

"Thank you, Joe." Max noticed the room was beginning to spin and reached for the bar.

"I wanna know the rest. Why on earth are you home? Chaz gave you the week off."

Max stood up, gripping the bar. "I left in the middle of the night. Left him a note."

Kaylie grabbed her arm and steadied her. "I'm gonna take you home with me tonight." She paid Joe for Max's drinks and thanked him, then walked Max out of the pub.

"He was giving up Thailand for me," she slurred. "I couldn't let him do that."

"Thailand?"

"And acqui—acqui—acquisitions. Everything he loved. Poof! Gone. And all because of me."

They arrived at Kaylie's car, and she leaned Max against the side as she opened the door, then guided her in. "If you're gonna heave, open the window," Kaylie instructed.

"I couldn't let him *poof!* because of me."

"You're not making any sense, Max, and I don't understand." Kaylie drove out of town, toward her house. "You like everything about him, but you don't want him to give up what? What's Thailand?"

Max closed her eyes.

"Are you asleep?" Kaylie asked quietly.

"No, I'm not asleep. How can I sleep when I'm this drunk?" Max opened her eyes, squinting at the bright streetlights. "Okay, so he was talking about for-e-ver. You know about for-e-ver? You have it with Chaz, only Chaz didn't have to give up Thailand and all the things that got his juices flowing to have his forever like Treat would have to do. What kind of name is Treat anyway? He is delicious, let me tell you."

Kaylie laughed. "You are so drunk, Max. Before the other day, I'd never heard you say two words about a man, and all of a sudden your mouth spilleth over. So, I assume by *got his juices flowing* you mean he would have to give up other women, and Thailand is some sort of reference to exotic women?"

"Locations." It seemed like the right choice. She missed Treat. Just talking about him made her loins ache.

"So, he has women in exotic locations and he'd have to give them up? Well, hell yeah, he'd better if he's going to have forever with you, but he didn't strike me as that kind of guy. I guess you never know. I mean, he's really hot."

"Hey, he's my hot guy."

"You left him, remember? Now he's anyone's hot guy."

"Shit." Max spun toward Kaylie. "What have I

done?"

As Kaylie parked the car in front of her house, she said, "You drank too much. We can deal with this tomorrow, after you're sober and thinking straight. It still feels like the story is a little off. I mean, come on, Max. Everyone gives up something when they get married."

"You're right. Actu-a-lly, I think I did the right thing. Now he won't resemble—reset—resemb. Hold on." Max covered her face, then shot a finger up in the air and said, "Resent me!"

"Okay, let's get you inside."

Chapter Twenty-Nine

TWO THINGS BECAME crystal clear to Treat as he sat by his father's bedside in the hospital. It was time for him to come home, and he desperately wanted to put down roots—with Max. He'd called her cell phone several times, and either she still hadn't checked the messages or she was purposely avoiding him, and every second that passed without hearing from her sent him spiraling further into an abyss of loneliness.

"Do you want to go to Dad's and get some sleep?" Savannah had been at the hospital when Treat arrived. When she'd first called him, their father had been having bouts of dizziness and chest pains. Within the hour, he'd had trouble breathing, and she'd brought him in.

"I'm not leaving." Rex was right, his father *had* needed him. He took his father's hand in his own.

"Rex is coming back in after he takes care of the

morning chores. I'm sure it'll be fine if you want to take shifts."

"Savannah, I'm not going anywhere." He didn't mean to sound gruff, but seeing his father in the hospital bed brought memories of his mother racing back to him. In her last months, she'd been in and out of the hospital too many times to count, and she'd looked just like Dad did now: small and weak beneath the sterile hospital sheets.

"Okay, okay. Dane finally got my messages. He's in Australia and he's taking the next flight home."

"Did you reach Hugh?" Treat clenched his jaw. He'd kill Hugh if he had some lame excuse not to come home.

"He's on his way, and before you can ask, Josh is on his way, too. He had to move his schedule around before he could leave," she said. She moved to the seat closer to Treat. "Do you want to talk?"

"No. I want the doctors to finish the goddamned tests and tell us what the hell is wrong with him."

His father stirred.

"Dad?" Treat rose to his feet as his father blinked the sleep from his eyes.

"Treat? What are you doing here?" He looked around the hospital, confused. "What the?" He looked down at his gown. "Aw, shit. Really?" He frowned at Savannah.

Treat breathed a sigh of relief to see his father hadn't lost his spunk. That had to be a good sign.

"You weren't able to breathe, Dad. What did you want me to do, let you die right there in front of me?"

Savannah asked.

"Wait. Savannah, you were at Dad's? Why? I thought you went back to New York."

His father's low, rumbly voice answered him. "Turns out Connor Dean's more than a client, and your sister here seems to have had a falling out with the man who isn't good enough for her family to meet but is apparently good enough for her to jet all over the world with."

Treat lifted his brows in Savannah's direction and held his palm out in question.

Savannah half shrugged, then turned away—her familiar *I can't talk about it right now* mannerism.

He couldn't focus on Savannah and Connor right then. He patted his dad's shoulder. "Dad, you should probably settle down. They're running all sorts of tests to see what happened, but they think it might have been your heart."

"*Pfft.* I saw your mother again; that's all. Your sister overreacted."

Savannah and Treat exchanged a worried look. Treat thought back to when he'd first arrived at the bungalow. He'd sworn his mother was nearby, and even now he wondered if she had been.

His father pushed the button on his bed and raised it so he could sit up properly. "Don't think I didn't see that look, you two."

"Dad," Savannah began. "We're just worried about you."

"Well, how about you worry about yourself a little

more. And you." He pointed at Treat. "Your mother is worried sick about you. What the hell are you doing about that sweet girl, Max?"

This time the look he and Savannah exchanged was one of annoyance.

Luckily, before they went any further down the mother road, the doctor came into the room. Dr. Mason Carpenter had been their father's physician for as long as Treat could remember. When he retired two years earlier, his son and partner in the medical practice, Dr. Ben Carpenter, had taken over.

Ben and Treat had grown up together, and Treat not only trusted his medical judgment, but he had always found Ben to be a loyal friend. He shook Ben's hand and pulled him into an embrace, giving him a strong pat on the back.

"Treat, good to see you," Ben said, his eyes shifting to Savannah.

Ben had had a crush on Savannah when they were younger. Now, as Ben drank her in, Treat remembered the summer after Savannah completed ninth grade and he and Ben had been home from college. Savannah had realized that her body was no longer that of a young girl and had flaunted it as such, much to Treat's dismay. Ben hadn't been able to take his eyes off of her then, and from the look in his eyes now, his feelings hadn't changed one bit.

"Savannah, you're still here."

"I'm not leaving anytime soon." She crossed her arms and narrowed her eyes at Ben.

Treat gave her a harsh glare. Their father had taught each of them better manners than that. Had she lost her mind?

"Don't mind her, Ben. She's been up all night," Treat said.

"Benjamin, when am I getting out of this place?" Hal asked.

Ben smiled and squeezed Hal's wrist. "Well, Mr. Braden, I have to ask you a few questions. What were you doing when your symptoms began? Savannah wasn't sure. Were you doing anything strenuous?"

"I told you. He was in the barn when I found him—"

"The last time I looked, honey, I was Mr. Braden. Now, he might have been talking to Treat, I suppose, but Ben here has been to medical school, and I can't imagine by the way he looks at you that he would mistake you for a mister."

Ben blushed.

Savannah stewed.

Treat laughed under his breath. *Yup, Dad. You're just fine.*

"To answer your question, I was in the barn with Hope," his father answered. "And, Ben, call me Hal, please. How many years have I been telling you that?"

"And were you brushing her? Mucking out the stall? What exactly were you doing?"

Treat had to smile at the way Ben ignored his father's request. Ben had told his father at least a dozen times that he had too much respect for him to call him by his first name, and his father still hadn't stopped grumbling about it.

His father set his mouth in a serious line and crossed his arms. Treat watched his father's biceps bounce to the same rhythm of his clenching jaw. Sitting up, with annoyance stewing just under his skin, his father no longer looked small or sickly in the hospital gown. He looked like he was ready to haul his butt out of bed and get back to work.

There's the dad I know and love. Thank you, God.

"Mr. Braden?" Ben urged.

Hal shook his head, then said with a grumble, "Oh, all right. But I don't want to hear any crap about this, you hear me, Benjamin?"

"Yes, sir. No crap." Ben flashed a knowing smile at Treat.

Ben had seen his father through every mood on the spectrum. He and his parents had enjoyed many barbeques at the ranch with his family, even though Savannah had never given him the time of day.

"I was talking to Adriana." He scanned his children's faces first, then his doctor's.

Treat knew his father saw exactly what he did on Savannah and Ben's faces— pity. He worked hard to keep that same look from being recognizable on his.

"Don't look at me like that. It doesn't matter what you think of it. Adriana was there, and she was watching over Hope the same way I was." He shifted his eyes to Treat and pointed a finger. "And you remember what I told you. She's worried that you're going to get so lost in your own little world of resorts and whatever the hell else eats up your time and forget about the thing that matters most." He patted his heart with his strong hand.

Ben drew his eyebrows together, and Treat held his palms up toward the ceiling, as if to say, *That's Dad for you.* But Treat couldn't lie to himself. His father's words ran through his head, stirring up the message he'd been giving himself all night. *Go get Max.*

"Mr. Braden, I don't doubt that you believe you saw your wife, or that you have ongoing conversations with her."

"Oh Jesus, really, Ben?" Savannah said with a sigh.

Treat touched her arm and nodded toward the chair. She sat down and crossed her arms and legs, bouncing her foot up and down.

"Hear me out, please, Savannah." Ben continued. "Your father had all the symptoms of a heart attack, but luckily" —he stressed the word *luckily* and looked at Savannah as he said it— "what he actually suffered was a case of broken heart syndrome."

"Okay, you know what?" Savannah rose to her feet and headed for the door. "I can't listen to this nonsense anymore. Treat, get me when...just get me after, okay?"

Treat went to his father's side. "I'm sorry, Ben. She's apparently had a rough time lately. Please continue." *I think I have broken heart syndrome.*

"Broken heart syndrome can mirror all of the symptoms of a massive heart attack, from difficulty breathing and chest pain to low blood pressure and even weakening of the heart muscle."

"That sounds like a heart attack. What's the difference?" Treat held his father's wrist. Feeling his pulse helped to settle his increasing worry.

"Well, BHS is also called stress cardiomyopathy, because it's caused by severe stress, usually emotional—extreme fear, anger, surprise. There are two major differences between a heart attack and BHS. The first is that most heart attacks occur due to blockages and blood clots forming in the coronary arteries. If those clots cut off the blood supply to the heart for a long enough time, the heart muscle cells can die, leaving the patient with permanent and irreversible damage. But with BHS, patients have fairly normal coronary arteries, like your father does, without the presence of severe blockage or clots."

Treat squeezed his father's wrist. *No blockage. No clots. Good arteries.*

Ben continued. "The second difference is that with stress cardiomyopathy, the heart cells are stunned by the adrenaline and other stress hormones, but not killed as they are with a heart attack. And as I'm certain we'll find with your father, that stunned effect gets better very quickly, often within just a few short days. So even if a patient suffers severe heart muscle weakness at the time of the event, the heart completely recovers within just a few weeks, and in most cases, there's no permanent damage."

"And that's what you expect with Dad?" *That's it. I'm definitely spending more time at home.*

"Yes, exactly. And from what we've seen with BHS,

there's no pattern of recurrence. It can happen, but we've never observed a second recurrence."

"So, you're saying I was too emotional and had a fake heart attack that weakened the heart muscle, but it'll repair itself and I'll be fine?" Hal asked.

"Yes, sir. And the damage to your heart muscles was minimal, so you should make a full recovery."

Hal started to get out of bed. "Well, then, I can go home and run my ranch."

Ben put a hand on Hal's arm. "Not so fast. We're going to watch you for the next few hours. We gave you some medication to lighten the load on your heart while you recover, and I'll go over the protocol with you before you're released. I want to monitor you for the next few hours, but then you should be good to go."

"So he should be okay?" Treat asked.

"Yes, but..." He looked at Hal. "Mr. Braden, you cannot go back to working the ranch like I know you want to right away. You should recover in a month or two, but during that time, I don't want you to do any strenuous work. Treat, can I count on you to ensure that he complies?" Ben ignored Hal's groan and the harsh stare he set on him.

"Of course," Treat answered.

"He's got his own life to lead, Benjamin. What kind of crap is that?" Hal lowered his voice to a grumble. "I'm a big boy. I don't need a babysitter."

"Of course you don't, Mr. Braden. I'm sure you'll go home and do exactly what I advise, because you were always so compliant with my father." Ben coughed and said, "Broken arm," at the same time.

Treat cracked a smile at his friend's levity and his father's simmering anger. Years earlier, his father had suffered a fractured arm, and instead of listening to Ben's father's medical advice, he was back on his favorite horse later that afternoon—and was back in the doctor's office two hours later, after the fracture had morphed into a full break and he'd needed a cast.

"Ben, thank you. I really appreciate you taking such good care of him." Treat shook Ben's hand.

"Do you want me to send Savannah in if I see her?" Ben asked.

"No need. I'm right here, and I heard all of it." Savannah walked in with her cell phone in her hand and suspicious red rings around the edges of her eyes.

Treat immediately knew his sister had been crying. He put his hand protectively on the small of her back when she came to their father's bedside.

"I'm sorry if I upset you, Savannah," Ben said.

She nodded, then took her father's hand. "So basically Dad needs to stop talking to Mom and stop worrying about us?"

Ben smiled. "Well, given that I don't think your father will ever stop doing either one of those things, no. For now we'll just go with something a little easier, like maybe talking out some of his frustrations instead of holding them in."

"I'm not talking to a therapist, if that's what you're saying, Benjamin. Your father would never ask me to do that," Hal said.

266

"Dad, you'll do whatever he tells you to do," Savannah said.

"No, Mr. Braden. I would never think of advising such a thing. My father schooled me well in the way of the Bradens. What I recommend is that when you are worried—or your wife is worried"—he ignored Savannah's eye roll and continued— "about something like your children, talk to them about it. Don't keep it inside. And if there are troubles with the ranch, talk it through with Rex."

"Or me," Treat added.

"Did I hear my name?" Rex came through the door, his eyes locked on his father's, then slowly met Treat's. "Talk what through with me?"

"I was telling your father that he needed to stop holding things inside, and if he has issues with the ranch, to talk them through with you...or Treat, I suppose," Ben said.

"Treat's never here," Savannah argued.

"Of course, Dad." Rex kept his eyes locked on his father. "You can count on me, and Savannah's right, Treat's never here."

"I will be from now on," Treat retorted. *Rex, my ass.*

267

Chapter Thirty

I SHOULD NEVER be allowed to drink again, Max thought as she reached for her throbbing head. It took only a few seconds for her to recognize Chaz and Kaylie's guest room. The combination of the pictures of the twins on the dresser and their happy little voices filtering into the room were hard to miss.

"Don't wake up Auntie Max," Kaylie warned them.

Max sat up with a groan. Flashes of Taylor's Cove came back to her, and she sifted through them and put the pieces of the previous night back together. She stood and held on to the dresser for support while the room circled her for a few seconds, then finally righted itself. She made the bed and straightened the throw rug that she must have pushed to the side.

Still wearing the same clothes she'd worn the night before, she went across the hall, washed her face, and rinsed out her mouth. She missed waking up with

Treat's heart beating beside her, his strong arms enveloping her. "Damn it," she muttered. She looked at herself in the mirror and fixed her ponytail, making a disgusted *tsk* sound at her puffy face. Then she said to her reflection, "No more of this. You made your decision, and it was the right one. Now hold your head up high and get into work. Do something productive." *Like pick up your car.* She groaned. She couldn't believe she'd put Kaylie out like that last night. With another irritated *tsk,* she went in search of Kaylie.

She walked down the hall in her stocking feet, and two adorably rambunctious toddlers raced toward her.

"Auntie Max!" Lexi said as she jumped into Max's arms.

"Auntie Ma-Ma-Max."

Max scooped Trevor into her other arm, then realized that either they'd both gained weight in the last month, or she was really worn out. She set them both down with a kiss on the cheek and a pat on the tush.

"Auntie Max needs coffee," she said, holding the side of her head.

"Lover girl walks," Kaylie teased. "Here. I heard you in the bathroom, so I was prepared." She handed Max a warm mug of coffee, which only made her miss Treat even more, and then two aspirin, which made her love Kaylie almost as much as she loved Treat.

The kids ran to their playroom, and she and Kaylie sat in the living room.

"How badly did I embarrass myself last night?" Max asked.

"Well, if you call telling my husband that you once thought you were in love with him but then realized you really just loved him like a brother embarrassing, then I'd say just a little. I found it hilarious. I have never seen Chaz unable to respond to someone before." Kaylie laughed.

Max covered her face with her hands. "Oh my God. I'm so sorry, Kaylie."

"For what?"

"For saying that. For Joe calling you to come get me. God, Chaz must hate me." *I ruined my career.*

"No, he took it in stride. Actually, I think he was glad. He always worries that you don't do anything besides work. When you went to Wellfleet, he was so happy. He said, 'I hope she finds him and he sweeps her off her feet. She deserves someone wonderful.'"

Max covered her face. "That's really sweet, but ugh...how humiliating."

"Oh, stop. Your worst drunken night is ten times more tame than my tamest drunken night."

"Thank you," Max said. "Whether that's true or not—and I don't want to know either way—thank you. I guess we should get my car."

"We already did," Kaylie said.

"Who's we?"

"Me and Chaz. The kids were up at, like, five thirty, so we buckled them in and picked it up. It was better than letting them wake you up, and they love to ride in the car."

"Kaylie, you're a godsend."

"Yeah, well, what can I say?" Kaylie pretended to fluff her hair. "But since I was your pick-up girl, I deserve to know about this whole Treat thing. Last night you were rambling on and on about other girls and Tahiti, or Thailand, or something like that. You made no sense at all, except for the part about you leaving in the middle of the night, which, I might add, was a pretty shitty thing to do."

"It was the only thing I *could* do. A guy like Treat can't give up everything he loves for someone like me. I don't do social calendars, jetting all over the world, and living out of resorts. And if he gave those things up for me, he'd eventually resent me for it." *I made the right choice, even if I can barely breathe just thinking about not being in his arms.*

"But you know how much it hurts to be left like that, Max." Kaylie shook her head, disappointment obvious in the look of disapproval in her eyes and the way she clenched her lips.

Max felt like she was right back in third grade, when she'd stuck out her tongue at her teacher and her father had given her that same head shake, the same baffled look.

"He did that to you and you about lost your mind, or did you somehow forget that when you were swept into the fated fantasy of love conquers all?" Kaylie left no room for misinterpretation.

"You're a real ballbuster," Max said.

"I'm not. I just don't think you have to hurt people to let them know you love them."

Max sat straight up. "That's *not* why I did it."

"Come on, Max. This is me you're talking to. I can spot love from a mile away, and whatever it is that has you running away from him is not very different than whatever caused him to do the same to you." Kaylie took Max's cup into the kitchen to get her more coffee. "The only question that remains is, how do you fix it from here?"

Max met her in the kitchen. "What do you mean? It's already fixed. I'm not letting him give up the things he loves because of me. End of story. Done."

"Right," Kaylie said with a roll of her eyes.

"I gotta get home and shower and change. I'm sure Chaz can use some help at work. Then I have to find my cell phone."

"Well, don't hurry too much. It's already one o'clock, so he's there for only a few more hours. Did you lose your phone?"

"One o'clock? Oh, Kaylie. I'm so sorry. You should have woken me up." Now I'm a drunken loser, too? *I better pull my shit together or I'll have to add* lost job *and* lost friends to keep my boyfriend company *on my* Things I've Lost list.

"Don't be silly. Want me to call your phone?" she asked.

"No, it's not in my purse. It's probably in my bags at my place. Kaylie, thank you for everything. I mean it. I'll make it all up to you."

"No need. That's what friends are for. But do me a favor. Please just tell me one thing. Did Treat have many women in Thailand?"

Max laughed. "Not that I know of. It sounded like he was negotiating on a resort there and then changed his mind because of me."

"The man knows how to create a fortune, that's for sure."

"He sure does," Max said in a flat voice. "You know I don't care about money, right?"

"Yeah, I know. But it doesn't hurt to know it's there," Kaylie said with a smile. "Security, Max. It does make life a little easier when you know you don't have to sweat every dollar."

Max grabbed her purse and found her keys on the counter. "Well, he and I won't be doing any sweating together, so for now I'll be sweating it out on my own." She gave Kaylie a hug. "I fixed the rug and made the bed."

"You didn't have to do that. I moved the rug last night in case you barfed."

"Oh my God, Kaylie. Anything else I should know?" *Can today get any worse?* Max needed a hot shower, a toothbrush, a gallon of water, and about thirty straight hours of sleep.

"Nope. That about sums up your night of debauchery. Let me know what happens with the man, and if you want to talk now that you're sober—but after you brush your teeth—call me."

Max smiled. "You're the best friend ever, you know that?"

"Yeah, I know."

TREAT AND SAVANNAH sat beside each other on their father's couch. They'd brought him home at nine o'clock, and he was asleep by ten. Now it was nearing midnight and Treat felt like he'd been running underwater for the past twelve hours. He hadn't heard back from Max, and he'd left enough messages that she surely had checked them by now.

Rex came in from the barn and joined them in the living room. "Where's Josh?"

"In the shower. Want a beer?" Treat asked.

"Nah, thanks. I think we need to have a family meeting." Rex sat in the chair next to their father's recliner.

Josh joined them a few minutes later. "Savannah, do you want a drink before I sit down?"

"Yeah, I'll take some wine. Red, please."

"I'll get it," Treat offered. He went to the kitchen. Anything to stop the pain of staring at his father's empty chair.

In the kitchen, he pulled Josh to the side. "You heard from Hugh?" He didn't want to ask in front of the others, knowing it would just lead to a brother bashing, and while Hugh probably deserved it, Treat didn't need one more thing to worry about.

"Yeah, he's almost here. Got hung up on a layover."

Treat put an arm around Josh. "Are you doing okay?" Josh was the most sensitive of his brothers, and he wanted Josh to know that he was there if he wanted to talk.

"Yeah, it scared me, though. I've never thought of Dad as someone who could get sick."

"Me either." Treat took a swig of his beer. "It scared me, too, but I think Ben knows what he's talking about, and if he thought this was anything other than stress cardiomyopathy he'd tell us."

"Do you believe in it? Broken heart syndrome?"

Hell yes. I'm afraid I'll be in the hospital next. "I don't know, but I do know that Dad believes he still sees and talks to Mom, and I think he just might."

"Yeah," Josh said. "Me too."

"Wine, please," Savannah called to them.

They settled into the living room, and for a while, they all sat in silence, nursing their drinks. Treat was surrounded by several of the people he loved most in the world, but with what his father was going through, his longing to see the others deepened: his father, Hugh, and Max. He wished Max were right there beside him, holding his hand. He didn't feel whole without her. His hand felt empty for the first time in his life. The truth was, he'd barely noticed his hands before the last few days with Max, and now his palms had become like empty souls, crying out for her.

The door opened, and they all turned toward it with a shush on their lips.

"Dad's asleep," Savannah said as she went to hug her youngest brother. "He's okay," she said to him.

Treat embraced Hugh. "You okay? Your trip all right?" He patted the back of his brother's leather jacket. Even though he was eight years younger than

Treat, tonight he could have passed for twenty-five instead of twenty-nine with his tousled, wavy black hair that feathered over his ears, badly in need of a trim, and his Levi's and Reeboks.

"Long, but I'm here, and that's all that matters." Hugh hugged his other two brothers and headed to the kitchen for a drink.

"Do you want me to make you something to eat?" Savannah asked.

"Nah. I grabbed a sandwich on the way here." Hugh sat beside Savannah on the couch and kicked one ankle up on the opposite knee. "So Dad's okay? What is this BHS?"

Treat explained what the doctor had told them.

"Sounds like it should be called BS to me," Hugh joked, his brown eyes flitting from sibling to sibling.

"Hugh." Treat used the same voice he'd relied upon when his brothers were out-of-control teenagers. It didn't always work, but it did right then.

"I just mean that I don't see why they call it that. Call it stress cardiomyopathy. Why does everything have to be about feelings?"

Treat leaned forward, and Savannah put a gentle hand on his leg. "Leave it alone, Hugh. Who cares what they call it? The point is, he needs to take it easy for a few weeks."

"Which is precisely what I wanted to talk about," Rex said. "I've been thinking. Maybe we should hire another ranch hand or two. I'm swamped and—"

"No need," Treat interrupted. "I'm gonna stick

around for a while."

"You have your own businesses to run," Josh said.

"Yeah, Treat. You've worked too hard to give it up," Savannah added.

"I'm not giving them up. I've thought this through. Rex, you were right. I should have come home sooner. I'll hire someone to do my overseas work and negotiating, and I'll have to travel only a few times each month." Just saying it aloud made him feel so much better. His dad's illness had been a sign. Maybe Hugh wasn't the only selfish one of the group. Treat ran away to escape his own demons, and it was high time he faced them.

"Treat, man, you don't have to do that. I can deal with it. I'll just hire a hand or two for a few weeks. We'll be fine," Rex said. His biceps flexed and unflexed, much like his father's did when he was upset.

"I know you can, Rex. This isn't about you versus me," Treat said.

"Is this about your girl? Max?" Josh's question didn't hold an ounce of resentment, as it might have if it had come from Rex.

Treat had been so scared that his father wouldn't pull through hour after hour while they waited for the prognosis, and he spent those countless, torturous hours thinking about Max's letter. And now, as he looked into the eyes of his siblings, he knew it was time to slay his own demons. His family deserved his honesty, and if he was ever going to try to win Max back, she deserved a man free from the weight of his past.

Treat took a deep breath, and with the image of Max's smile guiding him, he began. "I'd be lying if I said this has nothing to do with Max. I love her. I do. I love Max, but I realized that I can't be with her, or anyone else, until I get this off my chest. So to answer your question, this is really about all of you as much as it's about me or Max. Rex, you've been calling me on this for years, and I've deflected every jab, not because they were untrue, as I claimed, but because they were too true, and too hurtful, to admit." This was harder than he'd imagined. He dropped his eyes, grasping for courage. *You can't have an honest, happy relationship with a partner until you have an honest, happy relationship with yourself.* Max's voice brought the strength he needed to continue. "After Mom died, I failed you. Every one of you."

"What are you talking about? Jesus, Treat. You never failed us," Josh said.

"No, I did. I know I did. I never stepped up to the plate like I should have, and when it came time for college, and then after, I was relieved to move away, and as ashamed as that makes me, I need you to know the truth. The ranch was one big reminder of everything I didn't do—everything I couldn't do—for my family, for each of you." He blinked away angry tears.

"Treat," Savannah said, reaching out to him.

"Let him finish," Rex said. All eyes turned on Rex. "He's trying to tell us something. Let him get it off his chest."

"Thanks, Rex." Treat didn't know if Rex was waiting with bated breath for Treat to admit some sort of failure, or if he was just being a supportive brother, but it didn't matter which one was more accurate. He was thankful either way to have his brother standing up for his right to speak. "Anyway, I worked my ass off to prove that I was worth something, and I realized today that I'll never be the man Dad is." He pointed to his father's bedroom. "That man in there is a hell of a man, and I'm...I'm just a regular guy who never quite measured up to him." He'd said it aloud, and now he waited for the *I knew its* and the *It's about times.*

Savannah's arms were around his neck seconds later, her warm breath in his ear. "Treat, you have never let me down. You're everything to me, and you're every bit the man Dad is."

"Dude, you let me sleep in your bed, for God's sake. Dad would never have done that," Hugh said with a shake of his head. "You're anything but a failure. You saved me."

"And me," Josh admitted. "Treat, you were there every time I needed anything. You waited up for me at night and never let anyone bother me. You let me climb into your bed when I was scared, and you listened to me cry for weeks on end. Hell, you even gave me money for field trips."

"I had forgotten about that," Treat said with a smile. *Shit.* He realized that Dane wasn't there. It would have been easier to talk to them all at once, but since he'd already opened the floodgates, he might as well let the rest pour out. He'd have to talk with Dane alone after he arrived.

Treat waited to see if Rex would say anything at all, but Rex just cracked his knuckles, leaned his elbows on his knees, and looked at Treat with a stoic face. The familiar Braden biceps dance was in full speed.

"I'm not telling you guys this to fish for compliments. I'm telling you because it's haunted me year after year, and I don't want it to anymore. I'm ready to put down roots, and before I do that, I need to know that I've been honest with each of you. Rex, I'm sorry. You were right all along."

Rex got up and walked out the back door.

"Let him go."

Dad. Treat spun around and found his father leaning against the stairs. "Dad, you should be in bed."

"I'll go back to bed when I'm damned good and ready," Hal said.

"How much of that did you hear?" Treat asked.

"Oh, I reckon I heard all of it. All of it that mattered, anyway."

Savannah and Treat went to his side as he moved toward the living room, and he shrugged them off. He settled into his recliner and looked long and hard at his eldest son.

Treat had never felt so ashamed. It was one thing to tell his siblings, but a whole other thing to face the man who had raised him, who had poured his heart and soul into him, and to admit that he was a fake, a coward. He deserved everything his father was about to unload on him. He lowered himself into the chair beside his father's recliner, never breaking eye contact, and in a shaky voice he recognized as the eleven-year-old boy who must have been buried deep inside of him, he said, "I'm sorry, Dad. You tried so hard to raise me right, and I wanted to make you proud, but I know what I am, and I was too ashamed to stay home and run the ranch with you."

His father's mannerisms reflected Rex's, and for a minute, Treat feared he might walk out just like his brother had. Instead his father reached for his hand and squeezed it in his large, strong hand. Tears rose in his father's eyes, pulling forth tears in Treat's.

"Son, you are, and have always been, everything I ever hoped you'd be. You were barely eleven when your mama died, and barely nine when she first became ill." Tears streamed down his cheeks, and he made no move to wipe them away.

The pressure in Treat's chest nearly knocked the wind out of him. "Dad." He shook his head.

"No, son. You were everything this family needed, and there has never been a time that you haven't been." He patted Treat's hand with his other hand, then held his son's hand between his own for another beat. "You see the faces of your sister and brothers? Do you see the love in their eyes? They are who they are in large part because of you. You taught them about strength and family. You taught them about love, and even when you let your little scraggly brothers in bed with you, and don't think I didn't know about that." He looked at Josh and then Hugh. "You, Treat, and you alone, were giving them what I could not. The truth is, after your mama passed, she took part of me with her. I did what I could. I stepped up in every way I was able, but I'm just a man, like you and Rex, Dane, Hugh, and Josh. We're all just who we are, and who we are is Bradens. And Bradens always do their best. Not one of my children has ever let me down." He looked at Hugh, who had dropped his eyes to the floor. "Not Hugh when he didn't show up for the ranch's first auction." He looked at Savannah. "Not our beautiful girl, Savannah, when she snuck out of the house when she was fifteen, and you, Treat, you had to haul her ass back home. And you never said a word to me about it."

Savannah's eyes grew wide. "You knew?"

He just shook his head with a smile, then looked at Josh, who was listening intently. "And not your brother Josh, when he decided to design dresses for a living."

Treat watched his brother melt under his father's pride, and he knew that Josh had been waiting to hear that his whole life.

"The point is, Treat, you might have needed to cleanse your soul so that you could start a life without that gorilla on your back, but you gotta know that it was *your* gorilla. It was a monkey that was devised by a little boy's frightened mind and grew to a full-size gorilla that tried to weigh you down. While it might have weighed you down for a long while, you didn't let it take over completely because it wasn't real. I'm proud of you, son. That gorilla was just a figment of that little boy's imagination, and you finally saw your way clear to climb out from under it." He tapped the side of his head.

Treat went to his father and held him longer, and tighter, than he ever had. He didn't know if his father was right or not, but he appreciated every word his father said, and he knew that he would never let him down.

"Are you really thinking of putting down roots?" his father asked when they separated.

"Not thinking about it. I'm acting on it," Treat said. He looked at the back door.

"Now, that boy, he's got an even bigger monkey on his back than you did. Give him some time," his father said.

"I'm not sure what I did to him, specifically," Treat said.

"He'll let you know when he's good and ready," his father said. "Just like you did."

Chapter Thirty-One

BY SATURDAY AFTERNOON Max was finally rested and feeling more like herself—with a broken heart. She hadn't located her phone anywhere, and she'd called the airlines and finally the car rental company. They found her phone in the glove compartment of the car she'd rented and were sending it to her Priority Mail. She'd have it by Monday afternoon.

She flipped on her computer to check her work e-mails and saw a message that had come through Facebook. Max loathed Facebook; the idea of posting updates about what she did all day seemed an enormous waste of time, right up there with tweeting and getting manicures. Well, maybe a manicure now and then would be nice. She clicked over to Facebook, deleted the spam message announcing a great new diet plan, but before clicking off, she typed in *Ryan Cobain, Texas A&M*. Within seconds, her ex-boyfriend's photo was in front of her. She hadn't set eyes on him in years. She leaned in closer and clicked on his name. His Facebook profile page flashed on the screen. There he was, smiling at the camera. His long brown hair was cut short, and his face had thinned. If she didn't know him, she'd think he was a handsome, happy man. But she did know him. She looked into his green eyes and saw the same fiery mess of a man she'd seen the day she left. *Slay those demons,* played in her mind.

Her fingers shook as she clicked on the message icon. No way would he respond, but she had to try to slay the demon that was strangling her a little more every day that she was without Treat.

She typed in the chat box, *Hey. How are you? Thought I'd see what you've been up to. Max.* She hit return and then stared at the screen like it might come alive. Her body was poised to flee, or pounce; she didn't know which. She waited a minute. Two.

"That was stupid," she said to the empty room and went to the kitchen. A few minutes later her computer chimed.

Max froze.

She took two steps toward the computer, then stopped. *I don't want to do this. Yes, I do.* She took another step, then stopped again. *No. No, I don't.*

Another chime rang out.

Shit. She clenched her jaw and went to the computer. "It's not like he can see me."

She clicked on the chat box, and sure enough, there was a message from Ryan.

Hey, Max. How are you?

Her fingers hovered over the keys. She bit her lower lip and typed, *Fine.*

A second later his message came through. *Glad to hear it.*

What do I want to say? She shook her hands in the air as she thought, then hunkered down over the keyboard and typed, *Where are you living?*

The computer chimed. *Cheyenne, Wyoming. You?*

He was an hour and a half away. Max's hands stopped cold. What was she doing? She didn't want him to know where she lived, but somewhere in the back of her mind, she was already forming a plan.

She typed, *I'm in your area tomorrow for work. I'd like to come by and talk for a bit.*

He answered thirty seconds later. *Working all day. Where?*

He answered, *Cheyenne Crowne Inn. Off Central Ave. Can I stop by?*

He answered. *I never thought you'd speak to me again. Yes, I'd like that. I have things to tell you.*

Okay. 1:00?

He agreed, and Max closed her computer, her work e-mail long forgotten. She paced her apartment, thinking about the next day. Her heart raced and her mind ran in circles. She thought about asking Kaylie to go with her, but she knew Kaylie would just talk her out of it. She had to do this. She told Treat she had to slay her demons, and she'd be damned if she wasn't going to do it. She was Max Armstrong. She'd left Ryan once, and she'd carried the nightmare of him with her like a silent predator. After tomorrow, she hoped to never feel like his prey again.

Chapter Thirty-Two

TREAT'S BEDROOM DOOR swung open at five thirty Sunday morning, and Rex peeked in with a victorious smile, which promptly faded when Treat stood, fully dressed in jeans and a T-shirt and greeted him. "You're finally up?" He picked up his flannel shirt from the back of the chair, closed his laptop, patted Rex's shoulder as he passed him in the doorway, and headed downstairs.

They each filled a to-go cup with coffee and headed out into the cold morning air.

"You're gonna have to get me up to speed," Treat said.

"We've got the hired hands milking and moving. You and I are on fence repair. Something got into the back fifty and tore down a thirty-foot strip."

Treat climbed into the passenger side of the truck. "What got to it?"

Rex shrugged as he pulled onto the grass. "It

doesn't much matter now, does it?"

Great, an attitude before six a.m.

The truck ambled over the fields, and Treat waited for Rex to bring up what he'd said the night before. The silence between them was not particularly uncomfortable, but as it stretched a beat too long, Treat tried to break the ice.

"I checked on Dad. He seemed to be okay," Treat said.

"Good. Savannah's got him covered for the day, and Josh said he'd monitor his meds." Rex's cowboy hat was tugged down low. He kept his eyes on the field, never once glancing at Treat.

"You mind that I'm staying on for a while?" Treat asked.

Rex shrugged. He parked the truck and they began unloading the wood, wire, and supplies.

"Put 'em over there." Rex pointed to a grassy area on the other side of the broken fence. "We'll set up the sawhorses here and use that area there for the waste."

Treat did as he asked. He watched his brother pick up pieces of wood and throw them over his shoulder like they were toothpicks. Treat was a strong man, but even he had to admit that his brother had the bigger brawn and bulk. Where Treat had sleeker, though muscular, lines to his body, Rex's body bubbled with muscles in places that Treat wasn't even certain his body knew he should have muscles. Rex's long-sleeved henley clung to those bubbling muscles all the way down to his waist.

Instead of feeling envy for the brother who was clearly angry with him, Treat was proud of his younger brother. He'd spent his life taking care of the family ranch—and their father. That was something Treat hadn't been strong enough to do, and now, he realized, he was able to admit that to himself without feeling shame in its wake.

"You gonna help me or watch me?" Rex asked.

Treat grabbed his hammer and followed his brother's cursory instructions to a tee. He'd grown up helping with everything on the ranch from milking cows to fixing the siding on the barn. He was a bit out of practice, but it was all coming back to him. Each swing of the hammer brought with it memories of working alongside his father.

Working beside Rex also brought out the competitive side of Treat, and the need for instructions quickly fell away as he sawed the wood to perfect length, secured the wire into place, and pounded the poles into the ground.

When they headed into the house at lunchtime, Treat's chest and arms already felt battered and bruised. He gritted his teeth against the annoying pain rather than let his brother see it.

"Doing all right?" Rex asked as they drove toward the house.

"Just fine." Rex had a big chip on his shoulder. At some point, with Treat around more often than not, that chip was gonna get too heavy and come tumbling down, and Treat would be ready to catch Rex when he fell off balance.

After spending the day doing hard physical labor, Treat expected to feel a longing to return to his fast-paced, career-oriented lifestyle, where he was surrounded by creature comforts and a hard day meant securing a purchase for another resort. At the minimum, he'd expected to feel a strong amount of trepidation about changing the way he did things, but as they pulled up to the ranch and he mulled over the suggestion from his attorney to hire more of a front man or woman and handle negotiations via Skype, he found that his longing wasn't for more acquisitions at all. He longed to be with Max. The decision he'd made and the suggestion from the attorney both felt right.

"Looks like Dane's arrived," Rex said, observing the forest-green Land Rover in the driveway.

Great.

"Hey, I made you guys lunch," Savannah called from the kitchen.

They kicked off their work boots and were intercepted by Dane as he came down the hallway.

"You made it," Treat said, embracing his brother. He'd spent much of the night thinking through how he was going to tell Dane what he'd told his other siblings. He was sure that he'd heard it at least three times from his siblings by now, but no matter how uncomfortable it made him, Treat was going to do it himself, in person, man to man. And what better time than the present?

"You're kidding, right? It was a long flight, but I've

never missed an important family event." Dane said.

"Of course I was kidding. Come with me." He led the way outside with Dane on his heels, and they settled into two chairs facing the fields.

"I hear you're staying for a while," Dane said.

"Yeah. It's time."

"What about your resorts?"

"Nothing's gonna change except the amount of travel I'm doing and the number of new properties I'll take on." He looked at his brother relaxing in the chair beside him. His skin was tanned and his eyes were bright. He'd grown into a handsome man. Treat could hardly believe that he was pushing forty and Dane wasn't far behind. *How have the years passed so quickly?* One day they'd be gathering like this for their father's funeral, and it would most likely be in far fewer years than they'd all like to imagine. His father was strong, but no one was immortal.

"We met Max. Did she tell you?" Dane asked.

"Yeah." Treat smiled, shook his head. He still couldn't believe that she'd tracked down his father's address and had actually shown up. Then she'd shown up in Wellfleet. And now she was gone. *One thing at a time.*

"Pretty. Seems smart, a little shy, maybe? But I can see why you like her."

Treat's body went rigid. *She's mine.* He gave Dane a serious stare.

"You really like her, don't you?" Dane asked.

"I love her, Dane," he admitted.

Dane nodded. "I've never heard those words come out of your mouth before."

"I've never felt them before," Treat said. The truth tasted so sweet, almost as sweet as Max's kisses. "Listen, Dane—"

"Before you tell me, can I just say something I've been meaning to say for a long time?"

"Sure." Treat braced himself for a jab of truth. *I was never a good enough brother.*

"It's about Mary Jane."

Treat narrowed his eyes.

"Right, well..." Dane took a deep breath. "The truth is, I wasn't as hammered as I told you I was that night. I knew what I was doing."

"Why on earth are you telling me this now?" He couldn't stop his hands from flexing.

"Because the others told me what you said last night, and you need to know. I slept with her to feel like I was at least as good as you, Treat. Do you have any idea what it was like to grow up in your gigantic shadow?" Dane leaned forward, shaking his head.

"My shadow isn't so big, Dane."

"You have no idea. Anyway, it didn't work. I felt even smaller afterward than I had before, and I know that has always undermined our relationship." He looked up at Treat. "I'm sorry, bro. I've regretted it ever since."

Treat had never expected to hear anything even remotely close to what Dane had admitted, and because of that, he was at a loss for words.

"I thought you should know because I know that you worry about me and any of your women friends. You don't have to. I'm not that stupid kid anymore. I'd never do something as low or as demeaning as that to you or myself. Or to another woman. Mary Jane was a pawn to me."

"She wasn't to me." Treat's chest tightened at the memory.

Dane looked down. "I know, and I'm sorry."

Treat read the seriousness in Dane's voice and knew he'd been carrying that burden for a long time. He appreciated the guts it took for his brother to slay his own dragon, and in an effort to ease the moment, he flashed a mischievous smile and teased, "Are you trying to tell me that you won't try to tag Max with your giant spear?"

"Not an inch of it." Dane laughed. "Seriously, though, I'd never make the same mistake twice. Besides, there's a certain someone who I can't seem to get off my mind these last few months, so I might not be on the market for too much longer myself."

"Yeah?" Treat asked.

"Yeah." Dane leaned back in his chair and looked out at the beautiful mountains in the distance. "Yeah."

"So, they ratted me out to you already?" Treat asked, nodding toward the house.

"I had three calls by three in the morning," Dane said with a smile.

Typical Braden hotline. "Who didn't call?"

"Who do you think?" Dane nodded toward Rex's

truck.

"Right. I'm not sure what to make of things with Rex, but I'll just take Dad's advice and let him be. He'll talk when he's ready."

Dane got up to go inside and Treat held him back. Letting his siblings handle his admission for him was a cop-out. He needed to handle things himself if he was truly going to slay his demons with no regrets.

After their mother had died, most of his siblings had fallen back on tears and had crawled into their own shells for a while, but Dane had exploded. He'd gone from being sweet and even-tempered, like he was now, to an angry, petulant boy. Treat tried to talk it out of him, but there were times when he'd let Dane spew his fury far too loud, and he'd always wished he hadn't.

"I'm sorry, Dane. I was the oldest, and I should have been there more. When you were angry—so angry—I should have tried harder."

"I was a little off my rocker, huh?" Dane said with a sad look in his eyes.

"I think we all were. You know how much I love you, right?" There had never been any embarrassment wrapped around his love for his family, and today was no different.

"Never had any doubt." Dane stood and embraced Treat, then left his eldest brother alone to deal with the tears that had wet his cheeks.

Treat looked out onto the property and envisioned the memory of his mother waving from horseback in the field. *Treaty!* He hoped she'd have been proud of him, even with his faults. Her constant hospital stays toward the end of her life dulled his active memories. God, he hated those times. And finally, he remembered the day his mother had come home from the hospital and he'd known in his heart that she wasn't going to last very long. She'd become so frail. Her cheeks had lost their rosy glow months before. They'd become hollow, her arms and legs atrophied from her extended bed rest. He used to stand in her doorway when she was sleeping and just look at her, memorizing every feature as she slipped further and further away. One afternoon, when his father was in the field and the kids were out horsing around, she reached for him. He hadn't even known she was awake. He still remembered the roughness of the hardwood floor beneath his bare feet as he crossed the room. When he reached the bed and took her hand in his own, it startled him. He could feel each slender bone beneath her nearly transparent skin. She opened her eyes then and smiled, and in that breath, he saw the mother she had always been: virile, loving, beautiful. She was too weak to keep her eyes open, and they fluttered closed. He held on to her hand long after it had gone limp, hoping, wishing, praying she'd open those beautiful eyes again. He held her hand until his father's strong hands gripped his shoulders and dragged him away. *Mom! Come back! Please! I'll do better! I'll help you more with the kids! I'll help Dad on the farm!* He struggled and fought against his father's mighty grip until every fiber of his being was exhausted beyond repair and he collapsed into his father's waiting arms. When he woke up the next day, he ran to his mother's room. *It was a dream!* He pushed the heavy wooden door open. He remembered the creak, long and ominous, as the door came to a stop, revealing his mother's empty bed.

Chapter Thirty-Three

MAX HAD BEEN up all night, hoping and praying that she could carry out her plan, then second- and third-guessing it altogether. Twice she'd hauled herself out of bed to her computer and hovered over the keys, ready to nix the whole thing. In the end, she knew that if she didn't follow through, what happened between them would continue to haunt her forever, and she'd never have any chance of a lasting relationship.

She riffled through her clothes, looking for just the right thing to wear. Something that said, *I'm strong. I'm capable.* Her bedroom looked like a tornado had whirled through with jeans and skirts and slacks strewn over the bed and the floor. After two hours of shuffling, trying on, and shedding tears, she knew what she had to wear. She went to the front pocket of her suitcase, where she'd stuffed Treat's Provincetown Aids Support Group T-shirt. She brought it to her nose and inhaled deeply the scent of the man she loved but had set free, then slipped it on. Tucking it in was interesting, to say the least, since it hung almost to her knees. She'd finally given up and gathered the long shirt in her hands, tying the bottom into a ball at her waist, like she'd seen in television shows from the eighties. She threw a sweatshirt on over it and her most comfortable pair of jeans, then stared at her choices of boots and shoes.

Sneakers. In case I freak out and have to bolt.

THE CHEYENNE CROWNE Pointe Inn was built on the flattest piece of ground Max had ever seen. It stood alone among the parking lots and grassy lawn. *There's no place to hide.* She eased past the hotel, scoping it out, this place where she would finally confront her demons. The building looked like any other hotel, a few stories high, big windows, mostly curtained, and a circular drive that led to a covered entrance.

Why am I here?

Max turned around and drove by the hotel in the other direction, contemplating getting back on the highway and returning home. She crossed in front of the hotel two more times, until she was sure that the Cheyenne police would spot her and arrest her for stalking. *That would be just my luck.* She surveyed the parking lot again, and a shiver ran down her back. The hotel was too far off the beaten track; no one could see her there.

Oh no!

Maybe that was Ryan's plan. Lure her to a remote

location and do something horrible to her. He'd said he had something to talk to her about. Maybe that was a ruse. Wait—she'd contacted him. She was being stupid. They were in a public place. She'd be fine. She hoped.

She parked at the far end of the parking lot, giving herself plenty of time on the way in to change her mind and turn back. She held on to the edge of Treat's T-shirt beneath her sweatshirt. When she reached the entrance, she stopped to try and calm her racing pulse. She paced the sidewalk, then unzipped her sweatshirt so she could see Treat's shirt beneath. She pulled forward memories of the way he cared for her, the way he nurtured her. That's what she wanted, to be nurtured, to be healed. She had to go inside and do this—cleanse herself from the memories that stalked her like prey and pulled her back from every forward step she took.

Max took a deep breath and walked through the glass doors. The young dark-haired woman behind the desk smiled.

"Welcome to the Crowne Point Inn!"

Her high-pitched enthusiasm cut right through Max's anxiety like a knife, causing her to freeze in the middle of the floor of the large, open lobby. *Walk. Leave. Do something!* Her mind warred with itself, confusing her legs into frozen pillars. Was she insane? This was the worst idea ever.

She finally turned to leave.

"Max?"

Ryan's voice made the hair on the back of her neck

stand on end. She clenched her fists against the instant fear that grasped her nerves. *I can do this*. Max forced herself to turn and tried her best to feign a smile, but with the way her teeth were grinding together, she wasn't sure she pulled it off.

There he was. Why did his green eyes look friendly? That's not what he'd looked like at the end, in those weeks she'd spent stifled by his aggression. Now he was smiling like he was glad to see her.

He took a step forward, and again she had no control over her legs as they took a step backward.

"Max?" He wore a dark blue suit with a gold badge over his breast pocket that read RYAN COBAIN, HOTEL MANAGER, and he was walking—Directly. Toward. Max.

She willed herself to stand tall, and this time, her body obeyed. She looked down at Treat's shirt, now wishing she had dressed a little nicer. He had the edge on her in his nice suit, on his turf. *Wait! What am I thinking? I control this meeting, not him. Pull it together, Max. Pretend he's a sponsor—no, a salesman. That's it. He's a vendor who wants a deal, and I have to be strong. Stand my ground.*

Max felt her shoulders draw back and her neck stretch tall. She felt the familiar strength that she'd called upon so often with her career, the strength that began in her gut and traveled into her limbs. She took a step forward, then another, and extended her hand. *I can do this.*

"Ryan," she said in a frosty tone.

He took her hand and buried it within both of his.

She steeled herself against the initial jolt of panic, then allowed him to complete his greeting.

"So good to see you, Max. You look gorgeous, of course."

"Thank you."

He motioned toward a door beside the front desk. "Shall we go into my office and talk?"

Public. Stay in sight of others. "You know, I'd really like a cup of coffee. Is there a restaurant on site?"

"Sure."

She walked beside him down a wide hallway, shooting glances at him. He didn't seem nervous, and he wasn't acting sketchy. In fact, he seemed like the old Ryan—comfortable, confident. He led her to a small, dimly lit restaurant, where they were seated at a table off to the side.

"I was surprised to hear from you," Ryan said. He called over the waitress so Max could order a cup of coffee. The waitress brought Ryan a glass of water.

Max watched his mannerisms and found them to be reflective of the boy she'd met when they'd first begun dating. Gone were the jumpy eyes and fast, uncontrolled movements she remembered from their last months together. It was a mask; she was sure of it. *A game that he's just gotten better at.*

He said something she didn't hear. She was too busy remembering how he'd changed over the duration of their relationship. Had she liked him before he'd changed? She thought she had. She remembered fluttering in her stomach when she saw him, and when they'd moved in together, they'd been friends. Yes. She was sure of it. She *had* liked who he was at that time, before he'd changed.

"I'm sorry. What did you say?" she asked.

"I didn't think I'd ever hear from you again after—"

Max dropped her eyes, then silently scolded herself for doing it. This was her ball game. She called it; she controlled it.

"I surprised myself, quite honestly, but I wanted to...I needed closure." Max had thought of all sorts of ways to handle Ryan, and in the end, she fell back on her fail-safe: honesty.

"I tried to track you down for weeks, Max. Your parents wouldn't answer my calls. You, well, you never answered anything—calls, e-mails."

She wouldn't apologize for not returning his calls. She wouldn't apologize for anything.

"I finally found you in Colorado."

You tracked me down? Every muscle in her legs tensed with fear.

"You worked for that small film company, then a festival company. I've written you dozens of letters and e-mails over the years, but never had the courage to send them."

You stalked me. What if he'd shown up in Allure? What would I have done?

"In the end, I knew it was unfair to reach out to you," he continued.

Ryan kept eye contact with her, which she found

unsettling and reassuring at the same time. People didn't keep eye contact if they had something to hide. Why wasn't he acting like he'd done something so wrong to her that it had ruined her ability to have a real relationship? *Bastard.*

"I would have fled if I'd known you'd found me again," Max said with her chin held high.

"I don't blame you," he said. He dropped his eyes.

There it was. Finally. A little remorse?

"Max, I owe you an explanation and an apology, which I know will never be enough to fix what I did."

"I don't want to hear your excuses, Ryan. There is no excuse for what you put me through." *Then what do I want?* Tears of anger stung her eyes, and she refused to let them fall. Her voice rose despite her effort to remain calm. "You stole something from me, and I can never get it back. You stole my dignity, and you stole my trust."

"I know I did, and I've regretted it every day of my life."

Max didn't hear him. She was too busy formulating her next accusation. "You made me fear relationships and turned me into someone who..." What was she doing? She didn't come here to tell him what he'd *achieved.* She'd come here to tell him that she was fine even though he'd tried his best to tear her down.

"Max—"

"No, Ryan. I honestly do not want to hear your excuses. They're meaningless."

"Max, I was sick. Okay? It's not an excuse."

Max pulled her shoulders back. She was ready for

lies. She'd expected them. "Right, Ryan. I was there, remember? You weren't sick. You just changed. You stopped talking to everyone, stopped talking to me. You'd look at me with this cold stare sometimes, and it was like you had been hiding your meanness, or your hatred for me, for all those months, and then you just released them."

"Max—"

"I'm not stupid. I took the hint. I just took it one night too late. And I know it had to do with agreeing to move wherever I got a job instead of where you did. I've finally figured it all out—"

"Max!" His voice was deep and loud, startling her out of her rant.

"Max, I'm schizophrenic. They missed all the signs over that year or so. We all did. After you left, I fell apart. I spiraled out of control so badly at times that I was afraid to even go home."

"Schizophrenic?" Max had not seen that coming. She narrowed her eyes, looking for signs of deceit.

"Think about it, Max. My behavior changed. When I look back now, I see it. That night I...hurt you? It wasn't even you that I was seeing or yelling at. I was sexually abused when I was little, but I'd blocked it out. I was delusional. In my mind, it wasn't you I was hurting. It was the woman who had molested me."

"Oh, Ryan." All the bravado that had built up in her chest came tumbling down. "How did you find out?"

"One night I hurt someone else. Badly. She didn't call the police or anything, but she could have. In fact," he said with his eyebrows drawn together, "she probably should have. That's when I knew something was really wrong. I went home and told my parents that I wasn't going to leave their house because I was afraid of what I might do to someone else."

Max thought of Ryan's quiet, polite mother, and she couldn't imagine her hearing about what he'd done to her—or anyone else—which turned Max's stomach. She'd considered calling the police when Ryan had hurt her, but the shame of willingly allowing him to use that thing on her had held her back. Now she realized she might have saved the other woman from being hurt if she'd filed a police report.

"You hurt someone else?"

Ryan explained that he'd hooked up with another girl a few nights after Max had left him, and they'd gone back to her apartment off campus. While they were in bed, she'd taken the dominant role, and Ryan's memories had come rushing back. He told her that it was as if he'd blacked out. He didn't remember hitting the woman, or calling her names, and when he'd regained control, she had locked herself in the bathroom, bruised and bleeding. She told him that if he left, she wouldn't report him to the police.

"After being back home for a week or two, my parents began to notice—or maybe *accept* is a better word—the changes. My father tracked down psychiatrists and psychologists. He took me to just about every doctor he could find. They all made the same diagnosis, but he didn't want to accept it. Hell, I didn't want to accept it, but I also didn't want to be that person who hurt people."

"Should I have seen something? Did I miss a major sign? Was it triggered by the thought of moving with me out of state?" Max asked. *All these years I thought your anger was aimed at me specifically. What else have I misjudged?*

"No. It had nothing to do with that. They don't really know why I started recalling the memories, but I went through an inpatient program where they assessed and treated and reassessed. You know my mom. She was nowhere near prepared to deal with this. I've gone through years of therapy, and it took forever for them to find the right protocol of drugs to even things out. But you know, it's been a few years since they figured it all out." He shrugged. "And now it's just a part of who I am and who I will always be. Luckily, with medication, I'm not violent, and I don't have delusions anymore or anything. I just kind of live a regular life with all of that hanging over me." He took a drink of water, and then said, "Max, I'm not telling you this to gain your sympathy. I take full responsibility for my illness and my actions. But I am glad that you got in touch with me. I have been wanting to explain it to you and to apologize. I know you, Max, and I know you probably blamed yourself all these years. You're so sensitive. It's one of the things I loved about you. I'm so sorry. For those weeks, that night, and for all the nights since then that you've relived it. If I could erase it all from your mind and add your burden to mine, I'd do it in a heartbeat."

It wasn't me. It wasn't because he was going to move with me. The thoughts of her misplaced blame were quickly pushed aside and replaced with thoughts of Ryan, the boy she'd known before he changed, and the man he was, bravely sitting there with her.

"You must have been so scared." *As scared as I was that night.*

"Petrified. Imagine not wanting to live in your own skin. That's what it was like," he said honestly. "When I think back to how I hurt you for all those months, the awful things I said, and that night...and then, that other woman...I just wish it all never happened."

She saw in his eyes honesty and pain, and beyond that, she saw something else, too, that she had never expected to see again. She saw the young man who was her friend.

"Ryan, I forgive you." If anyone had asked her yesterday if she'd ever forgive Ryan Cobain, she would have said, *Never*, without hesitation. As she looked at him sitting across from her, not hiding behind his illness, not shirking the responsibility of having done those hurtful acts, but laying his life out for her like an open book, she felt the anger leaving her body, floating out with the words as they rolled off her tongue. "I do, Ryan. I forgive you."

He looked down at his lap, then up again. A little nag in the back of Max's mind worried that he'd look back with those cold, dead eyes—but he didn't. The same warm man who had apologized only moments before was right there in front of her, looking at her with empathy, honesty, and tears in his eyes.

"I can't tell you what that means to me," he admitted. "I didn't mean to get so emotional."

"How could you not? This whole thing is emotional. Those years were emotional. Do you remember what we were like when we first met? Everything had us on an emotional high." She smiled at the happier memories as they coasted through her mind.

"Yeah, I do." He wrinkled his brow. "Max, I have to ask, why now? After all these years, why are you just tracking me down now?"

Max touched her shirt. *Treat.*

"You don't have to tell me," he added. "It's none of my business. I was just curious."

"It's okay. I don't mind telling you. I met someone and, well, I'm not the same person I was when I was with you. After I left, I became stronger, self-sufficient." *But remained scared.*

"Wait. Do you put out your own trash?" he asked with a teasing smile.

"Yup." She grinned, remembering how she'd deemed that a *boy job.*

"Clean the toilets?" he asked with a smirk.

She nodded.

"No way. Wait. Do you ask for help in stores?"

"All the time. Gosh, I'd forgotten how shy I was. What a mess I was back then." She covered her eyes and shook her head.

"You were adorable, Max. I always knew how

strong you were. I never had any doubt about your strength or courage. You were destined to accomplish whatever it was you dreamed of. So, this guy, does he treat you well?"

Max thought of Treat. *He's what I dream of.* "We're not together right now. I...I ended things. It's a long story, but he stirred things in me that made me want him to take care of me, and I think that scared the shit out of me." Talking to the old Ryan was easy, comforting even. If only she'd learned years ago what she now saw so clearly. How different would her life have been? And if she hadn't come to slay her demons...She couldn't even go there. It was too painful to think of how close she'd come to turning around and going home.

"You do realize that it's okay to let guys do things for you, right? It doesn't mean that they'll hurt you. What I have is pretty rare, Max, and we were right at that age when it shows up. We're past that now. I don't think you have to worry about another guy going bat-shit crazy on you out of the blue." Ryan wasn't making fun of her. He was being honest. Again.

"Yeah, I see that now. For all these years I thought you hurt me because you resented me because you were the one to give up what you wanted to follow me wherever I got a job. I was sure of it. It's guided my relationships, or maybe I should say my lack of relationships."

"Max, I would have followed you anywhere. That's what relationships are, give and take. Compromises are essential." Ryan watched a petite redhead heading their way, and when she arrived at their table, he reached out to her. "Rachelle, this is Max." A warmth connected their gaze, and Max knew that Ryan cared for her.

Max smiled at the pretty woman. "Hi."

Rachelle put her hand on Ryan's shoulder. "Max, I'm so glad that you finally reached out to Ryan. He's told me a lot about you. I know how much you meant to him. He's worried about you for years."

He talked about me? "Oh, well." Max didn't know what to say. "I guess I've worried about me, too." Honesty won again.

"Rachelle and I met when I was in the inpatient facility. She was a nurse's aide then. She's an RN now, and she works at the hospital in town." He smiled up at her with pride.

The love in Ryan's eyes for Rachelle made Max think of Treat and the way he looked at her, touched her, and so wonderfully completed her. *I need to find Treat.*

Chapter Thirty-Four

BY DINNERTIME TREAT was exhausted. His father was feeling infinitely better and practically needed to be tied to his chair to follow Ben's order to rest. Every time his siblings turned around, their father was trying to get outside to the barn. Josh finally lured him inside by offering to watch a rodeo with him, and Treat sat on the front porch, watching Rex park the tractor in the barn.

They'd worked from sunup to sundown, and they still had evening chores to take care of. He had to give Rex credit. Rex was still running on full steam while Treat was sucking down coffee just to get a second wind.

The screen door opened behind him. "You still alive out here?" Savannah sat beside him on the top step.

"Barely. I had forgotten how labor intensive it was to run the ranch. I don't know how he does it."

"Yeah, he's pretty tough. So are you, you know.

Everyone is tough in different ways."

"I guess." Treat looked at Savannah. The spark in her hazel eyes had dulled. He'd assumed it was from his father's health issues, but he remembered what his father had barked at him in the hospital. "Everything okay with you? What was Dad talking about with Connor? Do I need to pummel him for you? Because I'm wondering if Rex might be a better person for that job."

She wrapped her arm in his and laid her head on his shoulder. "No one is better for that job than you. You've always been my protector."

The weight of her against him reminded him of Max. He'd called her two more times, and he was kicking around the idea of showing up at her apartment. He just wasn't sure that hounding her was the right thing to do.

"Way to skirt the question, Vanny."

She sighed. "It's complicated."

"Isn't everything?" Treat had replayed the night before Max left over and over in his mind, like a movie stuck on rewind, and he still couldn't figure out what Max was so afraid of. Every relationship meant compromise. He wasn't closing down shop. He was simply not going to acquire more overseas resorts. And now that he'd formed a plan, he wasn't even giving that up. He was just changing how he'd do business in the future.

"Yeah, I guess. Do you remember what Mom and Dad's relationship was like when you were younger? Before Mom got sick? I was too young to really remember. All I remember are trips to the hospital, being quiet when she needed to rest, and celebrating when she was feeling well. That would last a few days, a week, and then she was resting again."

Treat had often wondered how much his younger siblings really remembered about their mother. Hugh had been an infant, and he knew Josh had also been too young to remember, but Savannah had been four when their mother got sick, and he'd avoided talking about their mother, in fear of upsetting her.

"She was the most beautiful woman who ever lived, Vanny. She had this light about her that's so hard to describe. Mom was always happy. She used to yell at Dad when he'd try to toughen you up. I can still hear her." He raised his voice an octave. *"Hal, she's a girl. G-I-R-L. She doesn't need to know how to climb onto a roof and bang a nail. That's what men are for."* He laughed at the memory.

"She did?"

"Oh, yes. You were always treated like a girl by Mom. She'd want to dress you in frilly pink dresses and make your hair all pretty, and Dad would say she was raising a sissy."

Savannah pulled away from him and scrunched her nose. "Pink dresses? I can't even imagine. I loved growing up as a tomboy. I always thought Dad did such a good job with us."

"He did. So did she. She loved us like we were all precious. Even when we were bad. She would give it to you like fire for about a minute, and in the next breath, she was laughing and joking like you were a blessed angel who could do no wrong."

"Really?"

"Yeah. You know it was Mom who started the whole backyard grilling thing, don't you?" He watched Rex approach. His jeans stretched tight across his massive thighs, and his hat was still pulled down low. He looked every bit like the quintessential cowboy.

"I never knew why we did it. It's all I've ever known."

"It was Mom."

Rex stepped onto the porch and sat beside Savannah. "What was Mom?"

"She was the one who started the outside barbeque tradition," Savannah answered.

Rex took off his hat and ran his hand through his thick, collar-length black hair. He set his hat back on his head and wiped his face with his hand. "Remember that? She said we were only nourishing our bodies if we ate inside all the time and that we also had to nourish our souls."

A warmth softened Rex's hard exterior, and for a brief moment, Treat saw the sweet little boy Rex had been before their mother became ill. "Because that's what the sun, wind, snow, and rain were for," Treat added.

"I wish I'd known her then, like you guys did." Savannah tried to push the frown from her lips.

"You're just like her." Rex touched his sister's shoulder, then headed for the door. "You doing night chores with me?"

"Wouldn't miss it," Treat answered.

After the door closed, Treat and Savannah remained on the deck. It was nice, just being with his family, without donning a suit and tie, without needing to be "on" all the time. Treat had a lot to figure out, but he'd instinctively set up his resorts to function well without him on site, so he wasn't worried. He'd always made sound business decisions. *If only I could figure out what to do about Max.*

"Why did Max leave?" Savannah asked.

Treat picked up a rock from the lower step and tossed it into the yard, wondering if he was so transparent that Savannah could read his thoughts. "I'm not really sure. I'm still trying to figure that out myself." He wiped his palms on his jeans, wishing he could talk to Max.

"I really thought, after she came here, and then tracked you down at the Cape, that she was *the one*, you know?" She scooted closer to him again. "I want that for you. I want you to be with someone who adores you. Someone who would go anywhere to be with you."

"Then that makes two of us. Only I want Max to be that one. No one else. Just Max."

"So, why don't you go find her? Tell her?"

Savannah was goading him, and Treat knew it. She'd love nothing more than to spur him into action and stake claim on being the impetus for his actions forever. He smiled at her and touched her nose like he had when she was little. She smiled up at him. Her long auburn hair blew away from her face with the late-afternoon breeze, and for an instant, she was the spitting image of their mother.

"She wanted the distance between us. I can't keep pushing myself on her," he answered.

"Treat, you're such a fool. All men are. No matter what we say, we want the night in shining armor. We want Richard Gere riding up in his white limousine. We want Leonardo DiCaprio to tell us that he'll never let us go."

Why did Treat feel like she was talking about what she wanted and not necessarily Max or other women?

"Not when they tell you otherwise, Savannah. Don't women want respect? Don't they want us to respect their space so they can think clearly?" Savannah's energy was finding its way into his body, and he was actually wondering if he was wrong. Maybe he should go after Max.

"Nope. We want you to read between the lines."

"Read between the lines? She didn't leave much for interpretation." Treat had dissected every word Max had written, and still he came up empty as far as figuring out what to do.

"Trust me, big brother. Every woman wants her man to read between the lines, and because of that, she leaves a bread crumb trail."

"Savannah, do you want Connor Dean to follow your bread crumbs?"

A shadow passed through Savannah's eyes. "I'm not sure. Most of the time, I think I do. Sometimes, though,

I'm not sure if I'm only setting myself up to be hurt."

"Please tell me you don't mean physically hurt, because I'd hate to be known as the guy who killed Connor Dean."

"He's a butterfly, really. He's not a fighter." She pulled her hair over to one side.

"Well, you are a feisty thing. Is that the problem? That he's not a fighter?"

"It's just schedules and craziness." Savannah took his hand. "Let's analyze you instead. What exactly is the problem? What did Max say? I know you listened to her. You're the best listener there is. Besides Josh, I mean. He's really the best."

Treat poked her arm. "She said I'd resent her if I changed the way I did business."

"And you said you wouldn't, but she's convinced you will." Savannah rose to her feet. "Oh, brother of mine." She pulled him up by his hands. "You, my dear, are missing something. She definitely left a bread crumb trail for you to follow. You just have to find it."

"I'm a very wise and wealthy man, you know," he teased as they walked inside. "I'm pretty sure that if there were a bread crumb trail, I'd see it. In fact, I'd have seen it before she realized she left it."

Savannah opened the refrigerator and began taking out food to cook for dinner. "Don't fool yourself. You're wise when it comes to business, but maybe not so wise when it comes to the mysterious ways of women."

Chapter Thirty-Five

"KAYLIE, I NEED YOU." Max was almost back to Allure when she realized what she needed to do.

"Why, Max, I never knew you were into blond women," Kaylie joked.

"This is serious. I need help, and I need it now. I know I've been a big old pain lately, and I'm sure Chaz is not going to be pleased, but I need your help, Kaylie."

"Oh my God, you're serious." Kaylie's voice softened. "What happened?"

"Nothing. Well, something. Something big. But I can't go over it now. Can you meet me at the mall?"

"You hate shopping."

"No shit. That's why I need you. Please, Kaylie? I hate myself for sounding like a desperate, needy woman, but I am, so will you meet me before I change my mind?"

The situation with Ryan could not have been

anticipated, but, Max realized as she drove home, it couldn't have gone any better, either. The pieces were starting to fall into place, clearing a path for her to understand what she had misconstrued years earlier. Ryan hadn't been in control of his actions when he'd hurt her, and he hadn't made a cognitive decision to do so. And although she felt horrible for what he'd gone through, the fact that he hadn't been in control made her release from the guilt even more clear.

She'd been nurturing self-imposed guilt for all these years. The reasons that he'd hurt her had nothing to do with compromises they made in their relationship. She could no more take responsibility for causing his actions than she could for Treat wanting to change the way he ran his business in order to make their relationship work.

She'd messed up big-time, and now she was dead set on making things right.

"Be there in fifteen," Kaylie said.

"Meet me at Victoria's Secret."

"WHO ARE YOU and what have you done with Max?" Kaylie looked around Max's right side; then she peered around her left side. She spun in a circle with her hand shading her eyes; then she lifted up Max's arms and looked beneath them. "Max? Where are you?" she teased.

"Shut up before I change my mind." Max had purposely never stepped foot in a Victoria's Secret store before. She'd stayed away from places that encouraged the idea of women being seen as playthings. But now, as she walked through the brightly lit, far-too-pink shop, with half-naked mannequins donning barely there, sexy lingerie, she saw it all much clearer. The lingerie wasn't about being a plaything; it was about owning—and enjoying—her sexuality, not exploiting it.

Max was bound and determined to own Treat-worthy, seductive, take-me-all-the-way attire.

"Max, I'm scared," Kaylie teased.

"I'm getting Treat back, and I want a wardrobe that will turn him on. All of it, from my head to my toes." She looked at Kaylie with a serious face and said, "Kaylie, make me hot."

"Girlfriend, just saying that makes you hot." Kaylie dragged her to the rear of the store, where she fingered through racks of lacy lingerie, holding up corsets and camisoles, lace bras and barely visible thongs. "What are we talking here, a few nights, a weekend? Seasonal?"

Max held up her credit card. "Whatever it takes. Whatever you would wear, I want to wear. Then we're going to buy clothes to go on top of the naughty bits."

"Max, you're talking about a lot of cash. Are you sure?"

Max rolled her eyes. "I've never been more sure of anything in all my life. Besides, I've had the same jeans and shirts for years. I have a five-digit savings account that I'll never spend. For Treat? Definitely worth it."

"But you can buy a few nights' worth and just use those over and over."

"Kaylie, I want to be sexy all the time. I don't mean that I'll stop wearing jeans and T-shirts, but I want to know that what I have on underneath my jeans, seven days a week, is appropriate for making him lose his mind. I want to walk into my closet and find something that begs me to pull myself out of efficient Max and morph into seductress Max. I wanna have options. The guy has a social calendar. I want to make him proud."

That's all Kaylie needed to hear to let loose. Max tried on so many outfits that her head was spinning. She stood in front of the mirror in a pink, lacy baby-doll nighty. "Wow," she said. She turned to the side. "Look at my butt. And look at these." She grabbed her breasts and lifted them up. "They're kinda hot, huh."

"Steaming." Kaylie took the elastic from Max's hair, and Max watched as her hair billowed around her shoulders. "Now you're steaming hot and entirely too fuckable for him to turn away."

"Oh, turning away hasn't been an issue," she said with a coy smile.

They left Victoria's Secret with several large bags and sexy lingerie for every occasion. Kaylie took her hand and dragged her into Hot Allure, a trendy clothing store known for upscale and sexy clothing.

Kaylie and Max picked through the racks, plucking outfits off the racks and carrying enormous piles of clothes into the dressing room.

"You don't know how long I've been wanting to do this," Kaylie said. "This is like every girl's makeover dream come true."

"Now I feel like Julia Roberts in *Pretty Woman*. I really appreciate your help. I would never pick out half these things. I'm still not sure they'll fit." She held up a red formfitting dress that looked too thin to fit over one leg much less her whole body.

"It stretches. Trust me," Kaylie said. "I have an eye for fashion and figures and, girlfriend, we're going to feature your figure in fabulous fashions."

"What are you, on a fashion high or something?" Max laughed.

An hour and a half later, they collapsed onto a bench in the center of the mall, surrounded by bags of dresses, slacks, sexy skinny jeans, heels, lingerie, even accessories.

"Your man is going to be so excited. Every night of the week!" Kaylie squealed.

"Uh-oh. Kaylie."

"What? Oh no. You look like something awful happened. Did you spend more money than you meant to? I've done that. Should we return it all? Well, except the baby-doll nighty. Every girl needs a baby-doll nighty."

Max shook her head. "I have no idea where Treat is. I left him in Wellfleet, and my phone won't get here until tomorrow. His number is on my phone."

"How did you get his number last time?" she asked.

"I got it from Scarlet, but I don't want to bother her again."

Kaylie and Max both wrinkled their brows.

Kaylie took out her cell phone and started texting.

"What are you doing?" Max asked.

"I have an idea. He's Blake's cousin, so I'll text Danica. She'll ask him, and he'll know how to find out where he is." Kaylie looked up at Max while she waited for a return text.

"Thank God for the sister network," Max joked.

"Max, what was your plan? Once you got the clothes, what were you going to do?"

"I hadn't thought it out that far. I forgot I didn't have my phone. I was sort of thinking about calling him."

Kaylie's phone vibrated. "She said hold on a sec."

Max sighed and threw her head back. "How can I be so together at work and so disorganized with my personal life?"

Her phone buzzed again. "It's part of being a woman. We can't be perfect all the time." She read the text. "Girlfriend, fate is on your side. He's at his father's ranch."

"In Weston?" Max jumped to her feet. "It really is fate." Her eyes grew wide.

"Settle down, doe eyes. Now what?"

Max gathered as many bags as she could carry and started for the exit. Kaylie scrambled to pick up the remaining bags and hurried behind her.

"Max!"

Max held up her bags and made a beeline for the exit. Every determined step brought her closer to Treat. "Home. Shower. Sex it up. Ranch," she called over her shoulder to Kaylie.

Chapter Thirty-Six

SURROUNDED BY HIS FAMILY, Treat was beginning to see his life a little more clearly. Yes, he was successful—more than successful. He'd started with one resort and now owned twenty-seven, each one more successful than the last. Of course his father was proud. But there was also no doubt in his mind that he'd done it to escape his guilt. If it were not for Max, he might never have dealt with what had been hanging over his head for too many years.

Max hadn't returned his calls. Each hour that passed was like a slow, torturous draw of his fingernails from his nail beds.

"Dude, you gotta stop moping," Dane said as he patted Treat on the back.

"Moping? *Pfft.* I'm fine. Just worried about Dad," he lied. They'd had to wrestle their father back into submission more than a few times. The man was an ox and would probably outlive them all.

"Right. Like I can't smell woman troubles a mile away."

Treat shook his head, but he knew Dane could see right through his veil of denial. Hell, everyone probably could. You don't find a woman like Max very often; she was smart, competent, loving, and sexier than she could ever know. There was something else that he couldn't put his finger on, but he was pretty sure that it had to do with the fact that Max loved him—and yes, he was sure that beneath that feisty, stubborn exterior and her fears about relationships, she loved him—for him. Not for his money, or for what he stood for, or any of the other ridiculous reasons that beautiful women had clung to him over the years.

He carried apple cider out to the table, stopping when he caught sight of his father and Rex walking down by the barn. Rex had a pinched look on his face, and his father suddenly stopped walking and put his hand on Rex's shoulder. Treat could practically feel that secure weight on his own flesh. He knew the look his father was giving Rex, and he would bet the discussion had something to do with him.

He'd better go face it head-on.

Savannah touched his arm before he could take two steps. "Leave them," she said.

"I'm sure it's about what I said last night."

"No, it's not. Let them be."

Treat narrowed his eyes at his sister. "What don't I know?"

Savannah took the apple cider from his hands and set it on the table, ignoring his question.

"Savannah?" He stared her down. He'd be damned if his little sister would tell him what to do.

"Leave it alone, Treat," Hugh said as he approached from behind. He set plates and silverware on the table, then turned to Treat. "Rex seems tough, but he's not as tough as you might think. He's having a hard time with Dad's health issues."

Treat shot another glance at Rex, who was looking everywhere except at his father, while his father's stare never wavered.

"Why wouldn't he tell me? We worked in the field for hours, side by side, and all he did was snap at me."

Hugh shook his head.

"Would you tell you?" Josh asked. He brought the burgers to the table and motioned for everyone to sit down. "Think about it, Treat. He's here every day, slaving to help keep the family business alive, and suddenly you sweep in and expect him to just accept it. Meanwhile, the one person he loves the most lands in the hospital. It's a lot to deal with."

I failed him again? "So, what? I should have asked his permission to come back to my own father's ranch and help out? I thought it was what he wanted all these years."

His three siblings exchanged a look that said perhaps that's exactly what he should have done.

"All right. I get it. I'll talk to him." He started for the barn.

"Treat!" Savannah hollered. She came to his side and touched his arm. "He's hurting. Please don't push him. You know Rex. When he's ready, he'll open up to you. He always does."

When it came to his siblings, hurting them was the last thing he ever wanted to do. His father and Rex started toward them, and Treat turned away. Was he doing more harm than good by being there? What the hell was going on in his life? One day he was on a strong, straight path, and the next, the very foundation he built his world on was filling with fissures.

A few minutes later, Rex and Hal joined them at the table. Rex snagged a burger and bun, eyeing the rest of the food, and set to work building a massive dinner plate.

"Dad, you have a follow-up with Ben next week. I'll take you," Treat offered.

"I've got it covered," Rex said gruffly.

"Rex'll take me. Tell me what's happening with that pretty little gal I met," his father said, clearly trying to steer clear of the whole Rex situation.

Treat bit back the hurt he felt by his father's refusal and tried not to let the kick to his gut show on his face. He had to remember that healing himself was not the only priority here. He'd stirred the hornet's nest with Rex, and now it was his turn to wait it out—just like Rex had for the past fifteen years.

"Not much to tell, Dad. She's afraid I'm giving up my life for her and I'll resent her for it." He stabbed at the salad Savannah had dished onto his plate with a sisterly pat on his back.

"Since when have you sat back and waited for things to happen?" his father asked. "Where's that boy I raised who went out and showed those highfalutin, suit-wearing executives how to do things?"

Isn't everyone asking me to sit back and wait for Rex? And isn't that just what I'm doing for Max? Isn't that what Max wants? His father must have read his mind.

"Son, I've seen you pull out your cell phone more times than I can count. Do you love her?"

All eyes were on him. Treat put down his fork and looked at his family, and in their eyes, he saw so much support that it took the tension out of his gut and formed a cradle around his heart.

"Yeah, I do." He nodded, hoping they didn't notice the way his voice cracked.

"Then I don't see why you're sitting around here waiting for something to happen. Take that lame ass of yours and make it happen," Rex said. He followed that up with a big bite of his burger.

Treat's heartbeat sped up. What was he waiting for? He was giving her time. Time for what? To decide they weren't right for each other?

"It doesn't work that way with Max," he said. "She's...complicated. She's got stuff to deal with, and I don't want to push her in ways she might not want to be pushed." *Bullshit. I want to. I'm just afraid she'll run— again.*

"What are you afraid of, Treat?" Rex's eyes darkened, narrowed. It was a challenge, not a question, and he wasn't talking about Max.

"Nothing scares me, little brother. I'm here. I'm baring my soul and fighting the demons that have strangled me for years, which is more than I can say for you." *What the hell am I doing? I should walk away, not argue with Rex.*

His brother rose to his feet. "What's that supposed to mean? I'm here every damned day, taking care of the family business while you're out doing whatever you please. At least I didn't abandon Dad."

There was a collective gasp from his siblings. Treat felt his father's eyes on him.

"I never abandoned Dad. I built a life and a business," Treat retorted.

"Right. A life? You travel endlessly. You live a life of leisure while I hold down the real job."

"What's this about, Rex?" Treat rose to his feet, meeting his brother's stare. "No one made you stay. No one made you give up whatever else you wanted to do. Your whole life you wanted to be a rancher. I didn't."

Treat walked around the table, confronting his brother. Rex's breath was hot on his face, his nostrils flared, and his biceps jumped up and down to the pace of his fisting hands.

"I came home every single time you called, without fail," Treat said in a calm and even tone.

"No, you didn't."

"What are you talking about? Every time you called, I came. Every goddamned time." Treat had the urge to grab his brother's enormous shoulders and shake the shit out of him. Make him spit out whatever he was holding back.

Rex's index finger poked his chest so hard he took a step back. "You left. You abandoned the family, Treat. You abandoned me and left me to figure out how to hold things together."

"I went to college! What the fuck did you want me to do?" *Abandoned?*

"I was fifteen! What the hell was I supposed to do? Dane was a mess. How was I supposed to watch over the other three kids and take care of the ranch—and Dad? Fifteen, Treat. Fif-teen!"

His face grew red, and his eyes flashed with a rage that had Treat grabbing his brother's shoulders and staring down at him. "I never abandoned you. I went to school, Rex. College. It was what I was supposed to do. It was Dad's plan for me. I was doing what he wanted me to do, not abandoning him." The truth of his own words gave him pause. *It was Dad's plan for me. It's true. It was Dad's plan for me. How could I have repressed that?*

Rex twisted out of his grip. His body shook so hard Treat thought he might attack him at any moment. He readied himself for the blow that was sure to come as Rex took one fist in his palm and rubbed it hard.

Treat shot a glance around the table. His siblings were watching without so much as a flash of stress. They must have known what was eating at Rex. His father slowly rose to his feet but made no move to come any closer.

Rex's eyes shot darts; his venom-filled voice

pierced Treat's thick skin. "I called you a few weeks after you went to school and said I couldn't do it. Dane was out of control, Josh basically locked himself in his bedroom for weeks on end, Hugh was pulling away, and Savannah had disappeared for the weekend with her friend. I didn't know what to do."

"What? When?" And then he remembered. It seemed like a hundred years ago. Treat remembered the panicked call. It was a Saturday, and he was out with some girl. He couldn't even remember her name.

"You said Savannah went to some keg party and you couldn't find her. A goddamned party! I left my date and went back to my dorm and called every one of her friends' parents. I was going frigging crazy looking for her from a million miles away, and you called me a few hours later and said she was back home, that her friend had lied about it all to get her in trouble."

Treat took a breath and tried to bring his anger down a notch. "I thought it was fine after that."

Rex huffed, his rage bubbling beneath his skin. "Nothing was fine. You should have come home."

"How could I have possibly known? I was a kid, too, Rex. I was eighteen. What the fuck would you have had me do? Fly home and quit college? Give up everything Dad said I had to accomplish?"

They stared at each other, posturing, silently banging chests and measuring feathers.

"Boys!" Hal's stern voice broke their match. "You wanna blame someone? Blame me. I wanted Treat to excel. He was too academic and had too much to accomplish in life to run the ranch. He'd have had me buying up more ranches by the time he was fourteen if I'd let him, and maybe if I had listened to him, we'd all be even richer. And, Rex, you were born to ranch and you know it. The day you started walking, you wanted to follow my ass all over this place. You'd sit with me while I ran the finances and rode with me on every ride. You wanted this ranch, and you know you did. But it's a lot of responsibility, and I don't blame you for resenting your brothers—all of them—for taking off. But, Rex, I gave you the same choice I gave them. How many times did I say, 'Go out there and get your own ranch, or find something else that you want to call your own?'"

Rex looked away.

"When I'm talking to you, son, you keep your eyes on mine."

Rex met his gaze. "I didn't want my own ranch. This is family. This is where Mom is." He slid his dark eyes to Treat. "This is where Mom is," he repeated.

Treat knew what he was insinuating. "I didn't abandon you, and I sure as hell didn't abandon Mom."

"No, you didn't," his father said as he approached the two men.

To a stranger, seeing the two angry, muscular, confident men staring each other down would mean fists were gonna fly. To his family, Treat knew what they looked like. Two brothers at odds and finding their way back to each other.

His father stood between them.

Treat felt his father's hand on his back and knew his

other hand was on Rex's.

Hal lowered his voice and spoke in a serious, even tone. "You wanna blame someone for all of this? Blame me. I'm the one who led you all those years."

Rex's eyes shifted to his father, softened, then dropped to the ground.

"Rex, I'm sorry," Treat said. "I just didn't know. I was a kid trying to keep my own head above water. It's true; I did abandon everyone because I felt guilty, but you gotta know, if I had known you felt that lost, I'd have come running back. After Savannah came home, I figured it was just more of the same. The same grieving kids that I'd left when I went away to school."

Rex didn't look up for the longest time, and when he finally did, it was his father's eyes he met, not Treat's. "Sorry I ruined the afternoon, Dad. I've gotta go check on Hope." He headed for the barn.

Treat took a step toward him and his father held him back. "Leave him. This is how Rex operates. You remember this pattern, don't you? He'll work out his frustration. It'll take time, but now you know what's what. It may not be today, and it may not be next week, but at some point, this'll come out in the wash."

It wasn't the fight that had Treat so upset that every nerve was aflame. It was the truth of his brother's words wrestling with the truth of his own. Rex had said exactly what Treat had confessed to the other night, and now Treat realized that when he'd left, he'd been living up to his father's expectations in equal measure to escaping his own guilt.

Rex would eventually come around. Treat was home now. He might buy a place nearby, and he might have to travel and set up an office, but he wasn't going to abandon anyone ever again—including Max.

He couldn't eat. Rex was right. He'd been dicking around far too much where Max was concerned. He couldn't deal with Rex until Rex was ready, but he could damn well deal with his feelings for Max.

Treat stood from the table and threw down his napkin. "I've gotta go take care of something." Without another word from his family, he headed into the house.

A few minutes later, he was in the car, pulling down the driveway when Rex rode up on Hope and stopped in his path. Treat slammed on the brakes and jumped from the car. "What the hell are you doing? Trying to get Hope killed?" Treat yelled.

Rex settled Hope from her startled shuffle. "I know all that shit you said back there. I'm not an idiot."

"No. You're not," Treat said.

They stared each other down again.

"Just like you've been carrying that shit around with you all these years, so have I."

Treat nodded. Honesty was a bitch, and he wasn't about to get in Rex's way with some stupid comment.

"I know you didn't abandon me. Or Mom or Dad. I get that, and the truth is, I wouldn't have wanted you to give up what you were destined to do."

"Okay?"

Rex held on to Hope's reins. His bulging muscles contradicted the gentle apology he was handing Treat.

Treat had the overwhelming urge to hug his younger brother, but he was afraid to even move. Rex had a shell that was thick as a brick, and Treat knew just how much this breakthrough meant to their relationship, which might not be anywhere near normal for years to come, but this was a start.

Rex nodded. "I'm glad you're home, but I'm still running the ranch."

"Okay."

"You're far from in shape for this kind of grueling work. It'll take you months to get back up to speed—physically anyway."

"Agreed." Every muscle in Treat's aching body could attest to that, though it was his pride that was taking a beating at the hand of his kid brother.

"All right then."

"All right."

"Where are you going?" Rex backed the horse from the driveway.

"I gotta take care of some business. I'll be back to help with the evening chores."

Rex nodded. "Take your time, bro. Believe it or not, I'm glad you're back."

Treat ran one hand down the side of Hope's face, and swore he saw his mother's beautiful reflection in the horse's eyes, a smile of approval on her lips as she looked back at him.

Chapter Thirty-Seven

MAX SURVEYED HERSELF in the mirror one last time. Her hair was shiny and full. The skinny leather pants she wore might not be perfect for showing up at a ranch, but they were close. *Aren't chaps leather?* Although the knee-high, leather stiletto boots were definitely *not* appropriate. *Perfect.* She wanted Treat to stand up and take notice. She'd asked him to do one thing—one thing—and he didn't do it, and she'd be damned if she'd let that go. Even if she *was* the one who'd walked away.

She turned to the side to inspect her silhouette. Kaylie was right about the push-up bra. Who knew her boobs could look so perky? Or that a bra could make her torso look longer, slimmer? Wow, she could actually pull off *hot*.

Max tried her best to remain upright on the heels, and as she reached for the doorknob, her confidence began to fade. *I look ridiculous. He loves how I look no matter what I wear. What am I doing?* What was her goal? Treat. Treat was her goal, and she'd leave nothing to chance this time.

She opened the bedroom door and a bright flash sent her reeling backward as Kaylie snapped a picture. "What the hell?" She'd been so wrapped up in getting ready that she'd forgotten Kaylie was waiting for her.

"I couldn't help it!" Kaylie squealed. "I wanted to come in so badly, but I knew you would never let me dress you after letting me pick out all your clothes." Kaylie's eyes grew wide. "Oh my God, Max, you are sinful! Look at you. Not that you need to look like this, but wow. No man could ever turn you away looking like that."

She had to smile at Kaylie's supportive, overly enthusiastic comment. "Can I please just carry you on my shoulder? I'm so nervous. What if he's decided that I'm not worth it. I mean, I did just break up with him in not the nicest of ways."

"Max, one question. Take a deep breath, because this is really, really important."

Max did as she was asked and blew her breath out slowly. "Okay, what?"

"Are you one hundred percent sure that you want a guy who didn't come begging you to come back to him?"

"Why are you doing this to me?" Max asked, lowering herself to the couch. "Am I making a mistake?"

"I just gotta ask. I love you so much, and I can't see you get your heart broken again."

"I did tell him to love me through my insecurities. Why didn't he?" *It's the only thing I ever asked of him.*

Kaylie sat next to her and took her hand. "I'm not saying he didn't. He's respecting what you asked him to do. I just want you to think about him. All of him. What you like, what you don't like, what might be real and what might be fantasy."

Max chewed on her worries. Was she making a mistake? "I left him no choice, Kaylie. I told him I was done. I didn't really expect him to chase after me." She tried to remember what she'd written in her rushed note. "When I left, I didn't want him to, or at least that's what I thought. My whole life I believed that compromising to make a relationship work would lead to resentment."

"Are you insane? All of marriage is compromise. Who's living where? Who's watching the kids so one of us can do something else? Who's on top? Who gets to come fir—"

"Kaylie! I'm trying to be serious," Max huffed.

"I know. If that's really what was driving you to tell that gorgeous man not to follow you, then yeah, you really messed up. Just as long as you don't have any reservations about his love for you."

Max's cheeks warmed. She put her hand over her heart and said, "He'd give up anything for me, and I'll be lucky if he takes me back so that I can show him I'd do the same for him."

"Jesus. I hope I was never that swoony-eyed over Chaz. Okay, go. I'll lock up for you, but I want to use

341

your bathroom first." She looked into Max's room. "I'll even unexplode your closet for you."

Max kissed her on the cheek. "You're the best." On her way out the door, she stopped and turned back. "Thanks for asking me if I was sure. I've never really had a friend like you before."

"Yeah, I'm the best," Kaylie said with a toss of her hair. "Now get out of here."

Max ran down the stairs in her stiletto heels like she'd been running in them all her life. Her mind wrapped itself around one singular thought—reaching Treat.

Chapter Thirty-Eight

TREAT SPED THE whole way to Max's apartment. Traffic was light and he made it there in record time. He flew into the parking lot and took a cursory glance for Max's car as he ran for the steps, which he took two by two, feeling lighter on his feet than he had in years.

He knocked on her door twice, then twice more without waiting for her to answer. His heart thundered against his ribs. He had no idea what he'd say to her. He'd figure it out when he saw her beautiful eyes.

The knob turned. Treat held his breath as the door swung open.

"What did you forget?"

"Kaylie?"

"Treat?"

He looked over her shoulder. "Where's Max?"

A smile grew across Kaylie's lips. "She's heading toward your father's ranch."

"My father's—"

"Yes! Go! She just left ten minutes ago. Go!"

He bolted down the stairs and headed back toward the highway, spurred on by the knowledge that Max was coming for him.

BY THE TIME she pulled up in front of the ranch, Max had had plenty of time to mull over Kaylie's questions, and she'd driven herself into a relative frenzy. She had asked him to love her through her insecurities, and he'd promised he would. Maybe she was making a mistake after all. Maybe since he hadn't come for her, he didn't really love her like he claimed.

She parked the car and felt the anger building in her chest, battling with the love that was tugging at her heart. She hadn't given him a choice. She hadn't said, *Follow me. Love me.* No. Instead she'd been an idiot and written, *Please don't follow me.* Still, he should have known better. He should have figured it out, like she had when she'd gone to Wellfleet.

She watched one of Treat's brothers riding a horse across the field, toward her car. As he approached, she saw it was the one with the huge muscles. Not that any of them weren't cut from some incredibly sexy fabric that she'd never known existed, but this brother's biceps were the size of footballs.

He pulled up on the reins of the beautiful red and gray horse as Max stepped from the car.

"Max?" He ran his eyes slowly down her body with an appreciative nod.

Ugh! She had forgotten what she was wearing, and now, with the crests of her breasts saying hello to the world and her leather pants leaving nothing to the imagination, she felt like a fool, which only spurred on her anger even more.

"Rex, right?" she asked.

"Yeah, that's right. You just missed Treat. He took off to take care of some business."

Damn it. "Business?" *Why the hell isn't he taking care of fixing our relationship?*

Rex shrugged. "That's what he said."

His eyes roved to her breasts and remained there. Max cleared her throat, and he met her eyes with a nod of his head.

"Thank you," she said curtly and climbed back into her car. *Business? Business!* She snapped on her seat belt. And the way Rex had ogled her? She'd come out looking to entice Treat and now she looked like nothing but a tramp! If Treat were there, they would have recognized her sexy attire as the lure it was meant to be. *Damn it.* She jerked her car into reverse and slammed the pedal to the floor—she couldn't get out of there fast enough.

She felt the impact that sent her flying chest first into the steering wheel before she heard the crunching of metal on metal.

Shit. Shit, shit, shit. Dazed and shaken, Max blinked away her angry, scared tears and saw the rest of the Braden clan running toward her car. What the hell had she done now?

Rex yanked open the door. "Max? Are you okay?"

"Is she okay?" Max heard someone yell.

"Get away from her."

Treat?

"I'll get her," he said.

And there he was, yanking Rex from beside her door and pulling her gently into his arms. *Treat.* Max registered voices behind him, but she was still too shocked from the accident to think beyond being in Treat's strong arms.

"I'll call an ambulance."

"Wait. Let's see if she's okay first."

"What happened?"

"Max?" Treat's gentle voice was shaken and scared. "Sweetness, look at me."

She looked into his eyes as he pulled her to her feet.

"Are you okay?" he asked.

She saw his car behind hers, the front end smashed in by the rear of hers.

"Yeah, I think so," she whispered. Then, amid the shock, the worry, and his family members pawing at her, the anger returned, boiling in her belly and rising like heat into her chest.

"You said you'd love me through it." *What happened to my voice? Why am I whispering?* That won't do.

"What, sweetness?" Treat asked.

"You said you'd love me through it," Max repeated, this time a little louder. The confusion on Treat's face only pissed her off even more. She pushed away from him. Her chest was sore, but she could walk and stand

and, damn it, she could talk—and yell.

"You said you'd love me through it. I asked you, that night in Wellfleet, when I told you that if I got scared and those walls of insecurity went up, I'd need you to love me through it." *Why the hell am I crying?* "And you said you'd love me through anything, Treat. Anything! You promised. But you didn't."

"Max." He stepped closer, reaching for her.

She pushed him away.

"Uh-oh," Dane said.

His siblings stared at her. His father watched Treat. Max looked from his father to Treat and then back again. She didn't care if she was making a fool of herself, or if his father were sending him telepathic messages telling him she was a freak. She'd trusted him and he hadn't come for her!

"Max," he tried again gently.

She pushed him away again, trying to back into her car, which she couldn't drive away if she tried because she'd smashed into Treat's car. He grabbed her arm, keeping her from hiding.

"Max!" Treat finally said loud and strong, leaving no room for her refusal to listen. "I called you thirty-seven times in the last two days. Not once did you return my calls."

"Thirty-seven?" Savannah whispered.

"You—" Max fumbled for words.

"You had your say; now it's my turn. I tried to give you space. I tried to wait for you to come back. I called, and damn it, Max, don't you think that every call that went unanswered was like a slap in the face?"

"I didn't have my ph—"

"I don't want to hear your excuses. I want to finish what I started. I'm not giving up my life for you. I'm not giving up Thailand or anything else."

Max swallowed back the sobs that pressed at her throat. *He's done. Finished. It's over. This time for good.*

"Treat," Savannah cautioned.

Treat held up his palm toward his sister. "Let me goddamn finish." He turned back to Max, and when he spoke, his voice was a tender caress to her broken heart. "Max, I'm rearranging how things are done, not giving them up. I'm coming back to help my father on the ranch—for a while, anyway—and I do want to put down roots. But I don't care where, as long as you're with me. I will love you through anything, Max. I promised, and I always fulfill my promises."

He wiped her tears with a whisper of his finger across her cheek and moved in closer. "I slayed my demons, Max. All of them."

"You called me thirty-seven times?" Max's legs trembled from the accident and mostly from seeing Treat again. She relished his breath on her lips, his hands on her arms, and then the most intimate touch, as he reached up and pushed the hair from her shoulder. She closed her eyes. *I'm not going to make the same mistake again.*

"Open your eyes," Treat said with a smile. When he had her attention, he said, "You can push me away as much as you want from here on out, but I'm not budging. It's enough already. This is who we are. Treat and Max. Not Treat Braden and Max Armstrong, two separate people. It's us, not you and me."

Us. She swiped at the waterfall of tears streaming down her cheeks and shook her head. "I left my phone in Wellfleet."

"It doesn't matter," he said.

"I'll travel."

"What?"

"Whatever we need to do for your business. I'll travel with you. I can work from anywhere."

"Max, we'll figure all that out," he said.

She couldn't think straight. Everything was tumbling together. Treat loved her. He loved her! She was in his arms. It was real. This wasn't a dream.

Then Treat released her, and for a moment, the world stood still. Her eyes bounced from Savannah's to Josh's. Josh's eyes grew wide, and a smile pulled at the right side of his mouth. Dane put a hand on Savannah's shoulder, watching his brother with an intent and happy gaze. Max looked at Hugh, then Rex, still on Hope's back, grinning like a fool. It was the tears in Hal's eyes that drew Max's eyes back to Treat, only he was no longer standing before her.

"Max." He took her hand in his as he perched on one knee.

She gasped. "Treat?"

"Max, I would be honored if you would let me love you through the rest of your life. Through every insecurity and every argument."

The world stood still and her mouth went dry. She couldn't do anything more than stare at his beautiful face.

"Max?" he asked again. "Will you be my wife?"

"I...wife...? What if I freak out again?"

He stood and looked into her eyes. "Then I'll be there every step of the freak-out to make sure you're okay. To make sure we're okay."

"You want to marry me? After everything I did? After how angry I was? After I smashed your car?"

"Yes."

Savannah grabbed Josh's arm, and that little movement pulled Max from her stupor.

"You're sure?" she asked again.

"You are one stubborn, beautiful woman. Yes, I'm more than sure."

Max threw her arms around his neck. Her chest ached with the constriction of her muscles, but she didn't care. She wrapped her legs around his waist. "Yes. Yes, yes, yes!"

"I cannot wait to design her gown!" Josh exclaimed.

Treat's laughter filled the air, mixing with the cheers from his family and Savannah's giddy squeal. He lowered his mouth to hers and kissed the ache right out of her body, claiming her in a way she felt through her entire soul.

"Looks like we're gonna have a wedding!" his father said.

Treat lowered her back down to the ground and slipped a velvet bag out of his pocket. Looking her in the eye, he asked, "Max, just to be clear, will you marry me?"

"Absolutely, one hundred percent yes."

He slid the most gorgeous canary diamond ring on her finger, stealing the remainder of her breath from her lungs.

TREAT HELD MAX's trembling, soft hand in his and never wanted to let it go. In all the business dealings he'd ever handled, in all the resorts he'd acquired and the other businessmen he'd put to shame, never once had he felt the way he did at that very moment. It was as if the universe had righted itself, and he and Max were in the perfect place at the perfect time.

Rex pushed past Treat to hug Max. Treat didn't miss the full-body glance Rex gave her before pulling her into his arms. That was when he first noticed what Max was wearing. His body reacted instantly to seeing her in such a formfitting, sinfully sexy outfit. Unfortunately, with the way Rex was holding on to her, he assumed her figure had his brother reacting in the exact same way.

He tugged him away from Max by his collar. "Okay, back off. Get your own fiancée." He loved the feel of that word on his lips. *Fiancée.*

Savannah slid in between them and wrapped her arms around Treat. "Finally! I love her!" she whispered. "She'll keep you on your toes." She turned to Max with a wide smile and said, "I've wanted a sister for way too long," then pulled her in close.

Treat couldn't wait to get Max's hand back into his

own, where it belonged.

"Max." Hal wrapped his strong arms around her. "That was my wife's ring," he said with a nod at her hand.

Max touched the gorgeous stone. "Thank you for the honor of allowing me to wear it and share in the joy of one day being a Braden."

He nodded. "It was my wife's doing."

Savannah shook her head, but her beaming smile remained.

When congratulations had been doled out and they finally came together again, Treat whispered in her ear, "That outfit is going to make me do dirty things to you right here and now."

Max smiled. "Then it fulfilled its purpose."

Chapter Thirty-Nine

THE SOUND OF hooves on pavement called everyone's attention past the crunched vehicles and to the road. A beautiful woman riding a black stallion came to a stop at the end of their driveway. She flipped her long dark hair behind her back and settled her cowgirl boots into the shiny stirrups.

"Is that Jade?" Treat asked.

Rex spun around, practically salivating at the sight of her. "Jesus," he whispered.

"Looks like someone got the best of your cars!" she hollered. She wore a flowing white dress, hiked up and bundled across her thighs.

"Earl Johnson's girl?" Treat asked Rex. When Rex was in high school, he'd had an enormous crush on her. The Johnsons and the Bradens had been feuding for years, and Treat had always written that crush off as Rex wanting the forbidden fruit. But from the way Rex was looking at her, he could see that crush was still steaming hot.

Rex mounted Hope and looked over his shoulder at her, then turned away again. "One and the same," he answered.

Treat didn't miss the way his eyes narrowed as he drank her in, or the twitching of his biceps as he wrapped tight fists around Hope's reins.

Hugh looked up from where he was inspecting the damage to the cars and shot an uncomfortable look at Treat. Treat glanced back at the house. Luckily their father had already headed inside to dig up a bottle of champagne to celebrate Treat and Max's engagement. If their father caught them talking to a Johnson, they'd never hear the end of it, but being rude was not an easy thing to do to a beautiful woman. "Good to see you, Jade," Hugh said in a low, tethered voice.

"Not quite a Ferrari, is it?" she teased his racecar-driving brother. She looked at Rex and said, "Good thing y'all weren't on horses, huh?"

Rex's jaw flexed double-time.

"I think she's talking to you, Rex," Max said.

Hugh looked back at his brother and shook his head. "We'll be sending this wreck to your neighbor's garage," he said to Jade. Jimmy Palen owned the best body shop in Weston and owned the property on the other side of the Johnsons'.

"Jimmy'll be glad to hear that." Jade smiled, but Treat saw the hurt in her eyes when she looked at Rex again, who had ignored her comment. "See y'all around," she said with a wave, then galloped down the road.

When she was out of earshot, Treat smacked Rex's leg. "What the hell? You didn't have to be such an ass."

"I'll talk to a Johnson when hell freezes over." Rex gave Hope a quick jab with his heels and trotted off toward the barn.

"What was that all about? She was stunning." Max couldn't stop touching the ring on her finger.

"Hatfields and McCoys," Savannah teased. "He loves her." Savannah took Max's arm and they headed toward the house. "He just doesn't know it yet. Braden boys are thick that way."

Treat watched Savannah drag Max away, swearing that chartering that plane had been the best thing he'd ever done.

The End

Please enjoy a preview of the next *Love in Bloom* novel

Destined for Love

The Bradens, Book Two

Love in Bloom Series

Melissa Foster

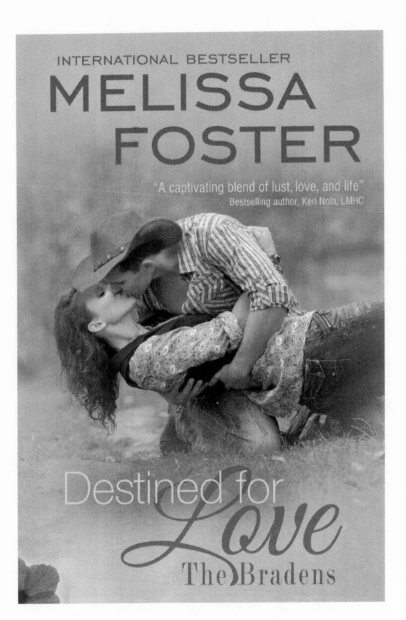

INTERNATIONAL BESTSELLER

MELISSA FOSTER

"A captivating blend of lust, love, and life"
Bestselling author, Keri Nola, LMHC

Destined for *Love*
The Bradens

Chapter One

REX BRADEN AWOKE before dawn, just as he had every Sunday morning for the past twenty-six years—since the Sunday after his mother died, when he was eight years old. He didn't know what had startled him awake on that very first Sunday after she'd passed, but he swore it was her whispering voice that led him down to the barn and had him mounting Hope, the horse his father had bought for his mother when she first became ill. In the years since, Hope had remained strong and healthy; his mother, however, was not as lucky.

In the gray, predawn hours, the air was still downright cold, which wasn't unusual for May in Colorado. By afternoon they'd see temps in the early seventies. Rex pulled his Stetson down low on his head and rounded his shoulders forward as he headed into the barn.

The other horses itched to be set free the moment

he walked by their stalls, but Rex's focus on Sunday mornings was solely on Hope.

"How are you, girl?" he asked in a deep, soft voice. He saddled Hope with care, running his hand over her thick coat. Her red coat had faded, now boasting white patches along her jaw and shoulders.

Hope nuzzled her nose into his massive chest with a gentle *neigh*. Most of his T-shirts had worn spots at his solar plexus from that familiar nudge. Rex had helped his father on the ranch ever since he was a boy, and after graduating from college, he'd returned to the ranch full-time. Now he ran the show—well, as much as anyone could run anything under Hal Braden's strong will.

"Taking our normal ride, okay, Hope?" He looked into her enormous brown eyes, and not for the first time, he swore he saw his mother's beautiful face smiling back at him. The face he remembered from before her illness had stolen the color from her skin and the sparkle from her eyes. Rex put his hands on Hope's strong jaw and kissed her on the soft pad of skin between her nostrils. Then he removed his hat and rested his forehead against the same tender spot, closing his eyes just long enough to sear that image into his mind.

They trotted down the well-worn trail in the dense woods that bordered his family's five-hundred-acre ranch. Rex had grown up playing in those woods with his five siblings. He knew every dip in the landscape and could ride every trail blindfolded. They rode out to the point where the trail abruptly came to an end at the adjacent property. The line between the Braden ranch and the unoccupied property might be invisible to some. The grass melded together, and the trees looked identical on either side. To Rex, the division was clear. On the Braden side, the land had life and breath, while on the unoccupied side, the land seemed to exude a longing for more.

Hope instinctively knew to turn around at that point, as they'd done so many times before. Today, Rex pulled her reins gently, bringing her to a halt. He took a deep breath as the sun began to rise, his chest tightening at the silent three hundred acres of prime ranch land that would remain empty forever. Forty-five years earlier, his father and Earl Johnson, their neighbor and his father's childhood friend, had jointly purchased that acreage between the two properties with the hopes of one day turning it over for a profit. After five years of arguing over everything from who would pay to subdivide the property to who they'd sell it to, both Hal and Earl took the hardest stand they could, each refusing to ever sell. The feud still had not resolved. The Hatfields' and McCoys' harsh and loyal stance to protect their family honor was mild compared to the loyalty that ran within the Braden veins. The Bradens had been raised to be loyal to their family above all else. Rex felt a pang of guilt as he looked over the property, and not for the first time, he wished he could make it his own.

With a gentle kick of his heels and a tug of the rein in his right hand, Hope trotted off the path and along the property line toward the creek. Rex's jaw clenched and his biceps bulged as they descended the deep hill toward the ravine. The water was still as glass when they finally reached the rocky shoreline. Rex looked up at the sky as the gray gave way to powdery blues and pinks. In all the years since he'd claimed those predawn hours as his own, he'd never seen a soul while he was out riding, and he liked it that way.

They headed south along the water toward Devil's Bend. The ravine curved at a shockingly sharp angle around the hillside and the water pooled, deepening before the rocky lip just before the creek dropped a dangerous twenty feet into a bed of rocks. He slowed when he heard a splash and scanned the water for the telltale signs of a beaver, but there wasn't a dam in sight.

Rex took the bend and brusquely drew Hope to a halt. Jade Johnson stood at the water's edge in a pair of cutoff jean shorts, cut just above the dip where her hamstrings began. He'd seen her only once in the past several years, and that was weeks ago, when she had ridden her stallion down the road and stopped at the top of their driveway. Rex raked his eyes down her body and swallowed hard. Her cream-colored T-shirt hugged every inch of her delicious curves, a beautiful contrast to her black-as-night hair, which tumbled almost to her waist. Rex noticed that her hair was the exact same color as her stallion, which was standing nearby with one leg bent at the knee.

Jade hadn't seen him yet. He knew he should back

Hope up and leave before she had the chance. But she was so goddamned beautiful that he was mesmerized, his body reacting in ways that had him cursing under his breath. Jade Johnson was Earl Johnson's feisty daughter. Jade Johnson was off-limits. She always had been and always would be. But that didn't stop his pulse from racing, or the crotch of his jeans from tightening against his growing desire. Fifteen years he'd forced himself not to think about her, and now, as her shoulders lifted and fell with each breath, he couldn't stop himself from wondering what it might feel like to tangle his fingers in her thick mane of hair, or how her breasts would feel pressed against his bare chest. He felt the tantalizing stir of the forbidden wrestling with his deep-seated loyalty to his father—and he was powerless to stop himself from being the prick of a man that usually resulted from the conflicting emotions.

JADE JOHNSON KNEW she shouldn't have ridden Flame down the ravine, but she'd woken up from a restless, steamy dream before the sun came up, and she needed a release for the sexual urges she'd been repressing for way too long. *Goddamned Weston, Colorado.* How the hell was a twenty-eight-year-old woman supposed to have any sort of relationship with a man in a town when everybody knew one another's business? She's thought she'd had life all figured out; after she graduated from veterinary school in Oklahoma, she'd completed her certifications for veterinarian acupuncture while also studying equine shiatsu, and then she'd taken on full-time hours at the large animal practice where she'd worked a limited schedule while completing school. She'd dated the owner's son, Kane Law, and when she opened her own practice a year later, she thought she and Kane would move toward having a future together. How could she have known that her success would be a threat to him—or that he'd become so possessive that she'd have to end the relationship? Coming back home had been her only option after he refused to stop harassing her, and now that she'd been back for a few months, she was thinking that maybe returning to the small town had been a mistake. She'd gotten her Colorado license easily enough, but instead of building a real practice again, she'd been working on more of an as-needed basis, traveling to neighboring farms to help with their animals without any long-term commitment, while she figured out where she wanted to put down roots and try again.

She heaved a heavy rock into the water with a grunt, pissed off that she'd taken this chance with Flame by coming down the steep hill. She knew better, but Flame was a sturdy Arabian stallion, and at fifteen hands high, he had the most powerful hindquarters she'd ever seen. Flame's reaction time to commands, and his ability to spin, turn, or sprint forward was quicker than any horse she'd ever mounted. His short back, strong bones, and incredibly muscled loins made him appear indestructible. When Flame stumbled, Jade's heart nearly skipped a beat. He'd quickly regained his footing, but the rhythm of his gait had changed, and when she'd dismounted, he was favoring his right front leg. Now she was stuck with no way to get him home without hurting him further.

Damn it. She bent over and hoisted another heavy rock into her arms to heave more of her frustration into the water. Her hair fell like a curtain over her face, and she used one dusty hand to push it back over her shoulder, then picked up the rock and—*shit*. She dropped the rock and narrowed her eyes at the sight of Rex Braden sitting atop that mare of his.

The nerve of him, staring at me like I'm a piece of meat. Even if he was every girl's dream of a cowboy come true in his tight-fitting jeans, which curved oh so lusciously over his thighs, defining a significant bulge behind the zipper. She ran her eyes up his too-tight dark shirt and silently cursed at herself for involuntarily licking her lips in response. She tried to tear her eyes from his tanned face, peppered with stubble so sexy that she wanted to reach out and touch his chiseled jaw, but her eyes would not obey.

"What're you looking at?" she spat at the son of the man who had caused her father years of turmoil. When she'd first come back to town, she'd hoped maybe things had changed. She'd ridden by the Bradens' ranch while she was out with Flame one afternoon. Rex and his family were out front, commiserating over an accident that had just happened in their driveway, resulting in two mangled cars. She'd tried to see if they needed help, to break the ice of the feud that had gone on since before she was born, but while his brother

Hugh had at least spoken to her, Rex had just narrowed those smoldering dark eyes of his and clenched that ever-jumping jaw. She'd be damned if she'd accept that treatment from anyone, especially Rex Braden. Despite her best efforts to forget his handsome face, for years he'd been the only man she'd conjured up in the darkest hours of the nights, when loneliness settled in and her body craved human touch. It was always his face that pulled her over the edge as she came apart beneath the sheets.

"Not you, that's for sure," he answered with a lift of his chin.

Jade stood up tall in her new Rogue boots and settled her hands on her hips. "Sure looks like you're staring to me."

Rex cracked a crooked smile as he nodded toward the water. "Redecorating the ravine?"

"No!" She walked over to Flame and ran her hand down his flank. *Why him? Of all the men who could ride up, why does it have to be the one guy who makes my heart flutter like a schoolgirl's?*

"Taking a break, that's all." She couldn't take her eyes off of his bulging biceps. Even as a teenager, he'd had the nervous habit of clenching his jaw and arms at the same time—and, Jade realized, the effect it had on her had not diminished one iota.

"Lame stallion?" he asked in a raspy, deep voice.

Everything he said sounded sensual. "No." *What happened to my vocabulary?* She'd been three years behind Rex in school, and in all the years she'd known him, he probably hadn't said more than a handful of words to her. She narrowed her eyes, remembering how she'd pined over each one of his grumbling syllables, even though they were usually preceded by a dismissive grunt of some sort, which she had always attributed to the feud that preceded her birth.

"All righty then." He turned his horse and walked her back the way he'd come.

Jade stared at his wide back as it moved farther and farther away. *Damn it, what if no one else comes along?* She looked up at the sun making its slow crawl toward the sky, guessing it was only six thirty or seven. No one else was going to come by the ravine. She cursed herself for not carrying her cell phone. She wasn't one of those women who needed to be accessible twenty-four-seven. She carried it during the day, but this morning, she'd just wanted to ride without distraction. Now she was stuck, and he was her only hope. Getting Flame home was more important than any family feud or her own conflicting hateful and lustful thoughts for the conceited man who was about to disappear around the corner.

She shook her head and kicked the dirt, wishing she'd worn her riding boots. The toes of her new Rogues were getting scuffed and dirty. *Could today get any worse?*

"Hey!" she called after him. When he didn't stop, she thought he hadn't heard her. "I said, *hey!*"

He came to a slow stop, but didn't turn around. "You talking to me? I thought you were talking to that lame horse of yours." He cast a glance over his shoulder.

Jerk. "His name is Flame, and he's the best damned horse around, so watch yourself."

His horse began its lazy stroll once again.

"Wait!" *Goddamn it!* She gritted her teeth against the desire to call him an ass and shot a look at Flame, still favoring his leg, softening her resolve.

"Wait, please."

His horse came to another stop.

"I need to get him home, and I can't very well do it myself." She kicked the dirt again as he turned his horse and walked her back. He stared down at Jade with piercing dark eyes, his jaw still clenched.

"Can you help me get him out of here?" Up close, his muscles were even larger, more defined, than she'd thought. His neck thicker, everything about him exuded masculinity. She crossed her arms to settle her nerves as he waited a beat too long to answer. "Listen, if you can't—"

"Don't get your panties in a bunch," he said, calm and even.

"You don't have to be rude."

"I don't have to help at all," he said, mimicking her by crossing his arms.

"Fine. You're right. Sorry. Can you please help me get him out of here? He can't make it up that hill."

"Just how do you suppose I do that?" He glanced at the steep drop of the land just twenty feet ahead of them, then back up the ravine at the rocky shoreline. "You shouldn't've brought him down here. Why are you riding a stallion, anyway? They're temperamental as

370

hell. What were you thinking? A girl like you can't handle that horse on this type of terrain."

"A girl like me? I'll have you know that I'm a vet, and I've worked around horses my whole life." She felt her cheeks redden and crossed her arms, jutting her hip out in the defiant stance she'd taken throughout her teenage years.

"So I hear." He lowered his chin and lifted his gaze, looking at her from beneath the shadow of his Stetson. "From the looks of it, all that vet schooling didn't do you much good, now, did it?"

Ugh! He was maddening. Jade pursed her lips and stalked away in a huff. "Forget it. I can do this by myself."

"Sure you can," he mused.

She felt his eyes on her back as she took Flame's reins and tried to lead him up the steep incline. The enormous horse took only three steps before stopping cold. She grunted and groaned, pleading with the horse to move, but Flame was hurt, and he'd gone stubborn on her. Her face heated to a flush.

"You keep doing what you're doing. I'll be back in an hour to get you and that lame horse of yours."

An hour, great. She was aching to tell him to hurry, but she knew how long it took to hook up the horse trailer, and she had no idea how he'd get it all the way down by the ravine. She watched him ride away, feeling stupid, embarrassed, angry, and insanely attracted to the ornery jerk of a man.

Melissa Foster

(End of Sneak Peek)
To continue reading, be sure to pick up the next
LOVE IN BLOOM release:

DESTINED FOR LOVE, *The Bradens*, Book Two
Love in Bloom Series, Book Five

"Contemporary romance at its hottest.
Each Braden sibling left me craving the next.
Sensual, sexy, and satisfying."

— *Bestselling author, Keri Nola, Psychotherapist (on THE BRADENS)*

LOVE IN BLOOM is a nine-book series

Check online retailers for availability

SNOW SISTERS

Sisters in Love
Sisters in Bloom
Sisters in White

THE BRADENS

Lovers at Heart
Destined for Love
Friendship on Fire
Sea of Love
Bursting with Love
Hearts at Play

Acknowledgments

There are so many people to thank for helping me bring this book to readers. There's a community of bloggers, reviewers, authors, readers, and friends that each deserve to be listed here, but I simply don't have space. My sincere gratitude goes out to everyone who has inspired, helped, and encouraged me though this exciting journey. I hope we can continue to inspire each other. Thank you all so very much.

My dedicated and efficient editors and proofreaders deserve a chocolate sculpture ten feet high for their energy and skills. Thank you Kristen Weber, Penina Lopez, Jenna Bagnini, Colleen Albert, Juliette Hill, and Marlene Engel. I'm so lucky to have you on my team. My beautiful cover was designed by Natasha Brown and formatting was handled by Rachelle Ayala. Thank you both for all you have done and continue to do for me.

Stacy Eaton, Amy Manemann, Emerald Barnes, Wendy Young, Christine Cunningham, Rachelle Ayala, Natasha Brown, Bonnie Trachtenberg, G.E. Johnson, and Kathleen Shoop—you are the best friends a person could hope for and I treasure every moment of our laughter, whining, wining **wink wink**, and trouble-making time together—virtual and otherwise. Sisters at heart...forever.

Thank you to each of my Team Pay-it-Forward community who have become like family. You're all so special to me and I am proud to be among your friends.

The name "Braden" was a gift from my good friend Russell Blake. Thank you for giving a name to the men in my head and then pushing me to make them ever bigger than life. I hope my readers will jump the fence and pick up your thrillers.

My writing life would not exist if not for the support and understanding of my mother, my husband, and my children. You rock my world and I love you all.

Melissa Foster is an award-winning, International bestselling author. Her books have been recommended by USA Today's book blog, Hagerstown Magazine, The Patriot, and several other print venues. She is the founder of the <u>Women's Nest</u>, a social and support community for women, and the <u>World Literary Café</u>. When she's not writing, Melissa helps authors navigate the publishing industry through her author training programs on <u>Fostering Success</u>. Melissa hosts Aspiring Authors contests for children, and has painted and donated several murals to The Hospital for Sick Children in Washington, DC.

Visit Melissa on her <u>website</u>, or chat with her on <u>The Women's Nest</u> or social media. Melissa enjoys discussing her books with book clubs and reader groups, and welcomes an invitation to your event.

Melissa's books are available on Amazon, Barnes & Noble, and most online retailers.

<u>www.MelissaFoster.com</u>

28559816R00231

Made in the USA
Charleston, SC
13 April 2014